Taylor slipped off her barstool and made a beeline for the rear exit. Ducking past a dark curtain, she hurried down a dimly lit hallway. A shape loomed in her path, and she drew up short. She gasped in recognition—the stranger with the dark, penetrating eyes and a five-o'clock shadow she'd spotted across the room. His hand closed firmly around her arm.

"You've either been keeping bad company, lady," he said in a low, smooth baritone that hinted at Southern roots, "or there are a lot of mean hombres who don't like you asking questions."

"Let me go!" she demanded in a harsh whisper. Talk about leaping from the frying pan into the fire! Though he wasn't actually hurting her, the stranger's grip was like steel, the calluses on his palm abrading her tender flesh.

"You don't want to go back in there, honey. Those guys are packing heavy iron."

"And there is some reason I should trust *you?*"

One of the men she was trying to escape brushed aside the curtain and stepped into the hallway. She spotted the metallic glint of a gun in his hand.

"That looks like a pretty good reason to me," the stranger said.

MAKE NO PROMISES

CHARLOTTE MACLAY

LOVE SPELL NEW YORK CITY

LOVE SPELL®

June 2006

Published by

Dorchester Publishing Co., Inc.
200 Madison Avenue
New York, NY 10016

ISBN 0-505-52649-2

Printed in the United States of America.

Visit us on the web at www.dorchesterpub.com.

ACKNOWLEDGMENTS

Thanks to George and Nancy for joining us on our adventure to the bottom of the world, and to my husband, Chuck, for taking such good notes.

As always, I couldn't have succeeded without the support, advice and friendship of my critique partners, Mindy Neff and Sue Phillips.

MAKE NO PROMISES

CHAPTER ONE

Santiago, Chile

"I regret I could not be of greater assistance to you, señorita."

The manager of the Hotel Magdalena spoke in the same ingratiating tone he'd used for the past hour, insisting that Taylor Travini's twin brother Terry had never been registered at his hotel. His shiny black suit, frayed at the cuffs, matched the equally shabby lobby through which he escorted her on the way to the monogrammed front doors. In the early 1900s this downtown Santiago hotel had been grand by Chilean standards, but no longer. Based on the guests loitering in the lobby, the establishment now served a slightly disreputable clientele. Taylor's brother never cared about posh.

She knew Terry had been here six weeks ago. He'd called her in California from his room. They'd talked for a half hour about his plan to travel to Patagonia and Tierra del Fuego at the southern tip of Chile on his much anticipated wildlife photography jaunt. She'd bemoaned the fact that she had decided to stay home in Sonora to develop a new promotional package for Travini Vineyards instead of flying south with him. They had shared so many adventures together, from climbing in the Himalayas to diving for sunken ships in the Caribbean; she should have joined him on this trip, too. For all of their thirty years, her twin brother had been her very best friend, and she his.

Instead of going with Terry on this trip, she'd wanted to impress upon their father that she had what it took to run one of the most successful vineyards in California. He'd barely glanced at her proposal before saying he would ask Terry's opinion when Terry returned home.

Hefting her backpack over one shoulder, Taylor acknowledged the hotel manager with a curt nod and shoved out through the heavy glass door. Sluggish street traffic edged through the summer heat and sweat prickled on her forehead. Diesel fumes tainted the air with exhaust from the ubiquitous yellow buses that carved their way through the canyons between modern high-rises and historic buildings, the latter revealing their age through peeling paint and chipped masonry. Horns blared as a river of small European-built cars, buses and taxis tried to switch places for no apparent reason.

She signaled the doorman to call her a cab. A short, squat little man of mestizo heritage, he wore a uniform with enough gold braid on his shoulders to outrank a five-star general.

Had Terry been with her, he would have chuckled about how putting on a uniform—any uniform—gave some people a false sense of power. The more braid and brass buttons, the more they would exaggerate their authority. In return, Taylor would remind Terry with a quick jab of her elbow not to make fun of the locals.

Still, she couldn't help but smile at the doorman's exuberant efforts to hail a taxi.

Her twin brother couldn't have vanished from Santiago without leaving a trace. Even if he hadn't stayed at Hotel Magdalena, he'd stayed somewhere. Met someone who would remember him. Someone who knew of his plans. There had to be some logical reason why he'd remained out of touch for the past six weeks. When traveling, they'd both made it a point to call home frequently.

Despite the warm day, a shiver of unease raised goose flesh along her spine. Surely she'd know if something bad had happened to Terry. They were as close as two people could be. And she'd promised their father she would drag her brother back home safe and sound.

Shaking off a feeling that could be a premonition or simply her concern about Terry, she glanced toward the street. The stream of cars parted, allowing a shiny black sedan with tinted windows through the fluid lines of traffic. The vehicle picked up speed as it headed for the hotel. With a sharp twist of the wheel, the driver swerved the car into the zone reserved for taxis. An instant before it lurched up over the curb, Taylor caught a glimpse of the driver. A dark, swarthy man, his eyes were focused intently on her. *Aiming* for her.

In a reflexive response honed while earning a black belt in karate, she dived out of the path of the oncoming car. Her backpack flew from her grasp as the vehicle passed within inches of her. She hit the ground in a tucked position, her shoulder and elbow connecting hard with the concrete, her hands scraping the rough surface as she rolled away. Behind her, she heard a cry and the characteristic thud of three tons of fast-moving steel making contact with soft human flesh. She looked up in time to see the sedan careening away down the street at full speed.

The doorman's body lay sprawled thirty feet from his post, his neck twisted at an impossible angle. Blood stained the garish gold braid of his uniform. Paradoxically, his cap rested unscathed on the sidewalk by the front door, as though waiting for its owner to return to his duties.

Bile rose in Taylor's throat and she began to shake. Her ears rang. She breathed great gulps of air through her mouth and her heart rammed against her ribs. Sitting on the ground, her hands stinging from her slide across the concrete, she bent her knees and put her head between them.

Why in heaven's name would anyone want to kill her?

As though in search of a talisman, something that would help her make sense of what had just happened, she fingered the smooth stone in the aquamarine pendant that hung around her neck. The birthstone necklace had been a present from her father when she turned thirteen, one of his rare gifts, and she treasured it with all of her heart.

Slowly she became aware of voices raised around her. Years of working with immigrant crews in the family's vineyards had given her fluency in the language if not a Chilean accent. But what these people were saying didn't make sense. Lifting her head, she tried to understand their meaning.

"She did it."

"I saw the blonde gringa do it."

"She shoved Julio in front of that car."

This last came from the hotel manager. His groveling manner was gone now. In its place was accusation and a fury that turned his narrow lips downward and his pockmarked cheeks fiery red as he incited the gathering crowd.

"No, that's not what happened." She struggled to stand. Her watery knees didn't want to bear her weight. Her right elbow, bruised by her dive to safety, throbbed. "The man in the car deliberately aimed—"

"*¡Homicida!*"

"*¡Policia!*"

As though their excited cries had reached the ears of the local police, sirens shrilled their arrival from all directions. An ambulance pulled up behind the police cars. Everyone seemed to be talking at once. Most of them pointed at Taylor or glared in her direction, the mob feeding on its own anger.

She was too numb, too stunned by what had happened to respond. She could only feel grateful when the ambulance driver draped a yellow plastic tarp over Julio's contorted body.

Did he have a family? He'd only been trying to call a cab for her. Should she offer some money to help with his burial?

"Señorita, would you please step over here with me."

The middle-aged police sergeant had dark, penetrating eyes and a bushy mustache that should have made him look like a cartoon character. It didn't. He was dead serious.

"Of course, officer," she responded in his language. She didn't want him to think of her as an ugly American who had no understanding or respect for his culture. "This is a terrible thing that has happened. I think the man who was driving the car—"

"May I see your passport, please."

She carried that in her waistpack, a leather pouch that made her feel a bit like a kangaroo. "The doorman was trying to call a taxi—"

"What is the reason for your visit to Chile?"

Feeling very uneasy about the police officer's attitude, she handed him her passport. "I've come here looking for my brother. He hasn't contacted the family in several weeks and—"

"Where are you staying?"

Her admittedly limited patience took a quick hike. "Look, sergeant, I was nearly killed here, and one of your own citizens was. What you need to do is look for that black sedan that hit the poor man, not waste your time questioning me."

"Where are you staying?" he repeated. His lips barely moved as he spoke. Or maybe his mustache camouflaged the movement.

She rolled her eyes. "I don't know. I hadn't had time to decide before that car—"

"Do you have friends in our country?"

"Only my brother. And he's missing. In fact, I'd like to file a missing-person report."

The officer's brows, which were almost as thick as his mustache, rose ever so slightly.

"Do you have luggage with you?"

"Of course. My backpack." She glanced around. The crowd of onlookers had been moved back from the scene, though they were still in shouting distance and appeared determined to see her hanging from a gallows before the next sunrise. She spotted her backpack mashed into a corner of the hotel entryway. It must have landed there when she evaded the car.

She indicated the spot with a tip of her chin. "It's over there."

"You will remain here, please."

The sergeant called over one of his lesser minions, a tall, slender man wearing an impeccably pressed uniform, to guard her while he retrieved her backpack.

Returning, he said, "You do not mind if I look through you personal effects?"

"Help yourself, officer. I've got nothing to hide. But I have to say your police work stinks if you think I'm responsible for Julio's death."

His dark eyes narrowed on her, and she had a moment of regret that she'd mouthed off. She was in a foreign country. This guy could basically haul her off and lock her up for no reason at all.

The menacing crowd continued to mutter amongst themselves as the sergeant methodically searched her backpack.

It occurred to Taylor that she could have dressed with a little more care when she left the States some twenty hours ago on the overnight flight to Santiago. For the sake of comfort, she'd worn old, faded jeans and a T-shirt with a Breakers Bay 10K-run logo. Her hiking boots were scuffed, her blonde hair laced in a single loose braid held with a scrunchie, and she wore no makeup. Not exactly an image designed to impress the local authorities.

But then, she hadn't expected anyone to try to kill her.

The police officer held up a small plastic bag containing white powder. "Miss Travini, do you recognize this?"

"No."

He opened a corner of the baggie and tasted the contents with his fingertip. The grooves across his forehead deepened. "It was in your backpack."

A sharp curl of anxiety twisted her midsection. "I didn't put it there."

"Ah, I see. Has anyone else had access to your backpack?"

Her gaze darted toward the onlookers. The hotel manager, who was standing inside the area cordoned off by the police, didn't meet her eyes.

"Any number of people could have put that in my backpack in all the confusion after the hit-and-run. Starting with Señor Emanuel, the hotel—"

"I'm afraid I must ask you to come down to police headquarters with me." The sergeant made a quick gesture with his head. Before Taylor could react, another officer had hooked her arms behind her back, and she was being handcuffed.

"Sergeant, someone planted that bag in my backpack. I don't do drugs. I never have."

The younger officer patted her down for weapons in a quick, professional manner that gave her the creeps. Then, none too gently, he propelled her toward the police car, opened the door, ducked her head and pushed her inside. The interior smelled faintly of old urine and fear.

She sat awkwardly on the seat with her hands behind her back. She suspected she was adding her own scent of terror to the perfume left by prior felons.

"I want to see someone from the U.S. embassy," she said when the officer slid into the driver's seat.

He ignored her.

CHAPTER TWO

In the Andes

A pair of hawks soared above the chalky white cliffs at sixteen thousand feet, circling through the air, rising with the currents and dipping again in an instinctive dance. They knew the maneuvers well, matching each other by feathering the tips of their wings or folding them back to pick up speed. Staying together.

Seeing any bird in this dry, parched landscape was rare. A pair even more unusual.

Above Rafe Maguire and the soaring hawks, the peaks were still iced with snow now tinted pink by the setting sun. Below, the valleys were shadowed by encroaching twilight. Rafe found little joy in the scenery; he felt only the sharp ache of loneliness that the sight of the mating birds brought back to him.

He led a group of twenty-two Chilean army recruits down a treacherous path better suited to mountain goats than men. Each one carried a hundred pounds of gear, which they had also carried up the mountain two weeks

9

ago. These young soldiers were the remnants of forty volunteers who had started six weeks of Ranger training. Half plus two had survived the grueling ordeal; the rest had surrendered to their own mental or physical weakness when the going got too tough.

Not a bad percentage, he thought. Comparable to his experience in the U.S. Army Ranger corps.

"Keep your ugly butt moving, soldier!" he shouted at a straggler. "In an ambush, they pick off the strays. Your ass will be toast." He grinned devilishly as the twenty-year-old struggled to catch up, making the youth sweat even harder.

The real test would come if and when these men came face to face with an enemy. Rafe wouldn't be there then. The training over, his work was done. They'd be on their own. Never again would he be responsible for another man's death. He wouldn't lead them into battle—or into an ambush.

He wouldn't be the cause of a woman's death, either, by not being there to protect her. He no longer made that kind of promise.

All he had to do was get this motley crew of exhausted soldiers safely down to the valley. After that, they could find their own war to fight. Rebels. Terrorists. Drug lords. He didn't care whom. He'd be back in Santiago sipping beer at the local pub.

Until the next time *el presidente* decided to hire him to teach boys how to fight.

Suddenly the weight of his own gear pressed down on his shoulders and his foot slipped on the rough shale. When would the cycle stop? When could he turn his murderous weapons into plowshares?

Not until I atone for not being there when Lizbeth and Katy needed me.

CHAPTER THREE

Taylor had once taken a tour of the Marin County jail in California as part of a school field trip. It hadn't smelled anything like this hellhole. Nor had the occupants been quite so . . . colorful.

After her personal effects, including her passport, had been confiscated, she'd been placed in a cell with six bunk beds and fifteen women. There'd been no effort to question her. She hadn't been booked or fingerprinted. No mug shot. And sure as hell no attorney or phone call to the embassy had been granted. Instead, she'd been unceremoniously ushered into this holding tank. The Chilean version of the Gray Bar Hotel had badly chipped green bars, a bare concrete floor and no windows.

We aren't in Kansas anymore, Toto.

Her cellmates were an eclectic group. Ranging in age from maybe fifteen to seventy, the dominant occupation she guessed was hooker. Petty thieves rounded out the bevy of not-exactly-beauties.

"Hey, chiquita," a woman with massive arms, hanging jowls and a whiskered chin called to her. "You overcharge some hombre and he turn you in? Or maybe he didn't like such a bony woman and he wanted his money back." Her laughter was like a timpani drum, vibrating between the concrete walls of the cell.

"There's been a misunderstanding," Taylor replied. "I'm sure it will all be worked out."

"Listen to that, sisters," the woman barked loudly, then hacked a cough. "Our little chiquita says she is innocent."

"She won't be innocent when I get through with her." The threatening words came from a woman with a pockmarked face bisected by a jagged scar down one cheek. She looked mean enough to have done the damage to herself simply to prove she was tough.

Taylor repressed a shudder of revulsion, consciously replacing the feeling with one of sympathy. It couldn't be easy for someone so disfigured to make any kind of a living in a country like Chile. Or even in the States. But maybe there she would have gotten pro bono plastic surgery.

Searching out a corner of the cell where she wouldn't have to watch her back, Taylor slid down to the floor. The incident at the hotel as well as the long overnight flight had taken their toll. Fatigue and ebbing adrenaline left her muscles aching.

"Any of you know how I could reach the U.S. embassy?" she asked.

They all hooted in response.

"Nobody cares about gringas who end up in this jail—except the guards," the heavyset woman said slyly. "They like a little fresh meat now and then."

"Wonderful," Taylor muttered under her breath.

With any luck, the sergeant or his supervisors were checking out her background now. They'd discover her family had a certain amount of clout, or at least some political influence in the States.

Taylor almost smiled, remembering how her father had stormed into the principal's office, totally intimidating the man, when she was about to be expelled for fighting in the girls' lavatory in seventh grade. "My daughter is a *lady!*" he'd bellowed. "She doesn't fight like a street urchin." She'd been so relieved that he'd come to her defense—however unwarranted, given the truth of the matter—that she'd given him a big hug, and he'd hugged her in return.

Except for that incident, which wasn't likely to show up on any record, her only brush with the law was a speeding ticket. That violation had come courtesy of the Viper she'd bought herself for her twenty-first birthday with the first installment of the trust fund her grandmother had left her. Taylor hadn't been able to resist testing the car's limits.

Her father had been appalled by both her choice of vehicle and the blot on her record. Her grandmother would have been pleased on both counts. Tata Travini believed a woman ought to sow a few wild oats before she married, and had made sure Taylor had the money to do it. Just as well, since thus far Taylor hadn't developed any serious marital prospects.

As the day wore on, prisoners came and went in a random procession escorted by khaki-clad guards with a combined IQ of twenty-seven, and enough body weight to sink a small destroyer. None called Taylor's name. Apparently the local goon squad had decided to let her sweat it out for a while before questioning her.

She closed her eyes, gritty with fatigue. As soon as she got out of here, she was heading for the nearest decent hotel to sleep and have a shower. Then she'd go to the embassy. Her brother was missing, for God's sake, and the Chilean authorities had locked her up without so much as a hearing. That wasn't the way for any government to treat an American citizen.

Her chest tightened, and tears borne of exhaustion and fear prickled at the backs of her eyes. What if Terry wasn't simply missing? What if he was dead?

She chased the thought away with a shake of her head. She'd find Terry—somehow—and bring him back home. He'd probably become so wrapped up in his latest adventure that he'd forgotten anyone would worry about him. When she found him, he would laugh about her making such a fuss.

After hours of nothing happening, the guards arrived with what masqueraded as dinner—a Saran-wrapped chicken salad sandwich on white bread. Or at least that's what she thought they were delivering.

Taylor accepted what was handed to her through a small opening in the puke-green bars, then returned to her roost in the corner. The bunks' mattresses didn't look all that inviting anyway. But before she could sit down and take her first bite, the scar-faced woman tried to snatch the sandwich from her.

Taylor reacted instinctively. She whipped around, catching the woman first with an elbow to her midsection, then hooked a foot behind her knee and gave a push. Scar-face hit the floor on her back, a whoosh of air escaping her lungs. The entire incident had taken less than three seconds.

Alert in the sudden silence that followed, legs spread apart, enabling her to react to a threat from any direction, Taylor waited for another attack. She was outnumbered by fourteen to one if they wanted to rush her. It wouldn't be a fair fight, but she wouldn't give up easily. *All over a stupid sandwich I'll probably have to gag down.* It made no sense.

Slowly, the jowly prisoner—the cell matriarch who had greeted Taylor so ungraciously upon her arrival—began to clap and smile her gap-toothed smile. Others followed suit.

"Looks like you met your match, *puta*," the heavyset woman cackled. "Chiquita got your number right off. Next time you better pick on somebody smaller than you."

With the feral look of a born predator, Scar-face struggled to her feet. Whatever sympathy Taylor had felt for the woman earlier evaporated.

"I don't want to fight you," Taylor said, not taking her eyes off the woman. "But I will if I have to."

The woman spat at her. The phlegm caught Taylor on the cheek. Repressing a shudder of distaste, Taylor wiped it off with her shoulder. Stalking to the far side of the cell, Scar-face targeted a teenage girl, yanking the pale adolescent off a top bunk and claiming it for herself.

Taylor wanted to go to the girl's defense, but suspected that would only make things worse. After Taylor was released, Scar-face would take her anger out on the teenager. That's what bullies did. In their youth, her brother Terry's slender physique and nonconfrontational style had made him the target of bullies more than once.

Taylor had been the one to inherit her father's big bones and Italian temper. Fortunately, over time, Terry had bulked up enough to hold his own. But he was still a pacifist at heart.

Returning to the relative safety of her corner, Taylor forced herself to eat the dry, tasteless sandwich. She was likely to need all the strength she could muster to deal with this ridiculous situation.

Eventually, the lights in the cell were dimmed. Beddy-bye time and still no sign of getting out. They were going to make Taylor consider the error of her ways until morning. She wrapped her arms around her bent legs and lay her head on her knees. Forcefully she conjured the image of the Travini vineyards. Rows and rows of peaceful vines stretched out toward the horizon. The mild spring air held the scent of sea salt from the ocean that was only ten miles away and the rich aroma of dark, fertile soil. New shoots budded on the vines, promising a good harvest come fall.

Dozing, Taylor was barely aware of her surroundings. Her cellmates turned restlessly on their bunks. Some snored. Others breathed heavily or mumbled in their sleep. One woman woke crying and quickly stifled her sobs.

She wasn't sure what warned her. The sound of a shoe scuffing concrete. A single breath drawn more deeply than others. A movement of air across her cheek.

Instinctively, she ducked her head to one side, covering it with her arm. Pain erupted in her biceps. She screamed and rolled away. The occupants of the cell came awake, complaining loudly.

It was too dark for Taylor to make out her assailant clearly. What she could see was the faint light from the hallway glistening off a hunk of metal held in her attacker's hand as she—or he—took another swipe at her.

She dived for the person's knees, but whoever was wielding the knife dodged away in a quick, agile movement. Unable to immediately get to her feet, Taylor pursued as best she could—her own three-legged race.

The cell door opened and banged shut. Prisoners screamed. Guards shouted to quiet down. The lights came on, blinding Taylor.

Finally standing, she wrapped her hand around her bleeding arm. Sticky liquid soaked through her fingers where she pressed them to the wound, and she could smell the metallic scent of blood. Damn, it hurt like hell! Thank God the blade hadn't been buried in the middle of her back.

Nothing inside the cell looked out of the ordinary. Most of the prisoners had been smart enough to stay in their bunks. Except Scar-face. She was standing across the cell, smirking. As though someone else had done her work for her, or tried to.

Taylor's stomach lurched and the blood drained from her head. For the second time in less than twenty-four hours, she could have been killed.

But why? It had to be more than sandwich-greed.

She'd traveled the world, including a good many remote areas, without a single violent incident. Until now.

Something sinister was happening here. She felt it like the slither of a water moccasin over bare flesh. She didn't intend to stick around this jail cell long enough for the snake to strike again.

CHAPTER FOUR

An unnamed island off the southern tip of Chile

Southern beech trees crowded the island's shoreline, their green foliage overlapping in a nearly impenetrable maze. Only a keen eye would spot the corrugated shack halfway up the hillside with its array of high frequency radio antennas on the roof, a second storage building virtually dug out of solid granite, or the wooden dock tucked well back into a natural cove.

In the unlikely event someone spotted the presence of activity on the island, either from the unpopulated mainland a half mile away or from a boat passing through the narrow channel, they would not live to report their findings.

Hamid Al Faysal and his ten associates would see to that. Allah willing.

A forty-two-year-old Saudi by birth, he had wildly curly hair now streaked with gray. But his body was still strong and youthful. He had trained in Yemen and

Afghanistan, led attacks of Chechen rebels against Russian soldiers, all preparing him for the day that would soon arrive. His moment of glory.

Allah be praised!

The furnishings inside the hut were sparse and illuminated only by a single bare bulb. Three sets of bunk beds with thin mattresses, a rudimentary stove and an eating table with six chairs were all that were necessary. At any given time, at least half of his men were on duty. Hamid rarely slept at all.

The heart of the hut was the radio, Hamid's single contact with the small cadre of Islamic fundamentalists in the Santiago and Punta Arenas areas, and those who had come from around the world to join him in the jihad. No telephones, no cell phones worked this far south of the equator in an almost totally unpopulated area; satellite communication was ill advised. Too easily intercepted.

The dials on the front panel of the radio glowed orange, the needle fluctuating with each word spoken or burst of static. Holding the microphone in one hand, Hamid listened carefully to his contact in Santiago until his associate finished his report.

"You must stop this woman," Hamid ordered, speaking in Arabic. Nerve endings twisted and knotted in his gut. Women should be locked in their homes, be there only to serve their husbands and raise their husband's sons. He would never understand American women, or why their men allowed such indecent behavior. If such a woman were his wife, he would beat her until she understood his wishes. And Allah's.

"We tried," the voice on the radio explained in a combination of Arabic and Spanish. "We had hoped to

19

arrange a tragic accident. Our man at Hotel Magdalena let us know of her arrival. But she is as quick and fleet as a cat. Then, when we arrested her . . ."

Hamid grew impatient as his man in Santiago continued to make excuses.

"Send her back to America," Hamid said when his contact finally finished his whining self-defense. "If she will not go willingly, then you must make other arrangements. We are too close to our goal to let a mere woman interfere."

"We understand."

"Incompetent bastards!" Hamid muttered as he switched off the radio. *He* would not have let a woman get the better of him!

Soon, he consoled himself, the infidels would understand the power of Allah. If Hamid had his way, women would be the first to get that message. The Taliban had understood the importance of keeping women in their place. Hamid would soon teach infidels an even more severe lesson. And it would come from a place they would least expect.

The door to the hut opened, casting a rectangle of misty morning light into the room. The gray-haired intruder wore a frayed Russian naval uniform and walked with an uneven gait. He dropped a thick operating manual on the table next to Hamid.

"It's all here. We'll be able to do just what you want."

Although Hamid couldn't read Russian, he flipped through the pages, glancing quickly at the diagrams and schematics. Yes, this would do, he thought, and smiled slightly. The outline of the known world would change with the knowledge this gave him.

And when that happened, those who had doubted Hamid Al Faysal would chant his praises in every mosque; his name would be on the lips of every freedom fighter, every martyr. No longer would his brothers chide him or his mother look away, for he would be the one to redeem his family's honor.

Allah be praised!

CHAPTER FIVE

"Captain, I was nearly run over by a hit-and-run driver and then assaulted by a knife-wielding maniac while in your custody." Taylor held her gaze steadily on the man seated across the desk from her.

"An assailant who you cannot identify," the police officer said mildly.

"Because your holding tank was dark. I was asleep, for God's sake. If I'd reacted a millisecond slower, you'd be notifying the authorities that an American was murdered in your jailhouse. That would be damn hard to explain, huh?"

"Not at all, señorita." Leaning back in his desk chair, the captain tented his fingers beneath his multiple chins, watching her with unwavering ebony eyes and offering not one ounce of sympathy.

To his credit, he and his men had gotten Taylor out of the cell in one piece after the attack and arranged to have a doctor stitch up her arm, after which she'd been allowed to change into a clean T-shirt. The numbness around her wound hadn't worn off yet, but Taylor expected it to burn like blue blazes when it did.

"Quarrels often arise between drug dealers," he pointed out in the same unemotional tone. "Fatalities happen."

"I'm *not* a drug dealer. I don't even *use* drugs." She didn't even like to take aspirin, for heaven's sake.

"The packet taken from your backpack tested positive for cocaine."

"That's nonsense. And if it's true, someone planted it in my gear."

The captain shrugged, unconcerned. "We get many young Americans visiting our country because they believe drugs are easier and cheaper to obtain here than in their homeland."

"I'm here looking for my brother. Not drugs."

He had a very high forehead, and when he raised a skeptical brow, it wrinkled his bald scalp halfway back to the narrow fringe of salt-and-pepper hair that formed a U-shape around his head. "So you have said."

Exasperated, Taylor blew out a long breath. "I'd like to have my things back, please. If you're not willing to take a missing person report, then I'll have to go to the embassy. They'll talk to me."

He slid a brown manilla envelope toward her, where she found the personal items that they'd confiscated plus her pendant necklace. Grateful to have her father's gift back in her possession, she latched it around her neck.

"I'm afraid you won't have time to go to your embassy." The captain glanced at his watch, a Rolex with a stainless steel band. A pretty expensive bit of jewelry for a government employee. "Your plane to San Francisco leaves in just over an hour."

23

"I'm not going back home!" she gasped. "Not yet. I have to—"

"Two of my men will escort you to the airport. When you are ready to board, they will hand over your passport and backpack. In the future, you will not be permitted entry to our country."

"You can't throw me out! I haven't done anything wrong. I need to find my brother. He could be in trouble."

"You are the one who is in trouble, señorita. We have enough difficulty with drugs in our own country without importing problems from *norteamerica*." He stood, which apparently signaled two of his cohorts to enter the office. "Please see señorita Travini to the airport and make sure she is safely onboard her flight home."

The Mutt-and-Jeff pair, dressed in long black jackets despite the summer weather, each grabbed Taylor by an arm.

"Ow!" she complained. "That's my bad arm."

Mutt loosened his grip. "My apologies, señorita."

Jeff was less gentle.

As he manhandled her out the door, Taylor concluded they gave the local police lessons in how to dislocate shoulders. She'd be black-and-blue by tomorrow, if not worse. And she still wouldn't know what had happened to her brother.

"Look, guys." If the captain's fancy Rolex meant anything, Taylor suspected bribery was an acceptable way of doing business in Chile. "I have some money with me and I can get more. I really need to get to the U.S. embassy. If you could help me out—"

Mutt looked interested. Jeff wasn't buying it. Evidently he was more interested in stuffing her in the backseat of an unmarked police car than lining his pockets with pesos. She would have to come up against the one honest cop in town.

Or maybe they'd already filched her money and ID from her waistpack. What they didn't know was that she'd done a lot of traveling, not all of it in developed countries. She always hid an extra stash of cash in the lining of her boots.

At least she wasn't handcuffed.

Thirty minutes later, she stepped out of the car onto asphalt where a hot breeze blew steadily across the Santiago airport parking lot. To the east, past the low hills that protected Santiago valley, the rugged, razorlike silhouette of the Andes rose into a clear blue sky, the highest peaks still iced with snow.

Mutt and Jeff escorted Taylor into the terminal building as securely as if they were two slices of bread and she was the lunchmeat in between. Their shoulders brushed hers as they walked in lock step. Jeff carried her gear in his off hand, too far away for her to make a grab for it and run.

Unarmed security guards wearing white shirts, dark pants and black Smokey the Bear hats leisurely patrolled the length of the busy terminal. Apparently the threat of terrorist attacks was less here than in the States, and they barely seemed concerned with thieves or pickpockets. Easy duty, she imagined.

Still, they might take serious note of a prisoner attempting to escape from police custody. If she could get away from Mutt and Jeff, she'd have to slip past these Smokies—which meant she didn't want to set off any alarms or call undue attention to herself. Then again, they were there to protect the airport and travelers, not stop ordinary citizens and visitors from leaving the premises; with a bit of luck their security training hadn't included classes in independent thinking and taking initiative.

At the ticket counter, Jeff handed Taylor her waistpack, including her passport. She noted her cash was still intact—surprise, surprise—as was her open-ended return airline ticket. Dealing with an honest cop certainly limited her options.

The clerk behind the counter made quick work of booking her on the flight, flashed a smile that included Mutt and Jeff, and wished Taylor a good trip. She slipped her passport back into her waistpack where it belonged.

As they walked toward the boarding gates on the third level, Taylor checked for exits. Those that went out to the tarmac were emergency only and outfitted with alarms. If she did manage to lose her attentive escorts, she didn't want to draw attention to herself by having bells and whistles going off all over the terminal building. She thought it possible that Gatsby, the local restaurant franchise, would have a back entrance. But if she was wrong, she could be trapped in a dead end.

The best way out seemed to be the way they'd come in.

They'd been waiting about ten minutes, along with a hundred or so other travelers, when the attendant invited those with young children to board the flight early. There were plenty in the crowd who qualified.

"Gentlemen," Taylor said. "I'm going to visit the ladies room before we board." She reached for her backpack.

Jeff didn't so much as flinch. "You can wait until you are on the plane." His voice was surprisingly high pitched and grating.

26

"Actually, I can't. Female troubles, you know. It takes forever before the pilot turns off the seatbelt sign."

A slight flush crept up his narrow cheeks.

Mutt gestured that it was okay for her to go.

Jeff still wasn't going to relinquish the backpack. So be it, she thought. There wasn't anything in it she couldn't replace. And she had her waistpack and her necklace.

With a nonchalant shrug, she turned and walked purposefully down the corridor toward the restroom. If she pulled a cut-and-run, her two pals would be on her in seconds.

Think, Taylor. As a kid she'd played enough kick-the-can with her brother and the workers' children in the vineyard to know how to slip past the guy who was *it*. Now was the time to come up with a creative maneuver to outflank her opponents. There were plenty of people around to create a diversion. A string of firecrackers would do it—*if* she had some, which she didn't.

A dozen women stood in line in the windowless restroom. Four more were washing their hands at the row of sinks. All six of the stalls were filled. She didn't have much time.

But she did have matches. Years of roughing it in the outdoors had taught her to be prepared for almost any contingency. Although she hadn't exactly planned for this one.

She slipped past the line, angling for the trash can overflowing with paper towels, some of them damp enough to create a heavy smoke. Glancing in the mirror to see if anyone was paying attention to her, she patted her hair. Her braid was half loose but repairs would have to wait.

Turning her back to the room, she unzipped one

pocket of her waistpack. Her fingers closed around a small metal container filled with stick matches.

With quick, sparse movements, she unscrewed the water-tight container's lid, retrieved a match, secured the lid again and struck the match. She lingered just long enough to be sure it had flared. Then she lowered the match into the trash can where it would catch the edge of a towel.

By the time she reached the end of the waiting line, the match container was back in her waistpack and someone had sounded the alarm.

"¡Incendio!"

Women screamed. A child started to cry. Those near the restroom entrance were nearly trampled as the women inside came running out, pushing and shoving their way through the crowd. Taylor added to the confusion by shouting, *"¡Peligro! ¡Vamanos!"* Danger! Hurry!

Standing back, Taylor stayed put until several women had made it outside. A janitor's cart left in an alcove by the doorway offered extra cover. Ducking down, Taylor shoved the cart ahead of her into the terminal waiting area. She made a hard right turn and kept the cart between her and the spot where she'd left Mutt and Jeff keeping an eye out for her. Her height—five-feet-eleven—plus her blonde hair, put her at a disadvantage. She was too damn easy to spot.

Running in a crouch, she pushed the cart along. By now the entire terminal was in an uproar. There was shouting and cursing everywhere. A security guard ran past her. Mothers called for their children.

Abandoning the cart, Taylor veered down an escalator to the baggage area. People were milling about, unsure of what to do. From behind her, Taylor heard Jeff's distinctive tenor voice shouting, "Stop that woman!"

She hopped over the rim of the baggage carousel and scrambled up the chute on all fours. To the surprise of a couple of slow-moving luggage handlers, she popped out next to their trailer. She didn't bother to introduce herself. Instead, she made for the fence surrounding the tarmac. With a running start, she grabbed the top in one leap, leveraged herself over and fell awkwardly to the ground on the other side.

Her breath sawed in and out of her lungs as she dragged in hot, dry air. Her wounded arm throbbed like hell. Her knee stung from her hard landing. Sweat sheened her face and pooled between her breasts, and her T-shirt clung damply to her back. If she could get to the U.S. embassy, they'd help her. She'd been falsely accused; her brother was missing. And way too many people had tried to kill her recently.

She eyed the area around the terminal, cars arriving to drop off passengers, pedestrians hurrying for their flights. Word of the fire—and the escaping prisoner—hadn't arrived here yet. But she had no more than a minute or two before it did.

An unattended taxi stood twenty feet away from her at the curb. Apparently the driver was taking a break.

She made a dash for the black-and-yellow vehicle, yanked open the driver's door and slid inside. She sent up a blessing to Antonio Ortiz, who had taken the gift of her virginity and taught her how to hotwire a car. She hoped she remembered the latter lesson as well as she had the former.

Moments later, she sped away from the curb, grinning. *Muchas gracias, amigo.*

CHAPTER SIX

Following the afternoon graduation exercises for the Rangers, Rafe had his driver drop him at the Bank of Chile downtown Santiago branch. Now he stood by the bank manager's desk waiting for him to complete the transfer of funds from Rafe's local account to his numbered account in Switzerland. Given Chile's inflation rate, it didn't pay to keep large sums of money in pesos. So when he collected his substantial salary for six weeks of turning boys into men, he sent the majority out of the country. He didn't need much to live on, anyway.

"Here you are, señor." The somberly attired manager handed Rafe a receipt that reflected his new bank balance. "We are always happy to be of service to you."

"Thanks." With barely a glance at the bottom line, Rafe shoved the slip of paper into his pocket. Money held little interest for him. Nothing much did these days, and hadn't for the past three years. When he'd lost Lizbeth and Katy, something had died inside him, too. He wasn't sure that part of him would ever come alive again.

From the bank he walked the few blocks to what passed for his home in Santiago. It was more like a place to store his gear between jobs. No one along the way took note of him. His Army fatigues, even without an insignia, and calf-high jungle boots discouraged idle conversation. He didn't wear a visible weapon but he was quicker with the ten-inch blade tucked into his boot than most men were drawing a handgun. And hidden inside his belt was a wire meant to garrote an unsuspecting enemy. In the States he'd probably have to register his hands as lethal weapons, too. That's what stealth training did for a man.

His apartment was on the second floor, above a garage owned by a mechanical genius named Igor Barerra. The guy kept vehicles running with the clever use of bailing wire, duct tape and stolen parts. He was an inspiration to a man like Rafe, who had bought his first car at sixteen for a hundred bucks, pushed it home and spent the next six months reassembling the guts in the summer heat of South Carolina.

At the moment, the garage doors were closed, Igor and his *compañeros* elsewhere.

The outside stairs were half busted, the wooden handrail wobbly. But the apartment had the advantage of a rear exit, something Rafe had learned to appreciate while dealing with the warring factions in northern Afghanistan.

The other precaution Rafe always took was to leave a *tell*—a piece of thread or strand of hair that, if moved, would tell him that someone had entered his apartment. Sometimes, for variety, he left two tells.

Whomever had entered his apartment while he was in the Andes had only spotted one of them.

Deliberately, Rafe backed down the steps he'd just

31

climbed. The intruder might be long gone. Or still inside. Whatever the case, Rafe didn't like surprises.

Circling to the back of the building, he kept close to the wall. His senses were on full alert. Listening. Watching for an unusual movement. Trying to detect an unfamiliar scent of perfume or cigarettes. It wasn't that he was paranoid, but he had made enemies over the years. So had the Chilean government. An American in any foreign country was a potential target.

Unsheathing his knife, he grasped the metal fire escape and crept up, rung by rung. When he reached the back window to his apartment, he paused and strained to hear movement inside.

Nothing. Maybe he'd been at this business too long. Maybe the tell had simply blown away.

Still careful, he raised the window and lowered one leg into the room.

"Bang! Bang! You're dead, Big Mac."

He rolled onto the floor and came up scowling. "Shit! You could have gotten yourself killed," Rafe complained, recognizing his visitor.

"With that toothpick you carry? Not a chance."

"How'd you know I was coming in the back way?"

"Because that's how I got in, too. *After* I left your second tell where it belonged."

Shaking his head, Rafe embraced Donovan Landry, his friend and fellow Army Ranger.

Rafe and Donovan—nicknamed Hacker because he was a whiz with computers—had been in a lot of firefights together. Despite his nickname, there wasn't anything geeky about the man. He was big and strong and could bench press Rafe's weight with one arm, or so it seemed when Donovan's strength was called upon. Like the time he'd lifted a slab of concrete off Rafe's chest in a raid gone bad in the Philippines that had been intended to rescue some missionaries who'd been captured by rebels. If it hadn't been for Hacker, Rafe would have long since been dead.

"So I'm getting a little rusty," Rafe conceded. Slowing down at the ripe old age of thirty-nine.

"Help yourself to a beer." Tipping his head toward the kitchen that was barely big enough for one person to move around in, Hacker held up his bottle of *cerveza,* the local brew. "My treat."

"You stocked my fridge with beer? Must mean you want something from me." Rafe rubbed at his week-old beard. He probably looked more like a disgruntled rebel than a government contract hire. Whatever Donovan wanted, Rafe wasn't interested. But he wouldn't turn down a beer.

He strolled into the kitchen and opened the ancient refrigerator. The enamel had worn off around the handle, leaving bare metal. "How'd you find me?"

"You can run as far as you like, buddy, but ol' Hacker won't let you hide forever. Not from yourself—or from your friends."

"Maybe sometimes a guy doesn't want to be found." He kicked the refrigerator door shut with his boot, twisted the top off the beer and took a long swig. The cold brew slid smoothly down his throat.

"Not one of the choices, Big Mac."

Rafe swung a straight chair around and straddled it, resting his arms on the back. "Those civvies you're wearing mean you've given up on Uncle Sam's largess and quit the business?"

"Not yet, but I'm working on it." He grinned a little. "Thinking of going into the private security business. It's a growing industry these days."

"I bet it is."

"I'll save a spot for you if you're interested—plan on setting up headquarters in the San Francisco Bay Area. Lots of shipping activity in the San Francisco and Oakland ports that needs beefed up security, and the traffic is growing everyday. The Coast Guard's way undermanned."

Harbors provided a target-rich environment for those who wanted to disrupt the U.S. economy. With his skills and experience, Hacker would probably make a bundle.

"Thanks, but no thanks," Rafe said. "There's nothing left for me in the States."

"There might be if you came back. A good job. Maybe a woman."

"I've got a job and I *had* a woman. I lost her." Agitated, and not willing to discuss his situation with anyone, Rafe pushed himself to his feet. He paced to the window to look out at the dreary view, an alley littered with debris and the backs of rundown buildings much like the one he called home. His mind flashed back to northern Afghanistan, the year 2003, and they had Osama bin Laden on the run.

In a pincer move, a battalion of Pakistani soldiers were moving into the mountainous area from the east. Rafe's company of Rangers had the southern flank, moving north at a steady pace along the line of advance with the hope that they could drive the terrorists into the waiting Pakistani army. The terrain was dry and rocky, the sun scorching hot, communication between the units difficult.

Lieutenant Sam Walker, a ROTC grad from Wyoming and a NCAA college wrestling champ, was Rafe's youngest platoon leader. A gung-ho kid who still needed some seasoning. Rafe had assigned Walker's 2nd Platoon to hold the left flank of the line and be ready to pivot to the center when the company engaged the enemy.

Checking every boulder, every dry creek bed big enough or deep enough to hide a man made for slow going, and all of it was uphill. The company had gone about two clicks when the 1st Platoon in the center of the line took incoming sniper fire.

Rafe's radio crackled to life—Lieutenant Abrams's voice, clear and calm. "First Platoon. Enemy position about one hundred feet above us with a clear field of fire about three hundred feet wide."

"Hold your position, First Platoon," Rafe ordered.

"Roger that," Abrams replied. "First holding."

"Second Platoon, establish a position two hundred feet up from current location."

Walker replied. "Second moving up."

Keeping low, Rafe zigzagged his way between boulders and over loose, crumbling scree to join up with his 2nd Platoon. He needed the best view he could of the terrain the enemy held.

A bullet whined past his head, and he dived for cover. Adrenaline had his blood pumping hard. He'd been in-country for almost ten months. Seven times his company had confronted the elusive al Qaeda and Taliban guerrillas. So far he hadn't lost a man. He intended to keep his record clean.

"First Platoon, see if you can keep 'em occupied."

Gunfire erupted from Abrams's platoon on his order.

Up and running again, Rafe spotted Lt. Walker and his platoon. The lead squad was all bunched up as they approached the dark opening of a cave.

"Spread out your men, Walker. Spread out!" he shouted.

His order came too late.

An Arab with a rocket launcher appeared at the cave entrance. An instant later, the rocket burst into the middle of Walker's lead squad. Two men flew into the air like toy soldiers discarded by an angry kid.

Machine gunfire crisscrossed the area. Someone screamed into the radio.

"I'm hit! Oh, God! My leg!"

Standing, Rafe poured AK-47 rounds into the cave opening. Above the entrance, tracers of returning fire scoured the hillside. White hot pain burned into Rafe's gut, inches below his flack jacket. He staggered back but kept on firing.

Another sear of heat blazed into his left shoulder and then a third into his thigh. With his one good arm he tried to aim his weapon. His bullets spattered into the ground as he sank to his knees.

On the radio, he heard Abrams calling for an air strike, Apache helicopters to bring in more firepower and a medivac rescue unit.

That was the last thing he remembered before he woke up four days later in a hospital in Frankfurt, Germany, his shoulder and thigh wrapped in bandages, gauze over the incision where the doctors had removed his damaged spleen.

He'd lost three men in that battle and had two others wounded. If he'd kept closer tabs on his green lieutenant, hadn't let the kid bunch up the squad, maybe nobody would have died that day. *If* he'd done his job. They gave him a damn medal anyway, a Silver Star to go with his Purple Heart, as if that would make up for the lost life of a tough kid who had dreamed of wrestling in the Olympics.

Later that same day they told him Lizbeth and Katy

had been killed, too. It was as though they'd been in the same battle, the same killing zone. He hadn't been able to protect those he cared about or those he loved the most. Rafe couldn't help but think it would have been better if he'd lost his own life on that boulder-strewn piece of Afghan real estate. Had it been possible, he would have willingly traded places with his wife and child.

Instead, the doctors had patched him up and sent him back to the States. He'd resigned his commission the day he was released from the hospital. The doctors said he had Post Traumatic Stress Syndrome; he should go home and see a shrink.

Without Lizbeth and Katy, he'd had no home to go to.

Rafe felt the weight of Donovan's hand rest briefly on his shoulder, bringing him back to the present.

"When you're ready to come back to the world of the living," the man said, "let me know."

Not fucking anytime soon. Rafe wasn't sure himself why he hadn't been able to get past the terror. The night sweats. The waking up screaming. Hearing the sobs of his wife and baby. Feeling bullets rip into his body. It had been three years, dammit! Rafe figured it was more like a bad case of cowardice.

"I've gotta get back to the General," Donovan said when Rafe didn't respond. "We're planning a joint exercise with the Chilean army. Lots of details to work out."

"I hear ya. Watch out for friendly fire."

Donovan chuckled as they clasped hands. In a war zone, friendly fire was sometimes the most dangerous because you didn't see it coming. Just as Lizbeth's death had blindsided Rafe.

"I should be around here for a couple of months. Call me if you need me," Donovan said. "For anything."

"I've got your number."

Donovan left by the front door. Rafe watched his friend jog down the street toward an old Jeep he'd failed to spot. In another time and place, that kind of carelessness would have gotten him killed.

Maybe it was time for him to throw in the towel here in Chile, face the demons that had been driving him for the past three years.

With a shake of his head, he turned away. He wasn't going anywhere. Except to Los Caballeros, a bar around the corner, a raucous place where the alcohol kept him numb and the noise kept his memories at bay. Memories that were still so sharp he could taste the blood in his mouth and the explosion of pain in his gut.

CHAPTER SEVEN

The wind at the airport whipped the hem of the shorter man's black jacket. His breath labored, rasping in his chest; his partner was nearly doubled over from the exertion of running after the American woman. A futile effort.

"Keep looking for her," he said, yanking his cell phone from his pocket and flipping it open. He punched in his boss's private number.

"*Sí.*"

"We lost her."

"What?" The man blurted out the word in a bark. "How in hell could she get away from the two of you?"

"There was a fire. In the confusion—"

"*¡Estúpido!* You should not have let her out of your sight!"

"*Sí, jefe.* She told us she had to go—"

"Listen to me, *mi amigo*. You must not allow that woman to leave Santiago. If she's not at the airport, check the bus terminal. Taxi stands. Hotels. Everyplace her brother was known to frequent. Find her and put her on a plane back to America. That is an order!"

The shorter man glanced frantically around the airport parking lot in the wild hope he could spot Taylor Travini, the blonde *puta* who was causing him so much trouble.

"Under no circumstances must she be allowed to reach Punta Arenas," his boss said. "If you fail me, your own life will be forfeited."

"If we find her and she will not go willingly? What then, *jefe?*"

"Then you must arrange to send her home in a box. *Comprende?*"

Yes, he understood. After today, it would be a pleasure to execute such an order.

CHAPTER EIGHT

Taylor drove through heavy traffic to a suburb northeast of Santiago and left the taxi parked and locked two blocks from the embassy, walking the rest of the way through a residential area.

Set back from the street and surrounded by a ten-foot fence, the embassy was built like a fortress, the brown-on-brown exterior architecturally uninspired. The American flag flying in the breeze and the spiffy U.S. Marine standing sentry duty at the gate were both reassuring, however.

Showing her passport, Taylor gained admission. In the spacious formal entry, with its sparse but tasteful decor, she felt severely underdressed wearing jeans and a T-shirt. Her mother, born to a prominent Italian family, had always been a stickler for propriety. Showing up at an embassy in anything less than a hat and gloves would have gone against the grain.

Despite the fact her mother had been dead for ten years, the lessons had been well-learned. Still, Taylor had never been that fussy about appearances. Now wasn't the time to begin. Before abandoning the taxi, she'd done what she could with a comb and lip gloss to give herself a semblance of respectability. The results would have to do.

After making multiple inquiries, she was ushered into the cubicle-sized office of a career government employee who looked as though he'd retired ten years ago—or at least had stopped working and no one had noticed. Dust an inch thick covered the stacks of files on his desk, as well as those that had spilled onto the floor. In small letters, his brass nameplate on the front edge of his desk read PETER PIPER PECKENBAUGH. It made one wonder what his parents had been thinking when they named the guy.

She took the one available chair and sat down. "I'd like to report a missing American citizen."

He stared at her through tiny oval glasses that didn't go well with his round face. The way he'd combed a few long strands of hair over his otherwise bald head didn't go well with anything.

"I assume you mean a citizen of the United States of America."

"Of course." Like, *duh?*

"In this part of the world, people are sensitive about the citizens of the United States claiming all of America for themselves. They will point out, with some pride, that they, too, are American. Albeit *South* American, but nonetheless—"

"It's my brother who is missing," Taylor inserted.

"—they are Americans. Chileans. Venezuelans. Brazilians. It is of interest to note that Canadians, who are also North Americans, go to great pains to separate themselves from those of us who originate from the

United States of America. We are not, as one might imagine, terribly popular in all parts of the world."

"I appreciate your lecture on world political geography, but I'm worried about my brother. We haven't heard from him for more than six weeks."

Behind the glasses that magnified his eyes several times over, Peckenbaugh blinked. "I see. How old is your brother, if I may inquire?"

"We both turned thirty last August. We're twins."

"Not identical, I gather."

"Um, no." She desperately wanted to roll her eyes but figured that would not sit well with Mr. Peckenbaugh. "Terry was on a nature photography trip. He's had some success in that business—"

"There isn't much wildlife in Santiago." He managed a faint smile. "Unless you count certain late-night establishments, which have acquired a reputation for a bit of anything goes, if you get my meaning."

Taylor did, and it wasn't funny. "Terry was interested in *penguins and elephant seals,* not nightlife. He was going to Patagonia—"

"Have you checked there?"

"Not yet. I stopped first at Hotel Magdalena where he was staying. I had hoped they'd tell me when he left and what his next stop would be. The last time I spoke with him, his plans hadn't firmed up yet. He was looking for a guide."

Peckenbaugh began to sort through dozens of slips of paper that filled one corner of his desk—messages that had to be a year old, given the tattered corners and faded pink forms. Finally he held up one that looked recent, peering at it through the bottom half of his glasses. "You're that Travini girl, aren't you?"

She bristled at being called a girl but let it pass. "Taylor Travini. From California."

"Yes. So I see." Setting the message chit aside, he lowered his narrow brows to look at her. "Ms. Travini, the United States of American does not offer asylum for drug dealers, even if they are our citizens."

"What? I'm not—" Trying hard not to lose her often volatile temper, she took a deep breath. "I assure you, Mr. Peckenbaugh, I am not now nor have I ever been a drug dealer. Or user. Someone planted a packet of cocaine—"

"American youngsters sit in that chair every day, young lady, and lie to me." His face began to turn red as though his blood pressure was rising. "Even my own son told me that same lie. That was before he died of an overdose in my arms."

Watching his eyes began to tear up, Taylor said, "I'm sorry for your loss, Mr. Peck—"

"I may not be doing you any favor, Ms. Travini, but I will not hold you until the local authorities arrive." Shoving back his swivel executive chair with some force, he stood. The movement caused the biggest pile of files to shake, and for a moment, the whole tower threatened to topple over. "I recommend you either return to the United States and enter a drug treatment program. That, or fade into the countryside if you insist upon remaining in Chile."

Taylor came to her feet, too. "You're not listening to me. I don't do drugs. What about my brother? He's missing! And besides, twice yesterday someone tried to kill me. I'm sorry about your son, but you can't just brush me off like this. Getting stabbed and practically run over is no small thing. It's . . . it's unAmerican! You're supposed to protect us."

The balding bureaucrat reached for the red phone that

was half buried under the files on his desk. "If I have to call security, I will be obliged to notify the Chilean authorities of your presence in the embassy. I suggest you leave now, Ms. Travini. For your own good."

Taylor wanted to argue. Hell, she wanted to leap across the desk and whap the stupid man upside the head. But that wasn't going to do her, or her brother, any good. She'd either be jailed or permanently evicted from the country. Then how would she ever pick up the trail to find Terry?

Her hands clenched into fists, she whirled and stalked out of the embassy. When she got home, she'd damn well make sure Mr. Peter Piper Peckenbaugh got in a peck of trouble over this with the State Department. If she had her way, his retirement pay would shrink to zipola.

But a voice inside her head contradicted that uncaring thought. Grief could change a person. Muddle their brain. Maybe she should give Peckenbaugh a little slack because of his son's death. She'd had to do that for her dad after her mother died. He'd loved Mama so much, he was never quite the same again. It was a love so deep, Taylor had always hoped she'd find a man who would someday care as much for her.

With a sigh, she considered her options.

If Terry had followed his plan, he would have flown to Punta Arenas in the south of the country before heading on to Tierra del Fuego. The local airline would have a record of his departure. Assuming she could get the airlines to reveal that information—Mutt and Jeff had left her plenty of money to use for bribes—she'd know when or if Terry had left Santiago.

The police were undoubtedly on the lookout for the stolen taxi by now. As a means of transportation, it had outlived its usefulness. She'd have to take a bus.

"You staying in town for a couple of days?" the Marine guarding the embassy asked after he gave her directions to the closest bus stop.

He was young, probably mid-twenties, and she smiled at him as she might a little brother. She wasn't generally flirtatious, and it always took her by surprise when a man hit on her. Oh, she knew she was attractive in a statuesque way that was often intimidating to men; she simply gave her appearance little thought, though. And the few relationships she'd had over the years had been tepid at best. She'd begun to believe she wouldn't ever meet a man who stirred her juices for more than a night or two. She'd adjusted to that reality with some regret—and moved on to focus her creative energy on making Travini Vineyards the most successful winery in northern California. She doubted this young marine would change her mind.

"I'm not sure yet," she said.

"Not many American girls traveling alone come through here. I know a couple of hot clubs in town with good music and drinks that aren't watered down. If you're interested, I could show you a good time." His ramrod-straight posture showed off his well-developed chest, and he turned slightly so she could get a good look at his corporal stripes. "I've got the evening free."

"Thanks. I appreciate the invitation. Maybe another time."

He looked so crestfallen, Taylor felt guilty for turning him down.

"Sure," he said. "Just call the embassy and leave a message for Skip."

Skip? Marines ought to be called Rock. Or maybe Hammer. A name that sounded tough.

"I'll do that." With a quick smile, she jogged off toward

46

the bus stop and felt his gaze following her until she turned the corner. Had the young man been ten years older, and she hadn't been worried about Terry, she might have taken Skip up on the invitation. Whatever the age, there was something very appealing about a man in uniform.

Riding a bus in any Latin American country was an adventure, particularly during rush hour. Although there was a very efficient subway system in Santiago, the embassy wasn't on one of the routes, nor did it go to the airport. Which left Taylor settling for second best.

She hopped onto one of the big yellow buses, this one so crammed with passengers she was stuck on the back step, unable to move all the way inside. Diesel fumes burned into her lungs, choking her and bringing tears to her eyes whenever the bus slowed. At ten miles an hour, the smell dissipated but the effort to hold on to the railing became more difficult as the bus jounced along. By comparison, the San Francisco cable cars with all their quaintness seemed like the world's greatest transportation system.

A tall, lanky man leaped onto the steps right behind her, straddling her with his feet on either side of hers. To her shock, he started to hump her as they got underway again. He forced the hard ridge of his arousal between her buttocks.

"*¿Es bueno, no?*" he announced with a throaty groan of pleasure.

"No." In disgust, Taylor rammed her elbow hard into his midsection and stomped her boot on his sandled foot. He grunted and fell off the bus.

Tires squealed behind her and horns blared.

She didn't bother to see if the pervert had safely avoided the oncoming cars.

¡El bastardo!

* * *

By the time she reached the airport, her hands were cramping from holding on so tightly and her legs were wobbly. She hadn't eaten anything since the dry sandwich in jail last night; she'd slept very little in the past forty-eight hours, and the strain was beginning to tell. The fog of fatigue muddled her brain.

Food first, she told herself as she passed the young Smokey the Bear security guards on duty at the terminal entrance. They didn't give her a second glance, which meant they hadn't been alerted to watch for an American woman who had escaped police custody that morning. Odd, really. If she were the cops, she would have put out an all-points bulletin.

Familiar food and lots of calories seemed the best choice to handle her hunger, so inside the terminal she ordered a hamburger, fries and a large Coke at Gatsby's. Gourmet, it wasn't. But she needed a jolt to her blood-sugar level in a hurry.

She picked an inconspicuous table off to the side, wolfed down half the burger, then downed a big swig of Coke. Most of the travelers were businessmen in coats and ties, carrying briefcases or laptop computers. There were families traveling together, the children excited to be going on a trip. Taylor remembered her father taking the whole family to Italy, to the village where his parents had been raised. She's been eight years old and unable to sleep for days, she been so full of anticipation.

As she looked around now, everything seemed normal. Life was good!

Until she noticed two men in black leather jackets, scruffy beards and muddy boots patrolling the concourse, methodically checking out every passenger, stopping every blonde female. Asking questions.

Shit!

The pair didn't look like cops to Taylor. They looked like something far more malevolent that sent a spurt of acid to her stomach.

She couldn't tell for sure if they were looking for her, but she couldn't take the chance of landing back in jail either. Or ending up in a place darker and more dangerous than a prison cell.

Only a sense of self-preservation made her think that's what those two men had in store for her. Like a wild animal chased to ground, she decided to rely on her instincts. Fighting wasn't an option. She'd have to flee.

Taking one last gulp of Coke, she slipped behind the Gatsby's counter. The line waiting for service was long. All of the employees were occupied with their respective duties, and no one seemed to notice as she ducked past racks of buns toward the back of the kitchen area. The place stank of French fries and old grease, and the humidity level was several notches higher than outside. She edged past a trash can filled with wilted lettuce and soggy buns. Not gagging became a high priority. Along with escape.

Her fear that this would be a dead end had been well founded. There was no exit. Apparently deliveries came through the front of the terminal. Now she was trapped in the back with no way out except past the two predators who were very likely looking for her. Maybe she'd stretched her luck as far as it would go.

But if she surrendered, she'd never find out what had happened to Terry. She'd looked after him since they were toddlers. She couldn't quit on him now, any more than he'd give up on her if their roles were reversed.

But dammit, she had no idea why men, who didn't remotely resemble your average cops, would be prowling around the airport scrutinizing blondes unless they were looking for her.

She found what appeared to be an employee locker room and spotted a white uniform shirt hanging on a hook. She pulled it on over her T-shirt. The fit wasn't great but it would do. Grabbing a matching cap from a nearby shelf, she curled her braid around the top of her head and covered it with the hat to hold her hair in place.

Brazen sometimes worked when planning failed. She'd simply hide in plain sight.

With her chin held high, she strode out of the kitchen, past the counter and into the main terminal corridor. No one stopped her. She didn't look right or left. Acting like she belonged improved her chances to escape, or so she told herself. If the baddies were going to nail her, she'd done all she could.

The escalator took her down to the main concourse, which seemed impossibly long. The fine hairs on the back of her neck stood rigidly at attention. At one point, a child dashed away from his mother and crashed into Taylor's legs, screaming when he fell to his knees. All she could do was right the youngster so he was steady on his feet, and then keep moving. Feeling like she had a target on her back, she had to dodge around a vendor selling cheap gold jewelry. He didn't view her as a potential customer and ignored her.

Questions bounced through her mind like grapes tumbling into a wine press. Where were those two goons? Was she the one they were after? Did they have something to do with Terry's disappearance?

Finally, she stepped out of the building into early twilight. The day's heat had ebbed only slightly. Lights blazed on the side of the terminal and lit up the surrounding parking lot. People hurried by without giving her a second look.

She wouldn't be catching any airline flight today, and her sense of frustration had her balling her fists. Unlike the hurdle races she ran in high school, in the rest of her life she hated people putting obstacles in her way. Generally, she found a way to overcome them.

For the first time since she arrived in Chile, fate seemed to be on her side. A bus headed back into Santiago idled at the curb. Only a few passengers were on board.

Digging some pesos out of her waistpack, she climbed into the bus, handed the money to the driver and found a seat by herself on the side away from the airline terminal. She scrunched down to make herself appear short.

As the bus pulled away from the curb, she noticed the two scruffy strangers come out of the building. They looked both ways, one of them pulling his jacket aside to reveal a gun tucked into his waistband. The taller of the two said something to a passing airport security guard. Taylor slid all the way down out of sight and sent up a little prayer of thanksgiving.

Her gratitude didn't last long, however. How in the name of heaven was she going to find Terry? The airline wouldn't give her any information about flight manifests over the phone. The embassy wouldn't help. Forget the local cops. They'd either lock her up or send her home. She didn't like either choice.

Rubbing her temples against a niggling headache, she tried to think about the last conversation she'd had with her brother. He'd stayed in Santiago a few days longer than he had anticipated. He'd been making plans to find

51

a guide to lead him through the glacier-filled area of Patagonia to the penguin birthing grounds. He'd been so excited.

And he'd found a local bar where he'd made friends.

She sat up straight in her seat. The name of the place was something about Caballeros.

Taberna de los Caballeros!

Grimly, she decided that would be her next stop. Assuming she could find the place.

When the bus pulled into the main station in the city, she shrugged out of her Gatsby's uniform and ditched the dorky little cap. Still, it didn't quite free her from the scent of soggy bread and old grease. *Yuck!*

As she swung down from the bus, her heart nearly stopped. There on the platform—looking the other way, thank God—stood one of the leather-jacketed men she'd spotted at the airport.

At a fast walk, she headed in the opposite direction and hailed the first taxi she spotted.

CHAPTER NINE

Rafe found a table opposite the bar, ordered a beer and a ham sandwich from Lola, the buxom Taberna waitress, then settled down to brood over his visit from Donovan.

You can run but you can't hide.

Rafe swore under his breath. Donovan had no idea how much effort Rafe expended to avoid getting involved with other people and their problems. Or how staunchly he resisted returning to the States and all the memories he'd have to confront there.

He glanced around the bar. On a Friday night it was busy. There were lots of regulars on hand, including the usual assortment of hookers searching for a guy with a boner and a few pesos to spare. The talk was loud and mostly friendly, until somebody got drunk.

After Rafe's first few visits to Los Caballeros, both the hookers and the regulars left him alone. Which was exactly what he wanted. The waitresses knew him, though. And they liked how he tipped.

He'd just finished his sandwich and washed it down with the last of the beer when the door to the pub opened one more time. He glanced at the newcomer and was slammed by a surge of lust like he hadn't experienced in years.

She was tall and leggy, with a figure that screamed for sweaty sheets and long, hot nights. The cut of her jeans would have marked her as an American even if her blonde hair pulled back into a single braid hadn't. She hesitated a moment at the doorway, probably to let her eyes adjust to the dim light and smoke-filled room, then strode across to the bar like she owned the place.

This woman was no demure Southern belle who made a man feel like she needed him. Instead, she was so self-assured, so gutsy, she'd walked into a seedy bar in a foreign country as though it was a club in L.A. He could almost feel her animal heat. Her pheromones overpowered the stink of stale beer and unwashed bodies. But she wasn't a hooker, of that he was sure. She didn't even seem aware that she was out of place. Or that every man in the bar was lusting after her.

So what the hell was she doing here?

CHAPTER TEN

Taylor approached the crowded bar, men sitting shoulder-to-shoulder, most of them drinking Royal beer on tap. Before she could speak, a slight man with greasy hair and crooked teeth eased off his stool and offered her the seat.

"*Gracias,*" she said with a smile. His neighbor, whose face looked like that of a boxer who had lost too many fights, shifted a bit to make room for her. From down the row of drinkers, she heard a distinctly feminine hiss of disapproval. She glanced into the mirror behind the bar. Only then did she fully realize the clientele was mostly men. The few women in the bar were flaunting their wares, their boobs pretty much flopping out of their low-cut blouses. Their skirts barely covered their tushes. *Hookers.* She wished she could tell them the johns were all theirs; she wasn't planning to go into competition.

The bartender arrived at her end of the bar. "*¿Señorita?*"

"Vino blanco," she said. In Spanish she added, "A local chardonnay, if you have one." Terry had told her Chilean wines were excellent, even those sold in neighborhood bars. After the past two days, she was more than ready to try one. If she'd traveled here with her brother, they might have stopped at a vineyard or two and taken home cuttings to try in California soil. But not this time.

The bartender returned, placing the glass of wine on the counter. Taylor took out a ten-thousand peso note and slid it to him, many times more than the price of the drink. He raised his brows as she took her first sip. Crisp. On the dry side. Slightly fruity. Very pleasant.

She set the glass down again and pulled a snapshot of Terry from her fanny pack, placing it on top of the peso note. "I'm looking for someone. My brother. I believe he was in here several times. Do you remember him?"

The bartender's gaze darted furtively to the big man next to her, then across the room to scan the rest of his patrons.

He leaned toward her, whispering, "Señorita, it is not always a good thing to ask questions in a place like this."

She took several more notes from her stash of funds but didn't place them on the bar. Bribery, she'd learned in her travels, was an art form. "I want to know that he's all right. If you can help me—"

He shook his head vigorously. "I do not remember this man you seek." He snatched the original note from the bar and returned to his other customers, leaving Terry's picture where she'd placed it.

The man was frightened, Taylor realized, but she had no idea why. Terry wasn't the sort who got himself into trouble. He was quiet, but friendly. A keen observer. He spoke the local language as well as she did and was used to traveling in all sorts of out of the way places, never so much as getting into an argument. What on earth had gone wrong this time?

Swiveling on her stool, she glanced around the bar in search of whatever—or whomever—was frightening the bartender. As she scanned the room, she was snared by a pair of cold, dark eyes. Drawn to them like a bee to a spring blossom. She sucked in a quick breath.

Sitting alone, he appeared relaxed. But Taylor sensed that was an illusion. He had shoulders muscled with the strength of iron that only came from constant physical exertion. Beneath his days-old beard, she detected an alertness, an intelligence that wasn't easily camouflaged. He watched her with a look that was just this side of predatory, yet she didn't feel threatened.

Given the European ancestry of most Chileans, he could have been a local out for a quick beer. But given the way he held himself, the aura of self-assurance, she pegged him as an American, despite the fatigues she recognized as belonging to the local army.

Call it chemistry or biology—or just as likely the lack of sleep—but she felt captivated by this stranger in a way that couldn't be denied.

"Señorita, perhaps I can be of service," the slender man who had given up his bar stool said to her.

Although the eye contact she'd made with the stranger across the room had lasted only seconds, it had seemed like minutes. She found it difficult to drag her gaze away to respond to the man next to her.

"I know many people in this town, señorita. If I were allowed to see the picture?"

"Ah, y-yes . . . ," she stammered, turning back to the bar and her neighbor. "He's my brother. Do you recall seeing him here?"

The tip of his cigarette dangled from his narrow lips, a half-inch of ash threatening to drop into his beer. "It is hard to tell. The light is so poor here. Perhaps if you were to come back to my room. I have some good wine and we could ask my amigos. They might know him."

Going anywhere with this dude sounded like a great way to get mugged. Or worse. "I don't think so. Thanks, anyway. I'm sure I'll find someone who remembers—"

Glancing over her shoulder, she looked for the stranger who had so affected her. His chair was empty. He'd left.

Automatically, her gaze swung to the doorway, and her breath lodged in her lungs. Mutt and Jeff were standing there, the two armed guards who had taken her to the airport. They were still wearing their long, black-leather jackets to conceal their weapons, and one of them had a cell phone to his ear.

Both were looking across the room directly at her as if they had been standing there for some time.

"*Shit,*" she muttered under her breath. She wasn't going to let these two goons prevent her from finding Terry. But ducking away from them here wasn't going to be as easy as it had been at the airport. Once burned, they weren't going to let her out of their sight a second time.

She leaned closer to the guy standing next to her and let her breast brush against his arm. "Señor, there are two men by the doorway. One of them is my uncle Raoul. If he catches me, he will make me go home with him and will beat me . . . and . . . and . . ." She forced a tearful quaver into her voice, suggesting she'd suffer even more unpleasant things than a beating. "If you will distract him for just a minute, I will leave by the back way and meet you at Hotel Magdalena. We can visit in my room."

Machismo was alive and well in Chile. Or maybe the guy was simply horny. He puffed out his chest like a boy pigeon strutting around the local park trying to impress a would-be mate.

"It will be my pleasure to discuss the situation with your uncle, chiquita." He winked and trotted off to confront Uncle Raoul.

As soon as he was between Taylor and the goons, she slipped off her bar stool and made a beeline for the rear exit. Ducking past a dark curtain, she hurried down a dimly lit hallway. A man loomed in her path, and she drew up short. She gasped in recognition—the stranger with the dark, penetrating eyes and a five o'clock shadow she'd spotted across the room. His hand closed firmly around her arm.

"You've either been keeping bad company, lady," he said in a low, smooth baritone that hinted at southern roots, "or there are a lot of mean hombres who don't like you asking questions."

"Let me go!" she demanded in a harsh whisper. Talk about leaping from the frying pan into the fire! Though he wasn't actually hurting her, the stranger's grip was like steel, the callouses on his palm abrading her tender flesh.

"You don't want to go back in there, honey. Those guys are packing heavy iron."

"And there is some reason why I should trust *you?*"

One of her former guards brushed aside the curtain and stepped into the hallway. She spotted the metallic glint of a gun in his hand. A long gun with a silencer on the end.

"That looks like a pretty good reason to me," the stranger said as he pushed her toward the rear exit.

Just as he opened the door, shoving her through, she heard the quiet *whup* of the gun and a bullet splintered the doorjamb inches from Taylor's head.

CHAPTER ELEVEN

The alley in back of Los Caballeros was as dark as the inside of a wine cask.

Her rescuer propelled Taylor past piles of smelly rubbish. They splashed through potholes filled with water and God knew what else. Their frantic pace startled an animal rooting in the garbage. The creature darted in front of them—a scrawny dog, ribs showing. One of the dozens of stray dogs she'd seen in the city since she arrived. Taylor stumbled, almost falling to her knees. The stranger's firm grip on her arm kept her upright, and they ran on.

Rounding a corner, they headed down another dank alley. Dark buildings loomed on either side of them. The scent of rotting garbage came in waves on the lingering heat radiating from masonry walls.

"Where are we going?" Taylor asked, beginning to gasp for air. Her boots pounded on the hard-packed dirt and her legs pumped as she strained to keep up with the stranger.

"Save your breath, honey. They're still on our tail."

Great! How did he know that? She couldn't hear anything except her own footsteps and those of the man running beside her. And the thundering of her heart. There'd been no more bullets zinging past her head, thank God!

She also noticed her stranger hadn't yet broken a sweat. His breathing was as easy as if he were out for a lazy morning stroll intending to stop for a cup of coffee at Starbucks. Obviously she'd been spending way too much time at the computer and not nearly enough staying in shape. But who would have thought she'd be chased around South America by two burly guys in black coats with guns?

They reached a dead end. A ten-foot high cyclone fence blocked their way.

"Up and over, sweetheart."

She didn't stop to argue. Grabbing hold of the fence, she started up. The next thing she knew, the stranger's hand was on her butt, shoving her up. For an instant, she was electrifyingly aware of the shape of his palm, the press of his fingers. Then she was over the top of the fence, dropping to the ground on the other side.

As lightly as an acrobat, he landed on his feet next to her. "You okay?"

She wasn't at all sure. He appeared unfazed by their brief but intimate encounter. Had she imagined her sensual reaction? Or was it fear-driven adrenaline, not libido, that had caused the sensation?

She swallowed hard. If he could ignore the tantalizing way he'd touched her, so could she. "I'm fine."

"I've got a couple of more tricks up my sleeve that are sure to shake our bad guys loose. Then I want to know why those two mobsters are after you."

"Mobsters?"

He didn't elaborate. Instead, he urged her down yet another back alley, this one past small industrial buildings. They crossed a street that was empty of traffic, then ducked into a doorway, stepping back into the deepest shadows of the alcove. They stood with shoulders nearly touching, waiting and listening to the quiet sound of the breeze whispering past the row of aging structures. The air carried with it the scent of dust, old motor oil and a pleasant masculine musk that could only be described as the essence of the stranger beside her. Sexy as hell!

Taylor was thoroughly disoriented by all the turns they'd taken. The sounds of the city were subdued. None of the big office buildings or pre-fab apartment complexes prevalent in the modern downtown section of Santiago were visible. She was lost. There wasn't a soul around in this deserted industrial area to ask for help.

Despite the warm night air, she shivered a little. If she had put her trust in the wrong man, she could be in big trouble.

"I think we're clear." The stranger visibly relaxed, although he remained alert. "You want to tell me now why the local Mafia has taken an interest in you?"

"I don't know anything about Mafia," she gasped. "Those two guys are cops."

"I don't think so. Those black jackets are the drug lords' uniform of choice around here. Meant to intimidate the innocent and scare the hell out of the guilty."

"Whoever they are, it's working." This guy was intimidating, too. Big and strong and very intense, his raven-black brows were lowered in concentration, his eyes narrowed. Not the kind of man she'd want to meet alone in a dark alley. In this case, she'd not only met him but run through alleys with him. And still she couldn't quite get over a surprising hum of sexual awareness thrumming through her veins.

"So tell me why you think the cops would be after you."

"Look . . ." She frowned. "Do you have a name?" If he planned to ravish her or chop her into little pieces, she wanted to know who she was dealing with.

"Maguire. Rafe Maguire."

"Taylor Travini," she said in return. "I arrived in Santiago yesterday morning looking for my brother. Before I could even get my bearings, a hit-and-run driver tried to kill me and then someone planted a couple of ounces of cocaine in my backpack. I spent a night in a jail cell with fifteen women and six bunks. Which was even less fun after somebody decided to stab me." Unconsciously she rubbed at the dull ache in her upper left arm. "Then those two goons took me to the airport to get me out of the country. I didn't want to go, not till I find my brother."

"Interesting story." His lips twitched ever so slightly in disbelief.

"You can laugh all you want, but every word I told you is true. And I certainly appreciate your helping me escape. But now, if you'll just point me in the direction of downtown, I'll be on my way."

"Not a good idea, Legs."

Her brows shot up. *"Legs?"*

He shrugged noncommittally, refusing to apologize or explain. But she knew from the glint in his eyes that her long legs weren't the only thing that had attracted his attention. She supposed she should be grateful he hadn't called her "sweet cheeks."

To her dismay, Taylor felt the heat of a blush rush up her neck and flush her face. Her height certainly didn't intimidate this guy. He was a good two inches taller than her five-eleven, which meant they were practically eye-to-eye. And lip-to-lip.

She suspected Rafe Maguire rarely backed off from anyone, man or woman. And he'd called her *Legs*.

"You're in pretty good shape, too," he added. "Not top condition, but not bad for a woman."

She bristled at that and had the urge to pop him one, just to prove what kind of condition she was in. Which wouldn't exactly be a polite way of showing her gratitude for his help. Continuing their conversation wouldn't do anything to help her find Terry, either. That was her priority.

So she stalked off down the street instead. He didn't follow her.

"Where do you think you're going?" he called, after she had taken a dozen paces.

"To find a hotel and crash. I'm beat."

"You're going the wrong way."

She halted. Turning, she hooked her wrist on her hip. "I forgot to leave a trail of bread crumbs so I can find my way back to civilization. You going to give me a clue? Or make me wander around until somebody shows up who is a little more accommodating?"

"I'll accommodate you," he said with a little too much innuendo. "At my place. You can crash there." He gestured directly across the street to a building that housed an auto repair shop on the ground floor, an apartment upstairs. "I'll even let you have the bed. I'll sleep on the couch."

"Your generosity is overwhelming." But his offer really was tempting. Now that she'd had a moment to think about it, she was bone weary.

He sauntered across the street toward his building. "Look at it this way. Whether those two goons are cops or local drug runners, you have ticked them off big time. They aren't going to stop looking for you anytime soon, and you can bet your pretty little behind that they'll be checking every hotel in town. So you might as well give them some time to cool off. They aren't likely to come looking for you at my digs." He stopped at the foot of the stairs waiting for her decision.

She hesitated. For her own peace of mind, she'd be better off at an impersonal hotel, not in the lair of a man who made her excruciatingly aware of her femininity—and a vulnerability she didn't care to admit.

She started across the street toward him. "I hope your accommodations are Auto Club approved."

He laughed, a low rough sound that bored holes through every bit of her reserve and raised her temperature by several degrees. Then she followed him up the stairs to his apartment.

CHAPTER TWELVE

Rafe hadn't considered his apartment through another person's eyes for a long time. Donovan's visit hadn't mattered. Now, with Taylor Travini in his living room, he gave the place a critical once-over.

The furniture was mismatched, the spindly tables sporting stained circles left by cold bottles of beer by a dozen prior tenants, the upholstery on the couch and chair wearing through in places. There weren't any pictures on the walls, no personal touches anywhere. It was as sterile and uninteresting as the day he'd rented the place. A bachelor pad fully worthy of the name.

He wasn't sure what impulse had made him bring her here; he'd only known the two men at the bar had meant her harm. He couldn't let that happen. Not on his watch.

Standing in the middle of the room, Taylor made a full turn. "Remind me to get the name of your decorator—so I can cross her off my list."

"I'm not here much."

"I can understand that." She lifted her nicely arched

brows, the same honey-blonde shade as her hair. "Where do you spend your time?"

"I do a little work for the Chilean army."

"Thus your khaki fashion statement?" Her gaze skimmed over his military fatigues from collar to jungle boots.

"My interior decorator moonlights as a fashion designer. You want anything to drink? Something to eat?"

Right on cue, her stomach rumbled. "That wasn't a ladylike answer, but it was an honest one. I had half a burger this afternoon. Last night they fed me a tasteless chicken sandwich in jail, and I had to wrestle some behemoth to get that."

"You win?"

She grinned. "Black belt in karate."

God, she was some strong woman! Physically and mentally. And smooth as silk. A real lady beneath that long, tall, sexy exterior.

But not his type, he reminded himself. He liked 'em small and shapely. Soft to the touch. Pliable. Like Lizbeth.

He motioned toward the couch. "Take a load off, and I'll see what I can stir up." Which was going to take some fast footwork, given his chronically empty refrigerator.

He found some eggs, which he scrambled with a little salami that hadn't yet turned green. He grated some cheese into the mixture and toasted a couple of slices of bread from the loaf he had in the freezer. He hoped she wasn't into gourmet fare because it wasn't gonna happen here. The coffee he brewed was dark and rich. That should make up for the lack of other epicurean delights.

Returning to the living room, he found her sitting on the couch, her chin on her chest, sound asleep.

"Hey, Legs," he said softly. "You better eat something or you won't be able to keep up with me."

She started and opened her eyes. An incredible shade of pale green, he realized. Like the top of a wave as it crashed onto the beach, the sun shining through the crest.

"Sorry," she said. "I didn't mean to fall asleep."

"No apology necessary." He handed her the plate of toast and eggs, then set the coffee mug on the scarred end table.

Hauling in a straight-back chair from the kitchen, he turned it around, straddled it and rested his arms on the back while he watched her dig into her meal. There was no phoniness about her. No coyness. She'd said she was hungry, and she ate like she meant it, relishing each bite in a sensual way that gave him ideas that were totally inappropriate under the circumstances.

He waited until she slowed down a bit before questioning her.

"Tell me about this brother you're looking for," he said.

She took a sip of coffee, then leaned back, studying him before she related her story.

As she proceeded to talk about her missing twin brother, her love and concern were obvious. Rafe experienced a twinge of envy. Raised an only child by a stressed-out mother and a mostly absent military father, he'd lacked the role models to teach him to care about others. Only when he'd met Lizbeth had he gained an understanding of what love really meant.

"Maybe Terry changed his mind and went to a different hotel," he suggested when she told him how the hotel manager claimed her brother had never been registered. "Magdalena doesn't attract many tourists."

"I talked to Terry twice at the hotel, the last time six weeks ago. I know he was there."

Rafe considered the possibilities, most of them not good. "Maybe he's already in Patagonia snapping his pictures."

"My brother has always been very faithful about checking in at home from wherever he is—we've both made a practice of that whenever we've traveled. He would have let me know if he was leaving Santiago. In any case, there should have been a record of him being at the hotel."

"Communication can be tough from that far south, in Patagonia and Tierra del Fuego. Cell phones don't exactly work there."

"He would have found a way to let me know he's okay."

Rafe had to respect her steadfastness when it came to her brother. "Have you talked to the local police?"

Her story got even more harrowing, and Rafe could do nothing but admire the way she'd handled herself, including her escape from the mafia goons. Damned hard to not be impressed with a woman who could hotwire a car.

"You sure you didn't bring that cocaine into the country, um, accidentally? It might have been left over from—"

"I've never, ever used drugs, Rafe. It would ruin my ability to properly taste wine."

He did a double take and frowned. "You're a discriminating wino?"

"For heaven's sake, no." Despite her difficult experience, she laughed lightly, a sound as bright and refreshing as a trickling waterfall on a blistering hot day. "My family owns Travini Vineyards in Sonoma, California.

We bottle some of the finest wines in the state. My palate isn't as educated as my father's, but I can still tell a quality chardonnay from swill."

"How about your brother? Is wine-making his business, too?"

A flash of emotion—regret or anger—turned her eyes a deeper shade of green. "My father is a bit old-fashioned. He believes the vineyard as well as the Travini name should be passed from father to son."

"But Terry isn't all that keen on the idea?"

"My brother will make a superb vintner," she said with passion—but less believably than her declaration of innocence.

Getting up, Rafe took her plate to the kitchen and returned with the pot of coffee, topping off her mug.

"Could your brother have gotten involved in the local drug trade somehow?" he asked. That would explain the mafia's interest.

"He doesn't use drugs any more than I do. But I suppose he might have stumbled onto something illegal. He didn't say anything to me about it, though."

The floor lamp cast a circle of golden light over Taylor as she sat at the end of the couch. Her hair gleamed with highlights, and Rafe wished he could loosen her braid, let her hair tumble down around her shoulders, comb his fingers through the strands to test their weight and silkiness. He pictured her above him, leaning over his naked body as they made love, her long hair caressing his bare chest—

With an effort, he crushed the thought.

"You're something else, Legs. You would have made a helluva Army Ranger."

Curious, she cocked her head. "Is that what you are?"

"Was. I resigned a couple of years ago." Three, to be

more exact. "It's getting late," he said, not wanting to pursue the subject further. "The bedroom's down the hall on your right, the bathroom's at the end. Help yourself to whatever you need. We'll talk more in the morning."

She stood and yawned again. "What I'd really like is a shower, if you don't mind. I feel grimy and—"

"Sure. Towels are in the cupboard."

"Maybe you've got an old T-shirt I could sleep in? Mutt and Jeff kept my backpack, and these clothes are all—"

"Mutt and Jeff?"

"The two goons who were after me."

He nodded. "I'll get you something."

The mental image of her in his shower made his groin ache and dogged his steps to the bedroom. God, it wasn't like she'd be the first woman to ever take a shower at his place. Or sleep in his bed, for that matter. But in the past he'd slept *with* his female houseguests.

Which wasn't going to happen this time. His libido would just have to shut the fuck up. So what if it had been months since he'd had a woman? And then only because a man needed release once in a while. The women he dated understood that. It was part of the deal. They had a mutually satisfying night and moved on. That's how it had to be with Rafe.

He doubted Taylor would understand. Or be the type to participate in a one-night stand. Besides, with her brother missing, she had other things on her mind. Not a quick tumble in bed.

He returned to the living room with an old khaki T-shirt and a fresh towel from the bathroom.

"Take your time," he said. "I'll clean up the kitchen and flake out on the couch when I'm done."

She met his gaze straight on. "I don't know how to thank you for—"

71

"We'll talk tomorrow." He knew the perfect way for her to show her appreciation, but he wasn't going to ask.

While she showered, Rafe washed the few dishes he'd dirtied and put them away. The water pipes groaned in a way that sounded a whole lot like a woman in the throes of great sex. As he listened, he envisioned the splash of warm liquid flowing over Taylor's shoulders and gliding down her full breasts to bead on her nipples. He imagined soaping her athletic body, rubbing his hands over her smooth back, measuring her slender waist and following the womanly curve of her hips. And then, one by one, he'd run his palms over her thighs and calves before letting his hand slip between her legs. She'd be moist and ready—

He slammed off the flowing water in the sink along with the uninvited images of Taylor in his shower.

Her story sounded legitimate enough. Somebody was certainly after her. But the local mobsters didn't go after a woman—a tourist, at that—without some reason. Things had changed for the better in Chile since the days of General Pinochet's dictatorship. The economy was flourishing, at least compared to most South American countries. Ordinary people weren't victimized as a rule. But there was a drug culture fed by greed, and pockets of rebels in remote regions. Neighboring countries sometimes spilled their problems into Chile. Still, it seemed unlikely either group would set out to kill Taylor on her first day in the country. Nobody made enemies that fast.

Whatever was going on, she'd be better off to go back home. Let the authorities, either here or in the States, deal with her missing brother.

Tomorrow he'd encourage her to either let him get

Donovan to intervene on her behalf with the government, or he'd insist she get on a plane out of town.

Later, when he decided Taylor had settled down for the night in his bedroom, Rafe ventured down the hallway. In the bathroom he discovered she'd washed out a few things. A tantalizing pair of white silk bikini underpants hung draped over the shower curtain along with her equally tempting bra.

Deliberately he fingered the smooth fabric of her undies, both innocent and provocative at the same time. He suspected Taylor was like that—filled with contradictions. Strong yet elementally feminine. A woman difficult to categorize.

He dropped his hand to his side.

Sending her back to the States as soon as possible would be the smartest thing he could do. For both of them.

CHAPTER THIRTEEN

The next morning, Rafe poured Taylor a cup of coffee and carefully explained that he would get her safely on a plane to the States, even if it took a contingent of Chilean Army Rangers to do it.

"I don't need a keeper, Rafe. Or a guardian angel. I can take care of myself."

"Right," he drawled. "Like you were so in control when those two hit men were after you last night."

"By now they've lost interest in me. Surely they have other things to do with their time than to chase me all around Santiago."

Rafe figured he'd be more persuasive if Taylor hadn't been standing in his minuscule kitchen, a mere two feet from him. Her honey-blonde hair hung loose past her shoulders and was softly mussed from sleep. She was wearing her jeans and the T-shirt he'd loaned her last night, her feet bare on the shabby linoleum floor. It was pretty damn obvious she wasn't wearing a bra, which was driving him nuts. Beneath the soft cotton fabric, her nipples were enticing nubs that practically cried out to be touched. He'd been wondering if she'd retrieved her silky undies from the bathroom—and hoping she hadn't. Which wasn't something he should be thinking about at all. Her safety was his number one priority.

"Come on, Legs," he said as reasonably as he could, trying to keep his gaze above her neck. "You know they'll be looking for you at the airport. You'll be dead meat if you show up there again."

"I need to know if Terry flew to Punta Arenas. If he did, I'll get on a plane and leave town. Mutt and Jeff and their friends will be glad to see me go."

"Only if you leave the country, not just Santiago."

Two slices of bread popped up in the toaster. In a graceful movement, Taylor snared them, then slathered butter across the toast. She took the first bite with the same relish she'd eaten his makeshift dinner last night. There was something carnal about her enjoyment of the elemental act of eating, and he had to wonder if she'd attack other physical activities with equal zest.

The thought sent a message directly to his crotch that was hard to ignore. Though he tried. *Hard* being the operative word.

Outside, morning traffic had picked up on the street, creating a hum of engines accented by the impatient honk of horns. Downstairs, his neighbor Igor had rolled up the door to his garage and begun work pounding out a dent in some hapless fender or other wounded auto body part.

"If I wear your shirt and borrow a hat, no one will recognize me," she said. "I'll be fine."

A muscle ticked in Rafe's jaw. "Sweetheart, you look so *norteamericana*, you scream 'Stars and Stripes.' A five-year-old could spot you from the end of the runway."

"Look, I appreciate your concern—and your help—

75

but you might as well save your breath. I have no intention of going home and telling my father that I wimped out on my brother."

"Even if it costs you your life?"

Her green eyes narrowed on him. "I have to do this, Rafe. It's my brother's life that may be in jeopardy." She ate the last piece of her toast with a finality that left little room for argument.

Rafe considered calling Donovan or using his military connections to check passenger lists in recent weeks. But he didn't like to use his influence and, since he didn't understand the situation with her brother and the local mafia, his raising flags might bring down more heat on Taylor. Not a risk he was willing to take.

He would have paced the floor but the kitchen was too small. She had him trapped, wedged into a corner of his own making. He'd foolishly invited her into his private world, let her past a door he rarely opened for anyone. She wasn't going to give up on finding her brother, and Rafe couldn't let her go on her own.

Which meant he was going to have to leave the relative comfort of his solitary life. At least until he could get Taylor on a plane back to the States, with or without Terry. He didn't much care either way.

"How'd you happen to visit Los Caballeros last night?" he asked.

She finished draining the coffee from her mug. "Terry mentioned the place to me. I thought someone might have remembered him and have some idea of his plans. Do you hang out there much?"

"When I'm in town." *And can't stand my own company,* he thought.

"Wait a minute. Maybe you'll recognize his picture. I

should have thought . . ." She set the mug on the counter and headed toward the bedroom.

Struggling against a growing press of claustrophobia, Rafe escaped into the living room. His apartment had never seemed so small, the walls and the outside world impinging on the life he'd made for himself. *Without Lizbeth.*

"Here it is." Taylor burst back into the room with an energy that seemed unstoppable, like a desert dust storm determined to envelop everything in its path.

He took the snapshot from her hand and had to drag his gaze away from her hopeful expression. She was so darn eager, so determined that everything would be all right. That she'd find her brother safe and sound. He hated like hell the gut feeling he had—that brother Terry might have run into more trouble than he could handle.

"Do you recognize him?" she asked.

A slender young man smiled up at Rafe from the photo. His coloring was the same fair shade as Taylor's but his face was narrower, his jaw slightly weak. His eyes didn't light with the same fire of purpose that Taylor's did. In comparison to Taylor's undeniable vitality, her brother seemed almost fragile. No wonder she acted like the guy couldn't take care of himself.

Rafe shook his head. "I've been out of town for six weeks on training maneuvers. I don't remember seeing him before that."

"Well . . . it was worth a shot."

Standing beside Rafe, their shoulders just brushing, the fresh scent of her hair teasing his nostrils, she gazed fondly at the image of her brother. "Once when we were about ten, we were hiking in the coastal redwoods. I'd gotten out ahead and Dad was right behind me. When we finally realized Terry wasn't with us anymore, we hiked back to the trailhead without finding any sign of him. Dad was fit to be tied. Said if I hadn't run off so fast, Terry wouldn't have gotten lost."

She looked off into the distance as though reliving the moment, and a tiny vee formed between her brows. "About an hour later, Terry showed up, happy as a clam. He'd rounded up every slimy, yellow banana slug in a two-square mile area and was going to become the world's greatest slug expert."

"Did your Dad apologize for blaming you?" Rafe asked softly.

"Well, no . . ." She blinked, apparently startled to find herself thousands of miles and twenty years past that incident, her father's behavior questioned by implication. "We were both so glad Terry was still in one piece, nobody worried about why he'd gone off on his own."

Which meant, in Rafe's view, that Taylor's father was a jerk. A ten-year-old girl shouldn't be held responsible for the stupid actions of her brother.

Neither should a thirty-year-old woman. And she didn't seem to realize her father was shafting her again.

"When Terry shows up this time," she said with a forced laugh, "I'm going to tie him to a very short leash. Meanwhile, I'm going to get dressed and head out to the airport. I can't thank you enough for—"

"I'm going with you."

She froze in midsentence. "You're what?"

"I'm going to take you to the airport. If we find out your brother flew to Punta Arenas, great. I'll see you off on the next flight. If not, I'll put you on a plane back to the States."

Her eyebrows flattened into a straight line. "In case you've forgotten, a couple of other schmucks tried shipping me back to the States. It didn't work out the way they'd planned."

"Yeah, but I'm a helluva lot smarter than they are." Or so he hoped.

CHAPTER FOURTEEN

Taylor's objections landed on deaf ears. Rafe was stubborn and opinionated, much like her father. Apparently he didn't think a woman could tie her own shoelaces without a man's help. Or make her own decisions.

A half hour later, as they clattered down the stairs from his apartment to the busy street below, she was still silently fuming. If he wanted to hang out with her because he had an urge to travel, she wouldn't mind the company. It was his high-handed arrogance she objected to. She'd gotten along just fine for thirty years without Rafe. Until last night, of course. And however much she might find him attractive, she could do without him and the distraction. She was going to find her brother. Whatever it took.

Rafe waved to a gaunt mechanic in the shop beneath his apartment. The leathery man wielded a small sledgehammer as though determined to reproduce a demolition derby in his own garage. The fender under attack bounced with each stroke of the hammer, and a skinny brown dog of indeterminate breed sleeping near the doorway wagged his tail once in a lazy greeting.

"*Hola, Igor. ¿Como estas?*" Rafe asked his neighbor.

"*Bien.*" The mechanic grinned broadly, cutting a knowing look in Taylor's direction. "*¿Que va?*" What's happening?

"I want to take this young lady to the airport. Have you got any wheels I can borrow?"

"You don't have your own car?" Taylor asked.

"Don't need one. The army usually furnishes a driver when I have someplace to go."

What was he, a general?

Setting his hammer aside, Igor scratched his head, his fingers running through strands of thinning gray hair. "Business is slow, sí? I would loan you this old rust-bucket, but the engine, she is cracked."

Rafe glanced around the area. "How about that stake-bed truck?" he asked, indicating a shabby Mazda truck with splayed wheels and half broken panels that was parked at the curb.

"I'll just catch a cab, okay?" Taylor suggested. From what she could see, that aging set of wheels wasn't likely to make it to the end of the block, much less the sixteen kilometers to the airport.

"The cabby would make a record of where he picked you up. I'd just as soon keep my name out of whatever mess you've gotten yourself into."

So much for Rafe trying to play the hero, she thought. Just as well. She preferred to be on her own, anyway. Nothing like having an attractive man around to muck up a woman's head. As tired as she'd been last night, knowing Rafe was only feet away trying to sleep on a too-short couch had contributed to a restless night.

"I'll walk into town and find a cab there. You won't have to bother—"

"Hang on," he told her.

"The truck, she belongs to my cousin," Igor said. "He is supposed to come pick it up today."

Strolling over to the truck, Rafe gave it a closer examination, glancing under the chassis and kicking a tire. Definitely a guy thing.

"It won't take me long to get her to the airport and come back. I'll fill up the gas tank on the way and add a couple of bucks for your trouble."

That seemed to tempt Igor, and he grinned again. "It is too bad such a pretty lady must leave our country so soon, *sí*? Perhaps she will return again someday?"

Taylor responded with a smile of her own. "*Gracias, señor*. It's nice that someone in Chile wants me to stay."

His leathery cheeks flushed when he realized that she'd understood him all along.

With a little more negotiation, Rafe cut a deal, and Taylor climbed up into the passenger seat. The truck's interior was in no better shape than the outside, and there was a decided hint of manure in the air. She rolled down the window.

The engine whined its objection when Rafe turned the key but finally caught, vibrating the truck from side to side like the old earthquake ride at Universal Studios. He tested the gearshift sticking up from the floor and eased in the clutch. The rubber boot that should have been at the base of the gearshift was missing, and through an inch-wide hole in the floor she could see the pitted asphalt beneath them. Finally, the truck lurched away from the curb.

"Cinderella's coach and four it's not," she commented.

"I'd say we've got three out of four cylinders working. Not bad for Igor's workmanship."

"Remind me to find a different repair shop next time I'm in town."

"Heck, it was probably only hitting on one cylinder when his cousin brought it in. Igor's a talented guy."

Taylor thought his admiration for the mechanic's skill misplaced. Still, the truck did run, and with some luck would likely get her to the airport intact.

Assuming Rafe managed to safely maneuver the vehicle through the early morning traffic. Cars, trucks, taxis, and buses all seemed to be vying for the same space on the downtown streets, missing each other by inches when they passed. As she watched the other drivers, Taylor remembered the man in the sedan that had tried to run her down. A swarthy complexion. A mustache, she recalled. And dark, beady eyes staring straight at her.

She shivered at the memory. She still didn't know why she'd been targeted.

Rafe came to a stop at a signal, letting the truck idle roughly while he waited for the light to change. Heat from the transmission rose into the truck's cab. Along with that, an unpleasant, decidedly earthy odor more potent than the smell of fertilizer crept in through the missing window between the cab and truck bed. Taylor wrinkled her nose.

"What do you suppose Igor's cousin uses this truck to transport?" she asked.

"I think he raises pigs. Probably takes them to market in the back."

"Oh, great!" Rolling her eyes, she covered her mouth and nose with one hand while rolling up the window with the other. A taxi would have been a smarter plan.

Chuckling, Rafe shot her an amused look. "Hey, I thought you were a country girl."

"Even spoiled grapes don't smell this bad. Roll up your window."

He did as she asked, but a teasing smile continued to play at the corner of his lips. She hadn't seen this lighter side of Rafe before and it brought a catch to Taylor's throat. Once past his macho exterior, maybe he wasn't such a tough guy after all.

"Are you saying that's a smell you enjoy?" she asked as they crossed the cement-lined river that bisected the city. A grassy park with lots of trees, walking paths and plenty of benches followed the course of the slow-moving water that flowed from the Andes to the Pacific.

"Honey chile," Rafe drawled, thickening the trace of Southern accent she'd detected earlier. "Where I grew up, sour mash and hogs just plain went together."

"So you're a redneck?"

"Born 'n bred in South Carolina. God's country, they say."

Taylor wasn't so sure about that, but it did explain Rafe's attitude toward women, a throwback to gentle Southern living where females were meant to be pampered and taken care of. That wasn't anything Taylor was used to—or appreciated. It had been hard enough to grow up in an Italian family that thought women belonged in the kitchen and were judged by the flavor of their tomato sauce.

"So what are you doing here in Chile?" she asked, more curious than she would like to admit.

"Training Chilean boys to kill bad guys."

"You're a cop?"

"U.S. Ranger. Or I was. Now I'm a civilian working freelance for whoever will pay me."

He didn't seem particularly thrilled with his work, leaving Taylor unsure of how she should react. His career did explain his mint physical condition, however, and meant if trouble came her way again she was in pretty good hands.

As they reached the divided highway that led to the airport and were able to increase their speed, anxiety began to gnaw at Taylor's midsection. Surely Mutt and Jeff had given up on her by now. What on earth could they or anyone gain by shooting her? It made no sense.

As they drove along, she watched the dry landscape and the sprawl of the city pass by; but her thoughts jumped erratically between her pursuers, Terry and the man sitting next to her. Given her history of brief and often tedious relationships, this seemed like an ironic time to meet a man who sparked her yearning for excitement. And for great sex. The way he did everything with such confidence, she imagined he'd be pretty terrific in bed. Not that she had a great deal of experience in that regard. Nor would she have a chance to test the premise, assuming she could pick up her brother's trail to the south.

When Rafe pulled into an angled parking spot at the airport between a new Honda Civic and an old pickup, Taylor forcefully set her provocative thoughts aside. Making sure her hair was well tucked up under the floppy rain hat Rafe had given her, she eased out of the truck. Before she'd gone two steps, he snared her by the arm.

"Let's reconnoiter before we go barging in there," he said. Her stomach did a little tumble at the renewed realization that *he* thought her pursuers might still be around.

Walking side by side, they strolled along the row of parked cars. She imagined they looked like a couple lingering over their good-byes. A well-suited couple with matching strides. She hadn't met many men she'd consider her equal, either physically or intellectually. To her dismay, she thought Rafe might be. But he was hooked up with the Chilean army; she was a California vintner. Their two worlds were practically at opposite poles, both geographically and philosophically.

"Let me know if you see anything that makes you nervous." He spoke in a low, intimate voice that slid across her flesh like a warm mist on an already hot day.

You make me nervous, but in a way that has nothing to do with getting shot at, she thought.

She forced herself to scan the parking lot and the entrance to the terminal. "Everything seems normal to me. No guys in dark coats packing guns that I can see."

"Okay. Let's take it inside. Stay alert and trust your instincts."

With the lightest touch at the small of her back, he urged her toward the terminal. The open construction of steel beams and glass made the building appear airy and light. But Taylor's attention was more on the warmth of Rafe's palm resting on her back than on the interior of the terminal.

Maybe if he hadn't been wearing baggy camouflage pants and a khaki T-shirt that emphasized his well delineated biceps, triceps and pecs, Taylor wouldn't have been quite so aware of Rafe as a man. His washboard abdomen didn't hurt the masculine image, either. A man's man, that was obvious. But also a man who a woman instinctively wanted to jump.

Which wasn't the instinct she intended to put into play. Self-preservation—at all levels—was the operative mode at the moment.

They strolled nonchalantly past the security detail at

the door. Once inside, Taylor swept her gaze over the ticket counters, lines of overweight businessmen, lovers embracing for their last farewell and mothers struggling to keep young children in tow. Her throat tightened at the sight of three-year-old twin girls circling their mother like maypole dancers, twisting their mother's skirt first one way and then the other. Their identical giggles were as welcome as raindrops on a parched summer landscape. She swallowed hard and looked away. No siblings could be closer than those who had shared a womb. No one owed more loyalty and love than one twin to another.

Spotting a man she took to be a supervisor, Taylor angled toward the LanChile airline counter.

"Excuse me," she said in Spanish as she slipped several U.S. twenties from her waistpack. "I wonder if you could help me."

The youngish gentleman turned toward her. "Señorita?"

"I'm hoping you can tell me if my brother flew to Punta Arenas sometime in the past few weeks. You know how younger brothers can be, so forgetful about—"

"Excuse us," Rafe said to the supervisor, taking Taylor's arm and dragging her away.

Her gaze snapped up, colliding with his. His pupils were dilated almost to black. "What are you doing? I just gave that guy a twenty—"

"Don't panic. Your black-jacket buddies just showed up," he murmured an instant before his mouth covered hers.

Don't panic? Good God! He'd kissed her before she'd had a moment to catch her breath. Panic, however, was not her first reaction.

Hot, jagged lightning seared through her at the initial

contact of his lips. Some part of her brain registered surprise that the entire electrical system at the airport hadn't burned out in that single instant. No lights. No circling baggage carousel. And certainly no operational control tower. This kiss was more than a diversion. Adrenaline swept through her veins. Fear mixed with arousal in a heady combination that left her heart pounding a hundred and fifty beats per minute and her breath staggering in her lungs.

His mouth shifted, making the kiss more intimate, and she knew something monumental was happening—to both of them. She craved the experience as a connoisseur longed for the next sip of a fine wine. She'd go anywhere, do anything, to sustain this intoxicating sensation.

Her hands cupped the back of his head, pulling him closer, and she dug her fingers into the neatly trimmed hair at his nape. He murmured something unintelligible as his hand on her hips pressed her into the hard ridge of his arousal. She thrilled at the sensation of his need. And hers.

With his tongue, he made love to her. Stroking, caressing, right in the middle of an airport terminal. With hundreds of people milling around. And she relished the wild, illicit experience in a way that no ordinary lovemaking had ever achieved.

She leaned into him, her breasts flattening against his rock-hard chest. Her nipples ached for even closer contact. For the feel of skin on skin.

Then suddenly he pushed her away.

She sucked in air, surprised and disoriented, standing there shaking, trying to remember where she was and why. Her breath came in gasps. So did his. But his jaw was tight, his sensual lips tense. His eyes burned with something that was closer to hate than sexual heat. And

Taylor suffered a double whammy of both regret and embarrassment.

"They're gone." The rasp of his voice was like a metal file scraping against her good reason. "Let's get the hell out of here."

CHAPTER FIFTEEN

The woman had vanished into the alleys of Santiago. None of his men had spotted her since last night, more than twelve hours ago, and Aquilar Mendoza, Minister of Internal Affairs, paced his office in the capital building. From his fourth-floor window he could see the public square where the people had celebrated the successful military junta led by General Pinochet in 1973. Nearby buildings were still pockmarked with bullet holes from that fierce battle.

As a young soldier, Mendoza had fought for Pinochet. He had admired the dictator's iron grip on the country and discounted all the rumors of torture and death squads as being necessary to maintain discipline in the country. Aquilar Mendoza had dreamed that he—the highest ranking mestizo in the government—would someday replace Pinochet and be *el presidente* himself. Had that dream come true, the power and wealth of all Chile would be his instead of in the hands of the current ineffectual president. A man who was little more than a college professor, for the love of God!

¡Un imbécil!

Mendoza had no desire to wait longer for his destiny to arrive. He had taken fate into his own hands by agreeing to collaborate with that crazed Arab, Al Faysal, and his Islamic zealots. When their mission was complete, Mendoza would step forward and snatch the reins of leadership for himself. He'd make it clear that only he could save the people.

His plan was in place to move thousands of his countrymen to safety. Into the chaos, he would be the one to step forward. The one they would trust. He would bring order; they would respond to his strong leadership. Though there would be collateral damage and loss of life, he would be acclaimed *el presidente!*

He could not let one determined, nosey American woman thwart his plans. Not when he was just two short weeks away from his coup d'état.

His men—local drug dealers, whom he had personally recruited and promised to well reward—had checked everywhere for Taylor Travini. It was as if she had fallen off the ends of the earth. Mendoza did not believe he would be that lucky. Like his fat mother-in-law, she would appear again at the most inconvenient time possible and ask too many questions.

Pacing back to his desk, he picked up the phone. He would have to warn his contact in Punta Arenas to be on the alert for Señorita Travini, if and when she arrived there. And to discourage her from traveling farther south.

He'd keep his men looking here in the city, too, and asking questions. If she was within a hundred kilometers of Santiago, they'd find her and run her to ground. She had to have help to elude his people so easily. That meant at least one other person knew where she'd gone.

All he needed was one informant. He'd get the answers he required. And he had to do that before the government dogs he intended to replace got so much as a sniff of his coup attempt.

CHAPTER SIXTEEN

The gears objected with the gnashing of metal-on-metal as Rafe turned the borrowed stake-bed truck off the main road from the airport into an older residential area south of central Santiago. Squat houses topped with corrugated tin roofs nudged up against each other, separated only by a narrow strip of barren ground and makeshift fences. The smell from the former porcine occupants of the truck drifted in through the broken cab window.

Taylor wrinkled her nose. They'd managed to get safely away from the airport and the black-coated gangsters, but now what? The relentless pursuit had shaken her. So had Rafe's kiss. The fact that it hadn't appeared to affect him annoyed her no end. Well, she could play it cool, too. She'd simply ignore the residual tingling of her lips and his stony silence.

He pulled to the side of the dusty road, bringing the truck to a halt. It coughed once, then quieted. Somewhere nearby a baby cried, and the heavy beat of a rock band on the radio pulsed out of an open window.

"Why are we stopped here?" Taylor asked.

"I've been thinking."

His hands rested lightly on the steering wheel, strong and deeply tanned, the nails trimmed short and even. With his Ranger training, those hands would be powerful enough to choke a man or drop him with a single blow. Taylor couldn't help but wonder if they could be gentle enough to arouse a woman, too. A little shimmer of desire rippled through her, suggesting it wouldn't take much in her case.

He turned toward her, his dark eyes intent, the stubble of his whiskers shadowing his angular face. "I think the best thing is for me to take you to the embassy. They can get you on—"

"I've already tried talking to those paper-pushers. If I go back, they'll turn me over to the Chilean authorities."

"I've met the ambassador a couple of times. If I can get to him, I'm sure he'll listen. He's not going to let those goons get their hands on you again. He'll make sure you're safely on a plane back to the States."

She leaned back and shook her head. "What about my brother?"

"You've got to let it go, Legs. If he turns up, great. Otherwise . . ." He let the thought dangle like a cluster of grapes ready to be sliced from the vine.

Taylor squeezed her eyes shut. How could she go home without knowing what had happened to Terry? She couldn't quit on him. But what other choice did she have?

"I think I should call my father, let him know what's going on." Idly, as she thought of the call she'd have to make, she fingered the aguamarine pendant hanging around her neck. Her father's gift. It meant so much to her, yet at the same time represented how he viewed her—a woman who should stick with her traditional role.

After a moment of hesitation, as though Rafe might be thinking of arguing with her, he unholstered his cell phone from his belt and passed it to her.

Sliding out of the cab, she walked to the front of the truck. A young couple walking hand-in-hand on the opposite side of the road gave her a curious look. She gazed down at the phone, her link to home. To her father.

This time, Rosa Lopez, their long-time housekeeper, answered the phone in her soft, patient voice. "Travini residence."

"Rosa. It's Taylor."

"Ah, *niña*. I am so glad you called."

Taylor detected a note of worry in the housekeeper's voice. "Is there something wrong, Rosa?"

"It is your father. He has not been well since you leave. The doctors say it is stress, and now he has a bad cough. I am troubled for him."

Taylor felt an ache in her chest. "I'm sure between you and the doctors, he'll feel better soon." His health would be improved, too, if she could find Terry and bring him home. "Could I speak with Dad?"

"Sí, of course."

A minute or two passed before her father came on the line.

"Travini!" Vincente Travini barked into the phone when he answered.

Taylor swallowed and licked her lips. "Dad, it's me. Taylor."

"About time you checked in." He coughed—a raspy, wheezing sound. "Have you found Terry yet?"

"No, there's been some trouble. I'm not sure—"

"Well, find him, damn it! And tell him to get his butt back here. You understand? I need him."

"I've been trying, Dad. He wasn't at the hotel—"

"Gus had a heart attack two days ago. He's still in the hospital and—"

"Is he going to be all right?" The news shocked Taylor. Gus Lopez had been their foreman for as long as she could remember. He knew as much about growing grapes and making wine as her father did, and had been a mentor and friend to Taylor while she was growing up. A big, burly man with a ready smile, she'd always thought of him as invincible.

"Yeah, yeah. He'll be fine. But he's not gonna be back to work anytime soon, and I'm sicker than a dog, and we've got pruning to worry about. Gus was already behind schedule—these damn wetbacks are nothin' but lazy s.o.b.'s. I need Terry back here on the double to supervise the work. He's been foolin' around down there takin' his useless pictures long enough."

She almost told her father she could do the job, and probably better than Terry could. The workers knew her, and they weren't all illegals. Pruning during the dormant season wasn't all that complicated. She knew how to choose the buds to leave on the canes, how to select the strongest fruiting canes, how to tie them to avoid damaging the buds. Gus had taught her.

But her father was sick. When he was ill, only her mother had been able to deal with him.

"Dad, Terry's missing. I can't—"

"What do you mean, he's missing?"

"I'm not sure. There's been some trouble and I—"

"Well, find him. I want my son back here where he belongs. I'm counting on you, Taylor Theresa. You be a good girl, now, you hear?" He coughed again.

"Yes, father," she whispered, her throat tight with a sense of failure as well as concern for her father. But he didn't hear her last words. The line had already gone dead.

She stood for a long moment simply staring off into space. The hard rock music still blared from a house down the block. A warm breeze silently shifted the tips of a clump of dry grass growing in the middle of a discarded tire in a nearby front yard. A scrawny mongrel dog trotted by, giving Taylor a wide berth. She fought the burn of tears in her eyes.

She'd find Terry, damn it! If that's what her dad wanted, that's what he'd get. She was as desperate to find her twin as he was. Maybe more so.

"So, what'd your ol' man say?"

Startled, Taylor whirled at the sound of Rafe's voice. He'd come up behind her and was standing too close, inside her personal space, making her feel uncomfortable. Edgy. And very feminine compared to his overwhelming masculinity.

"He's sick, and I'm going to Punta Arenas," she announced.

"Just how do you plan to get there?"

"I don't know." The airport was certainly out as long as the local Mafia used it as their hunting grounds and she was their prey. She swiped the back of her hand across her face. *Never let 'em see you cry,* her father had taught both her and her brother. "Since flying is out, I'll charter a boat."

She stepped around Rafe, making it a point that no part of her body or even her clothes brush against him. She couldn't handle the sexual sizzle that pulsed through her veins whenever he came too close. She climbed back into the smelly truck and reached for the door. He grabbed it, preventing her from slamming it shut.

Taking a wide-legged stance, he held the door open. "Maybe you haven't noticed. Santiago is a helluva long way from the ocean."

"I'll rent a car and go to Valparaíso." From studying the map with Terry before he left home, Taylor knew Valparaíso was the second biggest city in the country and the major port bringing goods into the country as well as handling exports. There had to be fishing boats nearby and a captain willing to make some extra money.

"You're going to rent a car with what?"

"I've got a credit card." She touched her waistpack, grateful she'd managed to hold onto that since she'd lost her backpack with a change of clothes. That was a problem she could deal with later.

"Terrific. You whip out your Visa one time, bells and whistles will go off all over the city. Those clowns who've been chasing you will show up in milliseconds."

"Then I'll pay cash." There was still money in her wallet. And in her boot.

"Are you nuts? You think your buddies haven't notified all the rental car outlets to be on the lookout for a sexy, six-foot blonde *norteamericana?*"

"Five-eleven," she corrected, while at the same time registering that he'd called her *sexy*. Warmth flooded her cheeks. "And I'll slouch if I have to. I intend to go to Punta Arenas. So are you going to drive me back into town or will I have to hitch a ride?"

"You are one stubborn lady, Legs. I'll give you that." He shoved her door closed and walked around to the driver's side. The truck springs gave under his weight as he climbed in and got behind the wheel.

She felt as though she'd won a small victory when he made a U-turn and returned to the highway, turning toward Santiago. But he was right. No matter what she did, the goons were likely to track her down. And she still didn't know why they were after her. Or why Terry had vanished.

Rafe maneuvered the truck through the heavy traffic on O'Higgins Avenue, one of the main roads through the city. No one had connected him or this half-broken-down truck to Taylor Travini yet, but he didn't like the way the mafia goons had flooded the city looking for her. Somehow she or her brother had stepped in some deep shit. He didn't like the idea of her trying to pull herself out on her own.

"You can let me out at the closest bank," she said. "I'll use the ATM, get some pesos and hire a cab before anyone can find me."

"No."

"Rafe, you're not going to stop me."

This lady was trouble with a capital T. He ought to just dump her at the embassy and let them sort things out. That's what they got paid for.

But he was so damn stupid, he wasn't going to do that. No, he was going for Hero of the Month, damn it all!

"I'm taking you to Valparaíso," he gritted out between his teeth.

"In this old truck?"

"You got a better idea?"

She sat back, not saying anything. Probably gloating. Or thinking he was a fool, which was damn near the truth. A sucker for a woman in distress. Particularly one with legs that went on forever and rounded breasts that filled out a T-shirt like nobody's business. A woman who'd tried to hide her tears after talking to her old man.

He remembered that even a hint of Lizbeth sprouting tears had torn him up. She hadn't cried often. It wasn't her style. Once when she'd been pregnant with Katy she'd gone postal when she burned dinner. That had been hormones. He hadn't had a clue how to calm her down. And when he'd shipped out to Afghanistan she'd lost it again, however much she'd tried to be brave. A soldier's wife. That was the last time he'd seen her and their baby girl. The image was etched into his memory with the acid of grief.

"Did you tell your dad that some really bad dudes were after you?" he asked.

"He was too sick to be interested." Her terse response told him more about her father than he wanted to know.

A lumbering '69 Oldsmobile changed lanes in front of him, and he slammed on the brakes. They didn't hold. He pumped them for all he was worth, finally slowing the truck. The driver of the ancient Detroit-made behemoth didn't appear to realize he had dodged a bullet.

When the crisis was over, Taylor said, "Are you sure this bucket of bolts can make it to the coast?"

"No. But I don't see as how we've got a choice. I don't want to raise any red flags by renting a car, either."

"All right, then," Taylor said in a snooty voice. "If you're going to drive me to Valparaíso in this crate, I'll pay you for your time and pay Igor's cousin for the use of his truck."

"I don't want or need your money, Legs."

"I insist. I always pay my own way."

He shrugged. "Whatever." He knew damn well he wouldn't take a dime from Taylor. That wasn't his style. Around a hundred kilometers separated them from Valparaíso, about sixty-two miles; he'd have to baby this ol' truck the whole way and hope to God that Igor was as good a stick-and-string mechanic as he thought.

Rafe thought about stopping by his place to pick up some gear, including his personal Colt .45 automatic that he kept stashed under a loose floorboard at the apartment. Taylor was facing some pretty tough customers and he wanted to be prepared if some goon should track her down.

But he didn't want to argue with Igor about keeping the truck. And it wouldn't be smart to involve the mechanic. The fewer people who knew Taylor's whereabouts the better.

There were other ways to get what he needed.

CHAPTER SEVENTEEN

By afternoon, the two men who were attempting to chase down the American woman had returned to Taberna de los Caballeros. The bartender claimed to know nothing about the *gringa* who had been in his bar. Even two broken fingers had not persuaded the man to tell them what they had wanted to hear. Perhaps he had not known the answers. Where had the woman gone? Who was helping her? She couldn't have escaped them on her own.

The two men began searching the neighborhood block by stinking block. They walked the narrow streets of the barrio through the heat of the day. They didn't dare return to Aquilar Mendoza without some news of the woman. Much was at stake. Perhaps their own lives if they failed.

"*Hola, amigo,*" the taller one called to a man whose head was under the hood of an old Toyota truck. His face was leathery and wrinkled with age, his hair graying and stringy.

"Sí? What is it I can do for you, señores?"

The shorter man showed the mechanic a picture of Taylor Travini that their boss had plucked off the computer. It amused him that the woman would be so stupid as to have her face where others could find it.

"Have you seen this woman?" he asked.

The mechanic's eyes darted between the two men. "Why is it you are asking?"

"Our reasons do not concern you."

A look of fear entered the man's dark eyes. He took a step back into the shadows of the garage. "I know nothing of this woman."

The smell of grease, oil and fear grew stronger as the two men followed the mechanic into his lair.

"You will tell us what we want to know, old man," said the taller of the two.

Although Igor tried to be brave, when the shorter man held his hand flat on his workbench and the other man brought a heavy wrench down hard across his knuckles, the pain was too much. His sobbed all he knew of Rafe and the pretty señorita and his cousin's truck they'd borrowed that morning.

When they released him, letting him sink to the hard concrete of his garage, he cried again because he had betrayed a friend. And a crippled hand meant he could not earn a livelihood.

The final, fatal blow of the wrench to his head was almost welcome. With his last thought, he prayed for forgiveness.

CHAPTER EIGHTEEN

A well-paved, two-lane highway led up and over the low range of hills that separated Santiago from the coastal region and the city of Valparaíso. The truck that belonged to Igor's cousin apparently had an aversion to going up. It ground along at the pace of a slow walk, dirty-gray exhaust billowing out the back and puffs of steam rising from the radiator in front. Taylor fully expected an explosion at any moment.

She glanced in the side mirror. A jagged vertical crack distorted the view to the rear. "It looks like we're the head of a long funeral procession." Twenty or more cars were strung out behind them. The road was just windy enough, and well enough traveled in both directions, to make it hard for a vehicle to pass.

"I'm getting all I can out of this ol' gal." Over the complaints of the transmission, Rafe down-shifted again. The car following them stayed well behind to avoid the exhaust fumes. And shrapnel, if the whole thing blew up.

"Maybe you can find a place to pull over and let some of those people go by."

He shot her a cryptic look. "If I stop this bag of bolts, I'm not sure I'll ever get her going again. Particularly uphill."

Getting stuck here seemed like a real possibility. Under normal circumstances, that wouldn't be a bad thing. Grapevines almost ready for harvest covered the rolling hillsides, part of the expanding Chilean wine business. Her fingers itched to pluck grapes from a cluster to test their firmness, and her mouth watered to taste the sugar content on her tongue. Of course, there were ways to accurately compute how much sugar the grapes held, but there was nothing like sampling them yourself and knowing just how sweet or dry the wine would taste when properly fermented. Just like there were limits to speculating about how a man would kiss—or make love. To be sure, you had to try it for yourself.

Rafe, she admitted, hadn't shown any inclination to do a little hands-on research with her. Beyond that one kiss, of course. Not that there had been much opportunity. But his lack of interest bothered her.

It shouldn't. She had other, more important problems on her mind. Like, if she would be able to find a skipper willing to take her to the tip of Chile. She'd had plenty of boating experience herself, and would be happy to take a boat out on her own, but the journey would require several days. Being alone might not be safe, particularly if pirates worked this southern coastline looking for vulnerable targets. They'd been known to board a boat, take whatever they could that had any value, then sink it with the crew and passengers onboard. Not a pleasant prospect.

"Have you ever been to Sonoma?" she asked, mostly to redirect her thoughts.

"Nope. The closest I've been was a stopover at Travis Air Force Base on the way to a Special Ops in the Philippines. They didn't give us much time to play tourist."

"The hills around Sonoma look a lot like this. Vineyards as far as the eye can see." Beautiful country. Both her home and her heart. A place where she felt she belonged. If only her father would recognize the vineyard and making wine were as much in her blood as his.

"What kind of grapes are they growing here?"

"Looks like they're raising a variety. Probably—"

A loud bang made her flinch and duck her head, as though a bullet had been shot in their direction.

Cursing under his breath, Rafe wrestled with the wheel to keep the truck on the road, his biceps flexing with the effort. Taylor clung to the door with one hand and the seat with the other as he struggled in a losing battle with gravity and a vehicle out of control.

Almost in slow motion, the old Mazda lurched off the gravel shoulder and down into a ditch, landing with a hard jolt. As the truck tipped to the right, Taylor fell against the door. The engine roared with more energy than it had shown in the past two hours, then Rafe switched it off.

"Hmm, that was a fun ride," Taylor commented as she tried to right herself.

"I always like to provide a lady an extra thrill or two," he deadpanned. "Keeps her on her toes."

She giggled. Good God, she *never* giggled. It had to be the stress of the past couple of days. And her exhaustion. "Well, you've certainly delivered." Between his surprise kiss and going into the ditch, it had been quite an eventful day.

A face appeared in the window on the uphill side of the truck. "Are you hurt?" the stranger asked in Spanish.

"Estámos bien," Rafe replied. We're fine. "But we may need some help getting the truck out of this ditch."

"I may need a crane to get me up from here, too," Taylor added. The truck was canted at a steep angle, making it an awkward climb to get out.

Once they were both safely on the ground, a cursory examination of the truck revealed they were in deeper trouble than they'd expected. Not only had they blown a tire, the front axle had broken on its dive into the ditch. The truck wasn't going anywhere soon, and maybe never again under its own power.

The good Samaritan shrugged, knowing there was little he could do, so he left.

Standing, Rafe scanned the area. The trail of cars that had followed them was gone, the highway suddenly deserted, and the curious folks who had stopped to gawk had vanished. There wasn't much to see except fields of grape vines.

"I'm open to suggestions," he said.

Taylor focused in on a two-story farmhouse with outbuildings standing on a rise about a half mile away. The owner of the vineyard, she suspected. A man who no doubt owned several vehicles and could be sweet-talked or bribed into taking them to Valparaíso.

"How 'bout I go have a chat with a fellow winemaker?" she suggested.

A grin kicked up the corners of Rafe's lips, softening his whiskered, rough 'n ready appearance and doing something wild and wonderful to Taylor's midsection. Her pulse rate spiked, unnerving her. The man didn't smile nearly often enough, which was lucky for her. She was already having trouble keeping focused on her goal.

"Good thinking, Legs," he said.

As though it were the most natural thing in the world, he took her hand, tugged her down into the ditch and up the other side, leading her between a row of grapevines toward the farmhouse. She was tempted to tell him she'd safely walked through vineyards a good many times on her own; he didn't need to hold her hand.

But darn it all, the feel of his calloused palm against hers felt too good to let go. The strength of his grip electrified her. Her reaction to this man from the moment she'd spotted him in the bar had been way too potent. Too visceral. He had her off balance. She wasn't like this. She could take men or leave them alone. Except, with Rafe her usual hands-off attitude had a hole in it as big as the one in the truck tire.

He kept up a pace that had her breathless. He covered the ground in long, even strides that had her struggling to keep up. She imagined he was a man who would keep her on her toes in every way possible, both mentally and physically. But her pride demanded that she not let him see how even his casual touch affected her.

The loud thump of a mortar exploded nearby, the sound reverberating in her chest. A flock of starlings rose helter-skelter into the sky.

In a move that was so swift it had to be instinctive, Rafe turned, grabbed her and threw her flat onto the ground, covering her body with his. He wrapped his arm around her head, protecting her. His weight pressed against her, chest-to-chest, pelvis-to-pelvis. She'd never been more aware of the length of him. His power and size. A perfect match to her physique.

"Don't move," he whispered hoarsely in her ear.

She wasn't sure she could if she'd wanted to. More than anything else, she felt terrifyingly, gloriously feminine.

"Don't make a sound," he warned her.

"Rafe?"

"Shh." He breathed the word against her ear. "We need to know how many there are, if they've got us surrounded."

"Rafe, no one is attacking us." She regretted more than she could say telling him the truth at this particular moment, from this erotic position.

"Shooting a cannon at us is considered an act of aggression where I come from."

"They're trying to scare off the birds."

For the length of two heartbeats, Rafe didn't move. Then he slowly rose up on one elbow.

"Scaring the birds?"

"So they don't eat the grapes."

"You know that for sure?"

She nodded, though her gaze drifted to his lips. Firm lips that were slightly full. Kissable lips she remembered so well.

"At Travini Vineyards we've switched to covering the vines with nets." Her throat felt tight and dry, her voice husky. "To keep the birds off."

She felt him relax and ease his position.

"Then I guess we shouldn't waste the moment."

For an instant she didn't know what he meant, and then his mouth closed over hers, hard and demanding. Need exploded in her. Blood rushed through her veins, heating every molecule of her body. It came in a tidal wave, a heady feeling as though she'd consumed too much alcohol. She staggered under the impact. Her breath came in gulps as she tasted the sweet flavor of his tongue, felt the roughness of his growing beard.

Reflexively, she wrapped her arms around him, threaded her fingers through his short hair, pulled him closer. She spread her legs, welcoming the press of his arousal at the vee of her thighs, and she hooked her legs behind his hips. Through two layers of denim, heat radiated from his center to hers.

His lips worked against hers. He spoke but she couldn't understand the words. She could only feel. And the feelings were sharp and mind-numbing.

Rafe pushed back from Taylor. The effort required every ounce of self-control he possessed. He was weak and winded, baffled by his reaction and infuriated he'd taken advantage of the situation. Her eyes, usually a pale green, had turned the shade of a deep forest, the pupils dilated. Her chest heaved and so did his.

He'd had no right to kiss her again. The first time, at the airport, had been necessary, a ploy to hide her from the goons. But even then he'd known, on some gut level, that he would kiss her again given the chance.

If only she'd gone to the embassy, this wouldn't have happened. But it had.

"I'm sorry." He eased his weight from her, cursing himself in the process.

"You're *sorry*? That you kissed me?"

"Yeah. I shouldn't have."

Her flushed cheeks deepened in color and her eager expression crumbled. She struggled to get the rest of the way out from under him. "Well, then, get off me, you big oaf."

"¡Muchachos! This is not the place for such things, not in my vineyard." Looking stern, a man of about sixty with a round face and belly to match marched down the row of vines toward them.

Rafe and Taylor separated as though they'd been shot from the same cannon that had frightened the starlings into flight.

110

"We apologize, señor," Taylor said in Spanish. "We did not mean any disrespect."

"We're on our honeymoon," Rafe added, "and well—"

Her jaw going lax, Taylor snapped her head around. "Honey—?"

"I'm afraid we got a little carried away," Rafe continued, ignoring her surprised reaction. "Our truck broke down on the road back there, and we didn't know what to do. So we . . ." The lazy lift of his shoulders looked anything but innocent to Taylor.

A knowing twinkle appeared in the farmer's eyes, suggesting he was a romantic at heart. "Ah, a honeymoon. Perhaps I can help you celebrate. My name is Rudolph Huhn, and these are my vines."

Rafe extended his hand. "I'm Rafe Maguire and this is my bride."

Sputtering, Taylor tried to object but Rafe drew her firmly to his side, holding her there with his arm around her shoulder. He had nerve! Telling this stranger that they were on their honeymoon, for God's sake. Which he'd done within seconds of apologizing for stooping so low as to kiss her. Damn his hide!

Whatever his game, she'd have to play along, so she forced a smile. But later she'd have plenty to say to her ersatz husband.

"Please. You must come up to my house. We will toast your wedding with my best vintage Merlot and then we will call someone to assist you with your breakdown."

"That's very nice of you, señor Huhn," Taylor said.

"Please call me Rudy, Señora Maguire. Otherwise you will make me feel like a very old man."

"You're not at all an old man, Rudy." She slipped out from under Rafe's embrace. "I understand you being protective of your fine vineyard. My father would feel the same way. Have you heard of Travini Vineyards?"

His full bushy brows rose. "A California house. Fine fruity red wines with a pleasant bouquet, but perhaps not quite as good as mine," he said with pride.

"I've been hoping to take some clippings back to California to see if your Chilean vines will grow as well in our soil as they do here."

"Ah, I would be honored to share some of my vines with such a lovely lady." He offered her his arm, which Taylor graciously took.

Rafe lingered a step or two behind the pair of wine aficionados. Apparently, good ol' Rudy had either not noticed the absence of a wedding ring on Taylor's finger, didn't care, or was so enamored of her that he'd gone foggy-brained. Rafe suspected the latter.

The way Taylor had taken over, with a flirtatious smile and a sway of her hips, annoyed him. So did the fact that it was Rudy's arm she had hooked onto instead of his. Hell, they were supposed to be on their honeymoon. She could have at least pretended some interest in him.

Though she'd sure given it her all during that kiss. He'd never met a woman quite that responsive—so instantly hot, he'd wanted to taste that heat, test the temperature in the hollow at the base of her throat and that creamy-smooth skin just below her ear.

But he'd known better than to test her self-control that far. Or his.

Walking behind the pair, he intentionally studied the sway of her hips, the ripple of muscle as her thighs moved beneath her snug jeans. While observing every notable detail, he listened as they compared grapes and production rates. He was more a beer and pretzels kind of guy. Fancy wines didn't do it for him. He couldn't tell a decent Merlot from a Sauvignon, yet these two seemed to have been weaned directly from mother's milk to wine.

Rudy ushered them into a wine-tasting area tucked between rows of huge metal kegs. Air-conditioning kept the barn-sized space at a cool, dry temperature of sixty-five degrees, and every inch of the concrete floor was spotlessly clean.

Bringing out a couple of bottles of red, Rudy poured them each a swallow and lifted his glass for a toast.

"May you enjoy many years of happiness, my new friends."

Rafe sipped; it wasn't bad. Smooth, with no medicinal bite to it. He was about to thank Rudy, but before he had a chance, the old guy had poured wine from the second bottle into clean glasses.

"And may you be blessed with many children to warm your heart and hearth in your old age."

Rafe wasn't entirely sure about that toast, but he went along for the ride. Taylor seemed to be enjoying herself. In fact, she offered a toast of her own with the next glass.

"To a good harvest at the Huhn vineyards," she said, lifting her wine again.

About the fifth toast, Rafe began to wonder if they were ever going to get out of there. "Sweetheart, we really need to be going."

"Of course, of course," Rudy said. "Let me call someone to see to your truck."

Taylor spoke up. "Actually, Rudy, we were hoping you might give us a ride or lend us one of your vehicles to take us to Valparaíso. We're hoping to charter a boat there." Cocking one brow, she glanced at Rafe. "For our honeymoon cruise."

113

With a troubled shake of his head, Rudy said, "I regret that is not possible at the moment. My son has taken our truck to Santiago, and his wife has the car. There is some event at church that she and my mother are helping the priest to plan."

"When will she return home?" Rafe asked.

He shrugged. "With women, who can tell?"

Hitchhiking was looking like their only option.

"I have only the tractor," Rudy said. "And my son's old Harley-Davidson motorcycle. I'm not sure either of those would get you to Valparaíso very rapidly, I am afraid. The Harley has been in storage for a long time."

"If you don't mind," Rafe said, "let's take a look at the Harley. It isn't much farther to Valparaíso, and that might do the trick."

"As you wish. But my son has not ridden his motorcycle in many years. His wife thought it was too dangerous, and I cannot be sure of its condition."

Stored in a metal shed behind the wine processing building, when Rafe removed its dusty cover he understood why Rudy would be hesitant to recommend the Harley to travel anywhere. Based on the cobwebs crisscrossing the motorcycle, generations of spiders had taken up residence in and around the vintage 1971 Sportster. The bright blue paint had faded, and the front fender showed rust where it had been dinged.

Nonetheless, as a kid, Rafe would have given both his arms and one leg to own this little beauty. Even now he'd love a chance to restore the old machine.

"Let's see how she runs." Using the cover, he wiped away the cobwebs, then checked the gas. It was empty, drained, which was good. If gas had been left in the engine, it would have long since turned to varnish, and the bike wouldn't have made it two feet before seizing and needing an overhaul.

He glanced toward Rudy. "Have you got some gas?"

The older man nodded. "But of course. We have extra for the tractor."

It took a few minutes to fill the small tank and prime the carburetor.

Rafe stradled the Harley, twisted the accelerator and kicked the starter. After one sputter, the engine turned over.

He grinned at Taylor. "Your carriage awaits, Cinderella."

She looked skeptical. "You sure you've got enough mice in there to pull us over the hill?"

"All harnessed and raring to go."

Rafe arranged with Rudy that they'd leave the bike at his friend's house in Valparaíso when they were done using it. Rudy or his son would pick it up in a day or two.

Just before they left the vineyard, Rafe called Igor to let him know where he could find his cousin's broken truck. The phone rang in Santiago but no one answered.

"That's odd," Rafe said.

"What's wrong?" Taylor asked.

He glanced at his watch. Almost three o'clock. "Igor doesn't seem to be home. He usually is at this time of day."

"Maybe he had to go shopping or buy some parts."

Rafe listened for one more ring, then disconnected. A troubling feeling pricked at the back of his neck. "Yeah. Maybe."

Or maybe the local mafia had traced Taylor to his apartment and questioned Igor. It was a possibility Rafe didn't care to contemplate but couldn't ignore.

CHAPTER NINETEEN

The deep-throated rumble of the motorcycle's engine was a deafening roar as they climbed up the highway to the crest of the mountains that separated Santiago from the west coast. Striking scenery flashed by in a blur on both sides of the road, but Taylor had little time to enjoy it. Instead, she concentrated on leaning into the curves as Rafe took the corners tight and fast, as though he were racing a clock. Speed seemed to suit him.

Unfortunately, comfort for the passenger was not one of the bike's best features.

Mounted behind Rafe, Taylor straddled the Harley, sitting on a rock-hard seat above the rear wheel. The machine vibrated between her thighs. The stiff suspension system meant she felt every rock and dip in the road. Intimately.

With her arms looped around Rafe's waist, she was also acutely aware of the breadth of his back, the pure muscled strength of his abdomen. No love handles there. The only thing that prevented her from cuddling up closer was the bundle of vine clippings in her lap. Rudy had wrapped the damp shoots in newspaper and plastic and given them to her to carry back to California and plant in the Travini Vineyards. The sweet man wanted her to report back to him on their success.

A truck roared by, going the other way, so close to the center line it almost clipped the motorcycle. A whirlwind of dust and gravel swirled on the road in the truck's wake. Closing her eyes, Taylor ducked her head, letting Rafe's back protect her from flying debris.

"You okay back there?" he asked.

"Too bad Rudy couldn't find his son's old helmet. A visor would be nice."

"It can't be much farther. We'll be there soon. Just hang on."

That's about all she could do. And she didn't like not being in control, both of the Harley and her emotions. As worried as she was about Terry, she didn't need the distraction Rafe presented. She certainly wasn't used to someone else taking charge, and she wasn't at all sure she liked being at the mercy of this macho road warrior. The persistent undercurrent of sexual attraction she felt did little to ease her mind.

Honeymoon, indeed!

She had the feeling that, when push-came-to-shove, they'd be like a bad mix of grapes, each one trying to overpower the other instead of blending flavors and styles. Of course they might also create a blend so unique that it would be blue-ribbon caliber.

No, the fact that she was intrigued by the possibility was only a result of her heightened emotional state over Terry's disappearance. As soon as she found a charter boat captain to take her to Punta Arenas, and she got away from Rafe, her libido would return to normal. She'd get back to business.

They crossed the ridge of the mountains. A few minutes later, they got their first view of Valparaíso. Rafe pulled the motorcycle into a scenic overlook and stopped.

Groaning, Taylor eased herself off the bike. "My butt is never going to be the same. I swear to God, it's numb."

Glancing at her rear end, the corners of his lips kicked up. "Looks to be in pretty good shape to me."

"Great. Then you can ride on the back the rest of the way into town. I'll drive."

He chuckled, low and husky.

Taylor made it a point to walk a few paces away, to the edge of the cliff overlooking the town. She wasn't going to react to his innuendo. At least, she had no intention of letting him know how easily he could raise her temperature.

The steep hillside dived down to the harbor below, houses painted in bright hues of blue, yellow and red clinging to every inch of vertical space. Urban sprawl took on new meaning when the only available land was on a thirty-degree incline, and the buildings were constructed roof-to-eaves almost as far as Taylor could see. It appeared as if each house were holding up the neighbor's house above it.

And then, at the base of the hillside, came the center of town where ribbons of roads snaked past multistory buildings that resembled the landscape of any midsized city in the States.

The urban center butted against a busy harbor. From this distance, cargo ships looked like toy boats pressed up against a long wharf where Erector-set cranes lifted matchbox-sized containers from the ships to waiting miniature trucks. Nearby, the fishing fleet was tied up to a smaller wharf, the boats looking even less substantial than the ocean-going freighters.

A breeze scented with sea salt swept up the cliff, teasing the hair that had come loose from Taylor's braid and shifting it in front of her face. Closer at hand, a pair of seagulls floated in the updraft, their synchronized slow dance requiring only the slightest movement of wings and feathers to keep them nearly motionless in the air.

Rafe came up beside her, resting his hand lightly at the small of her back. The heat of his palm warmed her through her T-shirt.

"Quite a sight, huh?" he commented.

She licked her dry, chapped lips. "Heaven help the people down there if there's a landslide. The whole town would slip into the harbor."

"Let's just hope that doesn't happen while we're around." With only the merest pressure of his fingertips at her back, he ushered her back to the Harley. "There's a *ascensores* not too far down the road. We'll take that into town."

"A what?"

"*Ascensores.* It's a funicular, a cable railway car that goes up and down. That's the way the locals get around these hillside neighborhoods. Most areas are too steep to walk."

"What do we do with the bike?"

"It'll fit inside. Those boxes are bigger than they look."

"Clever." Reluctantly, she swung her leg over the bike. She really did know how to drive a Harley. A college friend had taught her in an effort to tempt her up to his room and into his bed. The ploy didn't work. She doubted, however, that Rafe would give up his driver's position—or his control of any situation—for a single round of lovemaking. He'd be too tough a negotiator for that.

Before getting on the bike, he said, "When we get down to the harbor area, we'll find a place to stay."

She squinted up at him, his face a dark silhouette against the cloudless sky. "I plan to get going as soon as I can find a charter to take me south."

"You'll need some gear for the trip. We'll use the room as a place where we can regroup and make plans."

That did make sense, Taylor agreed. The prospect of living in this one pair of jeans and her T-shirt for a week or more wasn't particularly appealing. And she'd certainly need a warm jacket if she got as far as the Patagonia region. But she was determined to move on as quickly as possible.

In less than a mile, Rafe wheeled the motorcycle off the road at the upper terminus of a funicular. The two cable cars were about midway between their base stations, so he had a few minutes to make a phone call.

"Stretch your legs a little," he told Taylor. "I'll be right back."

Without waiting for her response, he walked to the other side of the wooden cable house and pulled his cell phone from its holster. Worried that he'd been unable to reach Igor earlier, he tried again. When he still got no answer, he gave up and punched in Donovan's number.

After the second ring, his friend answered. "Landry."

"It's me, Maguire."

"Hey! What's up, Big Mac?"

"I need you to check on something for me." As succinctly as possible, Rafe explained Taylor's situation and how he had borrowed a truck from Igor, whom he now couldn't reach. "I'd like you to go by the garage, see that everything's okay, and let him know his cousin's broken truck is about forty clicks this side of Santiago on Highway 69."

"Happy to do that, buddy. But I'm far more interested in this Taylor person. She sounds like trouble to me."

"Yeah. She is." In more ways than one. "But I can handle it." Like hell he could! With her arms locked around his middle for the past hour and her cheek plastered against his back, he'd been sorely tempted to drive off the road into a stand of trees and do something about the ache in his groin. Something stupid that she might not appreciate and sure as hell would make things harder for them both.

"Call me after you talk with Igor," Rafe said. "He'll probably be pissed I broke the truck, so give him a couple hundred bucks. That's more than it was worth this morning."

"I assume you're good for it."

"Yeah, yeah. I'll cover it as soon as I'm back in town."

Donovan laughed. "I'll hold you to that, Big Mac. And the beer will be on you this time, too."

"You got it." Rafe disconnected the phone and walked back to where Taylor was waiting. The rattle of stainless-steel cables announced the imminent arrival of the cable car.

"Did you explain to her why you'll be late for dinner?" Taylor asked, her green eyes sparkling with mischief in the bright sunlight.

"She promised to give me a rain check," he deadpanned. There was no woman waiting dinner for him tonight. There hadn't been for a long time.

He found them a room in a small hotel a block from the wharf. It was scruffy and old, but had the advantage of a back entrance, where he'd parked the Harley. He supposed the daughter of a mega-vineyard owner didn't usually stay anyplace this seedy. The double bed had a dip in the middle that resembled the Grand Canyon, and the doors on the armoire had been ripped off, leaving scars where the hinges had been forcibly removed. The bedside table where Taylor laid the vine clippings looked barely sturdy enough to hold the weight. On the plus side, there was an en suite bathroom, though the stained sink and tub weren't exactly inviting.

Taylor dropped heavily onto the side of the bed, making the springs groan in complaint. "Could you rent us a Caddie next time we have to go cross-country? Between Igor's old truck and that motorcycle—my body isn't used to that much abuse."

"I'll keep that in mind, Legs."

A little grin teased around the corners of her full lips. "So what's the plan, *señor jefe?*" Mr. Chief.

That I get out of here as quickly as I can before I throw you back on that bed and do exactly what my body has in mind.

"I'll nose around for possible charter boats," he said, "while you do some shopping. There ought to be some decent stores around here somewhere. Just remember to use cash. We don't want your mafia buddies tracking you down via your bank card."

Her smile faded. "You really think they're still after me?"

"Better safe than sorry." He shrugged. She, or more likely her brother, had stirred up some kind of hornets nest, and Rafe wanted to avoid poking at it again. "I'll be gone a couple of hours. Can you handle that?"

Her glare was enough to melt the buttons on his dress uniform, assuming he'd been wearing it.

"Why, little ol' me, I'll just bat my eyes if those nasty men show up. That's just sure to make them change their minds about hanging me up by my thumbs."

He didn't like her mimicking a Southern drawl. That cut too close to his beliefs that a lady ought to be cared for, taken care of. She probably thought he was a dinosaur. And maybe he was.

That didn't mean he'd throw her to the wolves so she could prove she was tougher or meaner than he was. Despite her objections, he'd take care of her as best he could. In his world, that was his only choice. He'd grown up knowing that. And then, when he'd failed Lizbeth and Katy, he'd vowed never to make that mistake again. When a woman was placed under his protection, he'd damn well do his best or die trying. Which included Taylor, stubborn as she might be.

"When you're walking around town, try not to be any more conspicuous than you have to be," he warned, though even the thought was a laugh. She'd stand out in either a crowd of beauty pageant entrants or a South Carolina hog-calling crowd, and everything in between. "We want as few people as possible to remember we've been here."

"Trust me. I'll be absolutely invisible, I promise."

He didn't believe that promise for a minute. But he had some business to attend to, and he didn't want her to be a witness. He'd done some covert work for the U.S. government; he intended to put his experience to work. Having her around would cramp his style. He also didn't want her to know about his concern for Igor until he got some answers.

For the moment, he'd have to trust her to stay out of trouble.

* * *

123

He found what he was looking for a few blocks away, a branch of the Bank of Chile. The bank manager was very obliging when Rafe asked to withdraw several thousand dollars worth of pesos from his numbered account in Switzerland. Rafe figured the mafia goons who were chasing Taylor knew her name but had no reason to connect him to whatever mess she was in. And it was going to take a lot of cash to charter a boat for more than a week.

As he left the bank, his cell phone vibrated at his waist. He flipped it open. "Maguire."

"I've got bad news, Mac."

Rafe listened intently as Donovan relayed what he had discovered in Igor's garage. When he finished, Rafe told his friend he'd be in touch, then disconnected. He swore under his breath.

Not only had he put Igor at risk by taking Taylor to his apartment, he'd left the local mafia a mile-wide trail that would lead right to Valparaíso and her. He had to assume they knew he'd borrowed the old truck from Igor; they'd be looking for it. And by moving money out of his Switzerland account at the local bank, he'd put a bull's-eye right smack in the middle of Valparaíso.

Everything had changed. Both he and Taylor were on the run now. And Rafe had a very personal reason to find out what the hell was going on. Nobody had the right to mess with a harmless old man and an innocent woman and get away with it.

Just in case, before Rafe took another step he called Rudy Huhn at the vineyard to warn him to get himself and his family out of the house. The old guy wanted to argue. Rafe did all he could to impress upon Rudy that his life could be in danger.

"One man has already been tortured and killed because he helped us," Rafe told Rudy as forcefully as he could. "I don't want you and your family added to the body count."

"I thought you two were on your honeymoon."

"We lied. Get your family out of there. Now!"

Rafe's next stop was a seedy saloon on the waterfront frequented by seamen from the freighters docked at the wharf. The hour was still early but already the room was smoke-filled and smelled of sour mash and unwashed bodies; a dozen rough-looking sailors lounged at tables or had bellied up to the scarred wooden bar. He already knew he wouldn't let Taylor go on without him. It was too damned dangerous. His guilt if anything happened to her would be too much. Forget she'd tried to *hire* him, for God's sake.

Rafe picked a spot at the end of the bar where he wouldn't be overheard by the other customers.

"What will you have?" the bartender asked in Spanish.

"*Cerveza*," Rafe replied, sliding a hundred dollar bill onto the counter and holding it there. "And information."

The bartender's black eyes widened, and he wiped the back of his hand across his mouth. "If you are after drugs, this is not the place."

"I need a handgun, an automatic, and the ammunition to go with it. I'm willing to pay a good price."

Slowly, the bartender shook his head. "This is a dangerous thing you ask."

With great care, Rafe pulled another bill from his pocket but didn't lay it on the counter. "The world is a dangerous place."

The man hesitated a moment longer and wiped his mouth again. "You wait here. I will make a phone call."

"Not to the *policia, amigo*," Rafe warned. "I would not be pleased if you double-crossed me."

"Never, señor. The call I make is to a man who is no friend of the *policia*." Rafe hoped the bartender's contact was an ordinary crook, not someone associated with Taylor's mafia buddies.

The bartender vanished into the back room. When he returned, he pulled a beer from the tap and brought it to Rafe. "My friend, he will be here soon."

"I'll wait."

As he sipped the beer, Rafe leaned back against the wall, keeping his eye both on the door and the other saloon patrons. He recognized there was a certain danger in relying on strangers. The bartender and his buddy could be planning to mug him for his money. But he didn't have much choice if he was going to keep this transaction quiet. A legitimate gun dealer would have to report his purchase. Given Taylor's situation, that was information Rafe didn't want shared with the authorities.

Surreptitiously, he unsnapped the strap that held his ten-inch knife tucked inside his boot and made sure it slid easily from its scabbard.

In less than ten minutes, the door to the saloon opened. A middle-aged man wearing a flannel shirt and baggy pants silently communicated with the bartender, then stepped back outside. Casually wiping the counter in front of Rafe, the bartender said, "My friend will meet you outside. He is waiting for you in his car."

Rafe nodded his thanks. He stood, leaving the hundred dollar bill on the bar, and went to find the gun dealer. After carefully checking the street in all directions, he stepped to the curb and slid into the backseat of a black Toyota. The man in the flannel shirt sat behind the wheel.

"What I have will cost you a great deal of money," the stranger said.

126

"Let's see the merchandise. I'll pay a fair price for a top quality piece."

He passed Rafe a heavily wrapped package. Inside, Rafe found a Sig Sauer .45-caliber handgun with a walnut grip in good condition. He tested the mechanism and sighted along the barrel. "How many clips have you got?"

"Three now. I can get you more by tomorrow."

Three ten-round clips should be enough unless he and Taylor ran into a lot more trouble than he could handle. "What's your asking price?"

Negotiations didn't take long. Within minutes, the package tucked under his arm, Rafe was back on the sidewalk, on his way to the dock where the fishing fleet was tied up for the night.

It took two more hours to get his plans in order. It was well after dark when he returned to the hotel and a very unhappy Taylor Travini.

She was planted in the middle of the room, standing with her legs spread wide apart, her arms crossed in front of her chest. With her hair hanging loose around her shoulders and a stubborn set to her jaw, she looked like Joan of Arc ready to lead her armies into battle.

"You sure as hell took your sweet time about doing whatever it was you had to do."

"There's been a change in plans."

"Like what?"

"I figure we've got an hour, maybe two, to get out of Dodge."

"What are you talking about?"

"Igor, the mechanic downstairs at my place, is dead."

That slowed her fury. "I'm so sorry. How? A heart attack?"

"He was beaten to death. Very likely by the same black-jacketed goons who've been after you."

127

CHAPTER TWENTY

Taylor couldn't catch her breath. Her knees felt weak, and it was all she could do to stand upright.

"They killed Igor?" Her question was whispered, her throat tight and raw with emotion. "Why? He was an old man. He wasn't a threat to them."

"My guess is they were asking everyone within blocks of Los Caballeros bar if they had seen a blonde American woman. Igor has always been a little protective of me and my visitors, and he was probably suspicious of your friends in those black leather jackets. Whatever they wanted, Igor didn't give it up easily." A muscle worked in Rafe's jaw, and she knew what was coming wouldn't be good. "They broke his fingers before they killed him."

"Oh, God . . ." Taylor sank slowly to the foot of the dilapidated old bed. If they had done that to a sweet old man, what worse things could they have done to her brother? Because she had no doubt that there was a connection between the two she didn't yet understand.

Rafe dropped a pile of packages she hadn't noticed he

was carrying onto the low dresser. "Don't quit on me, Legs. We've got work to do, then we're outta here."

"We have to go back to Santiago. Find out who did such a terrible—"

"I've got a friend working on it from that end. What we need to do, both of us, is locate your brother. He's at the center of whatever the hell is going on. We find him, we get the answers we're both looking for."

Staring at Rafe, she got the impression something had changed. He'd been willing to help her before. An inborn need to protect women, she suspected. Now, he'd taken his natural instinct to a higher level. He was determined. Whoever had killed Igor had crossed a line. Rafe was going to fight back. Now it had nothing to do with the money she'd offered. Assuming it ever had.

She drew a shaky breath. "All right. What do we do now?"

"I hired a charter for us. A very posh sport fishing boat. Two cabins. A fully equipped galley. Deck chairs and a promise that trophy-sized tuna will jump onto our lines."

"Sounds lovely, but I didn't have a leisurely fishing trip in mind. I need to get to—"

"With much fanfare, the captain's going to leave at first light," Rafe continued as though she hadn't objected to his plan. "And tonight in the local pubs he's going to tell everyone he knows that he's taking two crazy *Americanos* on a honeymoon fishing trip up the coast as far as La Serena."

"Rafe, we can't—I won't—"

"Meanwhile, we're going to change our appearance. No more blonde *gringa* and scruffy *Americano*." He pulled a razor, some scissors and a bottle of hair dye from one of the bags on the dresser. "Then we're going

129

to a small fishing village a few kilometers down the coast where I've arranged to buy a trawler that will take us to Punta Arenas. God willing."

"You're kidding."

"I'm dead serious."

From his expression, she couldn't doubt his resolve. Her gaze slid to the scissors, and a tremor of apprehension rippled through her midsection. "You said something about changing our appearance."

"As much as I think your long hair is sexy, it's gotta go. The color, too. You're too easily identifiable."

"I've always liked being a blonde." It was vanity, she supposed. And the fact that her father had always made a fuss about her hair. "The angels must have spun your hair out of gold," he used to say when she was little. But as she grew older, taller and stronger than Terry, her father had stopped talking about angels. All of the praise she'd sought had been heaped on her brother.

Standing, she picked up the scissors from the dresser, weighed them in her palm, tested the sharpness of the blades. "They say change can be good."

"Maybe you'll discover brunettes have more fun."

Her image in the smoky mirror above the dresser looked back at her as if she were already a stranger. She raised the scissors to make the first snip, and her hand trembled. "How short do you think?"

"Here. Let me." He lifted her hair at the nape, letting it flow like quicksilver over his palm. "I don't want you giving yourself a Mohawk."

She eyed him in the mirror. "Is hair-cutting one of the many skills the army taught you?"

"Just a sideline. When my wife was pregnant, she couldn't stand the smell of the beauty shop. All the chemicals made her sick. I was her last resort."

Everything inside Taylor froze. Rafe was playing macho soldier in South America, living like a bachelor, kissing her—albeit reluctantly—and all the time he had a . . .

"You leave your wife back in the States while you play soldier-boy?" she asked, carefully controlling her expression.

"In a way. She and our daughter are both dead and buried." Despite his blunt statement, Taylor could hear the depth of pain he carried echoing in each word he spoke.

"How long—"

"Three years."

"I'm sorry. I didn't—"

As abruptly as flipping a switch, Rafe's mood returned to all-business. "If we're gonna get out of here anytime soon, we've got to get moving. It'll be easier to cut your hair if you sit down on the bed."

Too shaken by his revelation to do anything else, Taylor did as she was told. On her brief shopping sojourn, she'd picked up a comb and brush as well as shampoo, basic feminine necessities and a change of clothes; she'd also washed her hair while awaiting Rafe's return. Now, as he brushed her hair, a shiver of both fear and anticipation rippled through her. She closed her eyes when he took the scissors from her.

Would she really be a different person with short, dark hair—perhaps more free to be who she really was and less the daughter who was always striving for her father's blessing?

Having Rafe cut her hair was a far more intimate affair than going to the beauty salon a few times a year for a trim. She sensed the masculine heat emanating from his body, imagined the warmth of his breath toying at her nape. As the scissors cut, she could almost feel the weight of the past lift away. Unlike Sampson when his locks were shorn, Taylor felt stronger by the minute, more able than ever to face the future. Together with Rafe, she'd find her brother and bring him home safely.

And then she'd consider which persona fit her best, the new or the old.

"That's it." His voice was low and husky, his tone arousing.

Opening her eyes, she saw a changed woman in the dusky mirror: still blonde, but evolving into someone she didn't quite know and could only wonder about.

She ran her fingers through her hair, fluffing the ends and feeling the absent weight. "Not bad for an amateur."

"You've got a lot of natural wave. It's . . . nice."

Meeting his dark-eyed gaze in the mirror, she felt an elemental response stronger even than the one he'd generated by his kisses. And perhaps just as foolish on her part. From the way he'd spoken of his wife and child, he was still grieving their loss.

"It will take me a few minutes to dye my hair. The color has to stay in for a while."

He took a step back, and she immediately missed the intimacy of what had just occurred, even the pain of grief he'd shared with her, however briefly.

"Fine. Do what you have to. I bought you an outfit that will go with your new hair." From a second bag he pulled out a full peasant-style skirt and a deeply cut white sweater that would emphasize the shape of her breasts.

"People are going to notice me in that sweater," she warned.

"It's called hiding in plain sight. They'll see you but they won't know who you are."

Neither would she. Wearing provocative clothes wasn't her style. Apparently it would be now.

She took the first turn in the bathroom, applying the hair coloring at the sink. Although the shade was supposed to be medium brown, it looked nearly black as she rubbed it in. The contrast between her wet hair and her eyebrows was noticeable, so she colored them, too, trying to avoid creating caterpillar brows.

Draping a towel over her shoulders, she vacated the bathroom so Rafe could shave. He left the door open so they could talk.

"Have you spent much time on small boats?" he asked as he lathered his whiskers with soap.

"Some family friends own yachts. I've crewed in a few sailing regattas in San Francisco Bay. Nothing very competitive, though. Mostly beer races."

Lifting his brows, he eyed her in the mirror. "Rich kid stuff, huh?"

"I suppose. But I do know enough to handle the helm and stay on course, and take a turn on watch, if that's what you're wondering."

The razor cut a swath through the shaving cream, conforming to the angular shape of his jaw. "The boat I got us isn't exactly in the same class as the fancy yachts you're probably used to."

"You have no idea what I'm used to, Rafe. Terry and I spent two months going up the Yangtze River in a dhow."

"In China?"

She shrugged. "That was his water fowl phase. He took some great pictures he was going to put together for a book, but the deal fell through. Come to think of it, I guess he's still in that phase, because he came to Chile for the penguins."

"And you went with him to China to keep him out of

133

trouble." Both of Rafe's cheeks were free of whiskers, and he began to work on his throat. The newly shaved skin looked smooth and pale compared to the deep suntan on the rest of his face.

"My brother's a lot of fun to travel with. He's got a great sense of humor. People love him. He makes friends everywhere."

"Except here in Chile," he reminded her.

"Apparently." That, in itself, made no sense. "Admittedly, there's a childlike quality to Terry, an insatiable curiosity that endears him to everyone he meets. He's never judgmental. He embraces the differences between people and accepts them. In turn, they welcome him into their hearts."

"That's a fine testimony to your brother. But maybe this time his curiosity took him somewhere he *wasn't* welcome. And he found out something he wasn't supposed to know."

"But what? Chile is a stable country. Very modern. It's not like some group is trying to overthrow the government."

"Maybe. Maybe not." With a towel, he wiped the remaining shaving cream from his face. "Maybe when we reach Punta Arenas we'll find the answer to that question."

"If you know something I don't, please tell me."

"All I know is that Chile has a standing army, and I train their Rangers to handle any contingency, from a foreign invasion to a guerrilla insurgency. Crazy things are happening all over the world these days."

When he tossed the towel onto the bed, she was stunned by the sharp angles and planes of his face, features etched by a master sculptor that had been hidden by beard. An exciting landscape filled with evocative

134

shadows hinting of hardship and endurance. Courage and determination.

Instinctively, her hand reached up to touch him, to feel for herself the texture of his flesh. The pliable nature of skin over bone, the sensation of her fingertips on his freshly shaved cheeks, and smell the minty scent of shaving cream.

"Taylor?"

Hastily, she dropped her hand to her side. "Shaving cream. You missed a spot," she lied. "On your left ear."

Using the towel, he wiped the imaginary soap away but his eyes never left hers. "Once we leave the hotel, I want us to only speak Spanish until we're alone on the trawler. The idea is to blend in with the locals."

"I understand." What she understood even more clearly was that they were about to embark on a week-long voyage, just the two of them. She didn't know what they'd find at the end of the journey or what might transpire during the long days and nights they'd spend together. But despite the possible dangers awaiting them, anticipation skated along her nerve endings like the shimmer of fine wine.

He gestured toward the bathroom. "Finish up, and then we'll get going."

Rafe retrieved the clothes he'd bought at a secondhand store, blue dungarees and a denim work shirt. When he'd changed, he tucked the Sig Sauer handgun in his belt at the small of his back. The Navy peacoat and black stocking cap he tossed on the bed, and would put it on as they left the hotel. With Taylor in tow, he'd look like a sailor off one of the freighters who'd found a girl and was hoping to get lucky.

Which was an easy fantasy to imagine but one he planned to keep in check.

A few minutes later, when she stepped out of the bathroom, he wasn't sure he wanted to give up the fantasy so easily. The white sweater clung to her body like a second skin, emphasizing the lush contour of her breasts; the skirt shimmered around her calves like water flowing over a smooth beach. With her hair a darker shade than normal, her sheen of innocence was gone, replaced by a subtle wildness. He had an urge to discover if that untamed aura was more than skin deep.

"I'm afraid my eyebrows didn't take the dye as well as my hair. The difference is really noticeable."

He drew a deep breath and shook his head, trying to dislodge the images that came to mind. "Legs, the last thing people will be looking at are your eyebrows."

She appeared momentarily caught off guard, and color rose on her cheeks.

Dragging his gaze away from her, he picked up the slightly worn duffel bag he'd bought and stuffed the jeans and T-shirt he'd been wearing inside. "You can put your change of clothes in this. You'll have to carry it in your lap on the bike until we get to Quintay, where the fishing trawler is docked."

"I could use some dinner. It's been a while since we ate."

"I asked the trawler's owner to have the larder stocked by the time we get there. Part of the deal. We'll eat on the boat."

He watched as she made space in the duffel for the grapevine clippings, then carefully rolled her clothes, including a warm jacket, packing them around what were little more than sticks. It took a true optimist to think those dead-looking vines would ever bear fruit again. Rafe could only hope her positive outlook would be rewarded, but given the circumstances and what had hap-

136

pened to Igor, he didn't have a whole lot of confidence. Forget fooling around with the wine-making business; he'd be happy if they found Terry, and if he could get Taylor and her missing brother safely out of the country.

Once she'd packed up their gear and strapped on her waistpack, Rafe pulled on his coat and carried the duffel downstairs, exiting by the hotel's rear door where he had left the motorcycle.

"Hop on," he said.

She eyed the bike dubiously, shrugged, then hitched up her skirt and straddled the machine. Rafe took an appreciative moment to admire the firm shape of her calves and her California tan from thigh to toe. Yep, her eyebrows were the very last thing any man would notice if they happened to be spotted.

He handed her the duffel, mounted in front of her and started the bike.

"You comfortable back there?"

"Just like home," she answered with a tinge of sarcasm as she adjusted her position. Her arms locked around his chest, and he felt the press of the duffel bag against his lower back where he'd jammed the Sig Sauer.

"How far is it to this town you're talking about?" she asked.

Gunning the engine, he twisted the clutch and wheeled slowly down the alley behind the hotel. "About fifty kilometers, thirty-five miles or so. The south side of the peninsula from here."

"I thought we were supposed to leave the motorcycle with Rudy's friend here in Valparaíso."

"We'll stash it someplace safe and let him know later where to find it." If the mafia goons tracked them to Valparaíso, Rafe wanted the guys in the black jackets diverted to follow the trail of the sport fishing boat. That would give him and Taylor a little breathing room and a head start going south.

The sun stayed up late this time of year in the southern hemisphere, but now it was slipping down to the sea, casting long shadows, as Rafe maneuvered the motorcycle up the steep and winding road to the crest of the coastal range he'd chosen to take rather than the *ascensores*. Each turn was a switchback, and there were dozens of them. A few vehicles passed them going the other way down to the city. Lights began to come on in the houses that lined the roadside, families settling in for the summer night.

Thinking of how far they'd come, of Igor's needless death, and how far they had yet to go to find her brother, Taylor shivered. Despite the comfortable evening air, a chill seeped into the marrow of her bones. Closing her eyes against the wind in her face, and her fears, she tried to picture her twin. His image came to her as clearly as if he were riding beside her. He smiled his encouragement.

"Come on, Tay-Tay." In her imagination, Terry's voice whispered his childhood nickname for her. "What's taking you so long? I'm gettin' some terrific pics down here."

"I'm coming," she answered with her heart, a heart that had pulsed in rhythm with his for the first nine months of their existence. "I'll be there soon."

They followed Highway 68 inland, the way they had originally come, then took the turn off to Quintay, a narrow secondary road that wended its way through yet another mountainous pass. By the time they arrived at the small fishing village, it was fully dark. Scattered streetlights glowed orange along the main street that led to the wharf.

Rafe cruised to a stop in front of an old wooden building with peeling paint and a faded sign that read QUINTAY PESQUERA—the local fish processing plant. He dismounted the bike first, took the duffel and cupped Taylor's elbow to help her off the Harley.

"The guy who is selling the trawler lives in the back. Remember, we're locals. Spanish only."

"*No problema.*" Taylor could think as fluently in Spanish as in English.

Slipping his free arm around her waist, Rafe ushered her toward the rear of the building. Even from outside, the smell of the fish processing plant overpowered the lighter scent of the ocean, making Taylor wrinkle her nose.

"Whew. *Eau d'fish,*" she murmured.

He gave her waist a squeeze. "*En español, querida.*"

She didn't have time to react to him calling her sweetheart, because they'd reached the back door. He knocked, and a masculine voice invited them in.

Inside, an old man sat at a table so roughly hewn that it was probably as ancient as the fishing village. In the light from one overhead bulb, his face resembled a poorly formed bunch of grapes from a diseased vine, his gray beard like mildew eating away at the bottom of the cluster. Taylor sensed he was ill and had been for too long a time. A cracked china saucer overflowing with cigarette butts sat on the table in front of him.

In addition to the old table, the only other furniture was a narrow cot placed against the wall, the blanket made of rough wool, and a wooden fruit crate standing on end with a hot plate on top.

"You brought the money?" the man asked, his voice gravelly and harsh, as though he'd strained often to speak over the sound of machines or the roaring sea.

Rafe pulled a wad of pesos from the pocket of his

Navy peacoat. "You fueled and stocked her?" he responded in Spanish.

"Said I would." All but salivating with greed or need, the old man eyed the money.

Rafe slid the pesos toward the old man. "I'll need the key."

The effort to shrug, to appear casual, seemed almost too much for the old man as he tossed the key on the table. "It is moored down the quay. *Reina de la Mar.*" Queen of the Sea. He reached for the money with a hand distorted by a combination of hard work and arthritis, drawing the cash to him like an alcoholic clutching a bottle of ninety-nine cent wine.

"If it's not as advertised, I'll be back," Rafe warned.

The old man caressed the stack of pesos with his fingertips. "I will be here, amigo. I have nowhere else to go."

"We got here on a motorcycle," Rafe said. "If I bring it inside and leave it with you, will it be safe until a friend picks it up in a few days?"

Again, the man fingered the money on the table. "Now that I am rich, I can afford to be honest, eh?"

"I'll take your word on it, compadre."

"You have it."

Taylor waited while Rafe went back outside and wrestled the Harley into a storage room the old man showed him. It looked like the space hadn't been used in years for anything other than gathering dust and mice droppings. Rafe said good-bye to the old guy and ushered Taylor down the wharf.

"That poor man," she said.

"The money will see him through his old age, unless he drinks it all up in the first week. In which case he won't have anything to worry about. He'll be dead."

Taylor knew Rafe's harsh prediction was probably

true, but she hated the prospect of a man who'd obviously led a hard life ending it there in that old building with no one to care for him.

"What about the Harley?" she asked. "You think he'll keep it safe for Rudy?"

"Until he runs through the rest of the money. Then he'll sell it to the first taker with a few pesos in his pocket."

Not a particularly encouraging thought. But maybe they could let Rudy know soon where they'd stored his son's motorcycle.

"I hope you're keeping a tab of all the money you're spending. I'll see that you're reimbursed when we get out of this mess."

"No need."

"Of course there's a need. I said I'd pay for your time. That goes for your out-of-pocket—"

"Shut up, Legs." He halted abruptly, turning on her. "This gig is as much mine as yours now. It got real personal when they killed Igor."

"I understand, but I still think—"

"Do whatever you want. I'm not going to waste time arguing." Taking her arm, he propelled her along the dock.

Arrogant, stubborn, pigheaded man!

Looking for the *Queen of the Sea*, they passed several large fishing trawlers tied to the wharf and bobbing quietly in the slow rise and fall of the harbor. Seagulls had found resting places for the night, the alpha birds choosing the highest perches above the boats' crow's nests, lesser gulls relegated to the top of pilings turned white by thousands of prior avian visitors.

Mounds of purse seine fishing nets and buoys covered with tarps or old rugs were spaced every fifteen feet or so along the dock. Bits of heavy twine from the fishing nets, empty wine bottles, soda cans and general trash littered the area. The smell of diesel fuel was thick in the air, and where the dock lights shone onto the water, swirls of oil and spilled fuel floated. Overhead, fingers of drifting fog veiled the stars.

"This must be it," Rafe said. He stood on the dock at the stern of a trawler much smaller than the others, REINA DE LA MAR in faded paint across the back. Even in the dim light, it was obvious the hull was rusty and the wheelhouse hadn't been painted in years. Fortunately, above the flying bridge Taylor noted a radar antenna, which gave hope that the old boat had been modernized sometime in the last century.

"That sport fishing boat you sent off on our honeymoon without us would have been nicer."

He tossed the duffel bag onto the deck. It landed with a thud. "Not if your shadow men track it down."

"True," she murmured as she gingerly crossed the narrow plank that served as a gangway to the wheelhouse. Pulling open the heavy door, she found the light switch and flipped it on, revealing strictly basic equipment—a radar set, an ancient radio and a newer global positioning device. Varnish had long since worn off the helm, leaving bare wood, and the captain's chair appeared to be listing toward the port side due to one short leg.

"You really know how to treat a girl right, don't you?" she said. "Everything first class."

An amused half-smile lifted one corner of his lips. "I'm glad you appreciate the finer things. The good news is she has four hundred and fifty horses and can make ten knots, maybe more on a good day."

"Hmm. I'm going to check belowdecks."

"I'll see if I can get this old crate going. Then we'll cast off."

The galley was larger than she expected, with a four-burner stove and a gimbal-mounted table that could seat six. The small refrigerator had been stocked with eggs and bacon, the pantry cupboard with canned soups and stews, fresh loaves of bread and jelly. A couple of six-packs of beer had been thoughtfully included in the larder, three bottles of local wines and one bottle of brandy. Not exactly gourmet fare, but adequate supplies to see them through for several days.

Beneath her feet she felt the low rumble of a powerful engine starting.

Turning, Taylor went back up to the wheelhouse. Rafe stood at the helm, straight and strong, his shoulders broad, his feet wide apart, looking for all the world as though he were the captain of a giant seagoing vessel. She felt the now familiar tingle of anticipation about what would come.

"Can you handle the helm while I cast off?" he asked.

"Sure. Aren't we going to turn on the running lights?"

"Not till we get out of the harbor." He stepped aside so she could get to the helm. "Keep her hard against the dock until the lines are free. When I give the signal, ease out into the center of the channel. No more than two knots. We'll take this slow and easy."

Clicking her heels together, she saluted. "Aye, aye, captain."

He cocked his head, appraising her in a way that made her want to squirm, despite his often arrogant ways. "You make a damn cute deckhand, sailor. Just don't give me any lip."

She imagined doing something wild and wicked with

her lips and his, but thought better of mentioning the idea. Besides, they were going to be in close proximity to each other for the next five or six days, minimum. She didn't dare start something she wasn't willing to finish.

He left the wheelhouse. She familiarized herself with the controls. The radar screen glowed green, sweeping an outline of the other boats tied up at the wharf and the hillside behind the fishing village. From her position at the helm, she had a three hundred-sixty degree view of the surroundings through a wrap-around set of windows. Nothing moved except Rafe as he untied one heavy line, tossed it onto the deck, then jogged to the other end of the boat.

The second line hit the deck followed by Rafe. "Take her out," he ordered in Spanish.

Taylor pressed the throttle forward. As the deep-throated engine responded, she gripped the helm lightly, the wood smooth in her palm. On her command, the boat eased away from the dock and turned a few degrees to port.

By the time she had the boat at midchannel, Rafe joined her in the wheelhouse, bringing with him the duffel bag, which he tossed down to the galley. Coming up behind her, he looped his arms around her waist and watched over her shoulder as they made their stealthy departure, heading in darkness out to sea. At the entrance to the fishing harbor, a buoy clanged its bell, rocking rhythmically in the swells to welcome or say farewell to those who were moving on to new harbors.

Rafe's breath warmed the sensitive column of her neck, and she wondered where or what their final destination would be.

CHAPTER TWENTY-ONE

As Rafe stood with his arms around Taylor, he watched the obstacles vanish from the radar screen until they were beyond the harbor and into the open ocean. He hated to let go of her. Her hair smelled faintly of apricot shampoo and was feathery light against his cheek. The inviting juncture of her neck and shoulder was a lure few men would be strong enough to ignore. The smooth skin was made for kissing. For tasting.

A coil of frustration tightened in his gut. This was no time for his libido to get out of hand. The journey had just begun. They had a long way to go. Throwing sex into the mix could only mean trouble later.

Though, somewhere deep inside, Rafe had the feeling it wasn't just lust he was experiencing, but something more profound. He was even less sure he was ready for that. If anything, it made him feel disloyal to the woman he'd vowed to love forever.

"Take her up a few knots. We'll see what this old tub can do."

She eased the throttle forward. The hum of the engine

rose in volume; the vibration of the deck increased. With the hold empty and with only an eight-foot draw, the old trawler rode high in the water. It pitched up and down over the swells instead of plowing through them, like a larger ship with a deeper keel would. In heavy weather the ride would be pretty rough.

"Take a heading of a hundred ninety-two degrees, south-southwest," he said when their speed reached ten knots. "We'll stay about twenty miles off shore. Keep the coastline on the radar. If we run into any trouble, we'll be within shouting distance of a safe harbor and help."

She swung the helm to port and the compass responded, taking up the new course. The trawler wallowed as the sea changed, then settled down to the new rocking motion.

"Hundred ninety-two degrees. Aye, captain."

He squeezed her around the middle. "At ease, sailor. With a crew of two, we don't have to be quite so formal."

"Just demonstrating good seamanship, captain," she teased.

"In that case, sailor, how 'bout you go below and scrounge us up something to eat. I'm starved."

She slanted him a look over her shoulder. "That sounds exceptionally sexist to me. One woman in the crew, and she's the one who has to do the cooking?"

"Okay. So we'll take turns. Can you handle it up here while I go below?"

"I'm fine. This isn't exactly a racing yacht, more like a bathtub, but I can keep her on course."

"Great. I'd prefer that some passing freighter doesn't ram us because we're running without lights. I'll take care of that first, then dinner."

A minute later, Taylor listened to Rafe's footsteps descend the companionway to the galley. There wasn't much to see outside. The running lights illuminated only the faint outline of the bow as it cut through the water, stirring up phosphorous plankton. The stars were dim and there was no moon. The radar showed nothing but an irregular coastline on their port side and empty sea on the starboard. They were alone.

Gooseflesh crept down her spine. Twenty miles from shore with dangerous men very likely in pursuit of them, or they soon would be. She suddenly wished Rafe had commandeered a speedy destroyer bristling with guns instead of a rusty fishing trawler that still carried the scent of its former occupation. Surely any Army Ranger worth his salt could have arranged that.

Suddenly, something struck the window with a bang right in front of her. In a reflexive action, she ducked and let out a startled shriek. An instant later, Rafe flew up the gangway from the galley brandishing a gun.

"Get down!" he ordered.

Taylor's eyes widened, and she straightened. "Where did you get that?"

Half crouched, his gun extended at the ready position, he glanced around the wheelhouse. "In Valparaíso. I thought I heard a shot."

She eyed the weapon cautiously. She and Terry were basically pacifists. Clearly, Rafe wasn't. Under the circumstances, that was a good thing. But she hadn't been aware he had a gun, and he hadn't thought to tell her.

"I think a bird hit the windshield. Sometimes land birds get confused and are attracted to the light on passing boats. Anyway, it startled me. I'm sorry I screamed."

He lowered the gun. "I suppose you're going to tell me the same thing happened to you when you and your brother were cruising through China in the dhow."

Her lips twitched ever so slightly. "No, actually the first time it was in the Mediterranean."

Shaking his head, he slipped the handgun into the waist of his jeans. "I'll go check on dinner."

"Wait. You take the helm a minute. I'll see how badly the bird is hurt."

"Did you go around rescuing wounded animals when you were a kid, too?"

"Sometimes," she admitted with a smile. "Besides, Terry would shoot me if I didn't try to help the bird. Figuratively, of course. Terry isn't into guns."

"Maybe he'd have been better off on this trip if he were."

She hesitated a moment, then stepped away from the helm. "I'm hoping that's not the case."

Shoving open the door, she stepped outside. The sultry breeze blew warm and fresh in her face, and she breathed the ocean air deeply. Santiago sat at the same latitude south of the equator as Los Angeles did to the north, and the weather patterns were similar, although the seasons were reversed. As they continued toward the tip of Chile, the weather, even in summer, would grow colder the closer they got to Antarctica. Where Terry had been heading, there were glaciers that calved big chunks of ice right into the sea.

She found it lying on the deck; still stunned, the brown bird was slightly larger than a sparrow and stared at her with blinking yellow eyes. Terry would no doubt know the species, but she wasn't as good at identifying birds.

"It's okay, little lady." Gingerly, taking precautions not to injure the bird further, Taylor picked it up. "I'll find you a box or something for tonight, then we'll let you go in the morning when you'll be able to find land. How's that sound?"

The bird chirped its agreement—or disapproval; Taylor didn't know which.

Walking aft past the big winch used to haul long fishing lines, she found a storage locker filled with odds and ends, including an empty cardboard box. She carefully placed the bird inside and folded the top closed.

"You'll be fine now, little lady."

When she got back to the wheelhouse, she found it empty. Alarm shot through her. The boat was still on course but Rafe was gone.

"Rafe!" she shouted, a little bubble of panic pressing against her breastbone.

"Down here," he called from the galley. "I was afraid our stew would burn."

She exhaled in relief, and set the box on the floor in a corner of the wheelhouse. "Don't you think someone should be driving the boat?"

"I engaged the auto pilot." Carrying a tray with bread, two bowls and wineglasses, he came up the stairs from below.

The scent of beef stew made Taylor's stomach growl with hunger. "If that stew tastes as good as it smells, I'm going to sign on to be the California distributor."

"I doctored it with a little Merlot. Figured it couldn't hurt."

Taylor discovered it did better than that. Sitting in the captain's chair, balanced on its uneven legs, she consumed her entire bowl of stew plus two slices of crusty French bread. Rafe ate standing up, leaning back against the counter that held all the electronic gear. He seemed to be at one with the rocking motion of the boat—comfortable and at ease, as he appeared to be in all situations.

"Where did you learn to be such a good sailor?" she asked.

"I spent the summer after high school graduation working on a salmon boat out of Alaska. Made some damn good money for a kid."

"If you were so experienced, why didn't you join the Navy instead of the Army?"

"My dad was Army. A Ranger. He would have rolled over in his grave if I'd enlisted in the Navy."

"Is your mother still alive?"

"Nope. Mom died while I was in college."

"I'm sorry. Brothers and sisters?"

"No. My parents put all their eggs in one basket, metaphorically speaking."

And now that his wife and child were gone, Taylor realized he had no one left to love.

Downing her last sip of wine, she said, "If you can make canned stew taste this good, I vote for you to do all the cooking."

His lips hitched into a half smile. "Oh, no you don't, Legs. We had a deal. You get the breakfast detail."

"I'll probably burn the eggs."

"Wouldn't be the first time I've eaten burned eggs. Hell, I've lived for weeks on cold C-rations that I had to carry on my back and been glad to have 'em."

"You've been in a lot of battles?" From the haunted look she sometimes saw in the corners of his dark eyes, she imagined he'd seen more death and destruction than any man should have to witness.

His dismissive shrug was barely perceptible and not in the least believable. "It's what Army Rangers do, go from one hot spot to another."

"Why'd you join the Rangers in the first place?"

"Following in my old man's footsteps, I guess. Thought I could make a difference."

"Did you?"

His forehead furrowed and he seemed to consider his answer before he pushed away from the counter. "I got some good men killed who shouldn't have been." He reached for her bowl and put it with his on the tray. "I'll clean up the dishes, then take the first watch while you hit the sack. You can use the captain's cabin, such as it is. I'll take one of the bunks in the crew's quarters when it's my turn."

He'd sailed so fast past his remark about getting men killed, she'd had no time to react. Clearly he didn't want to pursue the topic. She'd go along with that—for now. But she was darn sure some of the pain she'd seen in his eyes stemmed from the deaths of those men he'd spoken of with such feeling.

"Okay," she said. "How do you want to handle the watches? Four hours on and four hours off?"

"Fine," he said.

"You'll wake me?"

"Sure."

She eyed him suspiciously. "We need to be a team, Rafe, or this won't work. I can carry my part of the load."

He halted at the top of the stairs to the galley, one hand on the railing, the other holding the dinner tray. Without looking at her, he said, "I've been going solo for three years, Taylor. I'll get you to wherever you need to go. Hopefully we'll find your brother, and I can get you back to the States in one piece. Beyond that, I'm not making any promises."

She drew back as though she'd been slapped in the

face. She hadn't been looking for commitment. Or even a relationship. Yet he acted as though she'd crossed some unseen line.

Rarely had she been so attracted to a man. It hurt that he'd blow her off, particularly since his kisses had been more than platonic. Or so she'd thought.

She took a crust of bread she'd saved and knelt beside the cardboard box. Little Lady needed to keep up her strength if she was going to fly all the way back to shore in the morning.

Opening the flap, she peered inside. When you open a box—or probe too deeply into a person's life—sometimes there's something scary lurking inside. Maybe Rafe wasn't ready for someone to take a deep look at what was haunting him. Or why.

Chapter Twenty-two

Taylor woke slowly. The gentle rocking motion that had finally lulled her to sleep had changed. Trying to ignore the tug of sunlight on her eyelids, she burrowed further under the covers.

Sunlight!

Blinking, she sat up. Sun slanted through the porthole onto the captain's bed. Outside, it caught the tops of white caps, turning them gold in the morning light.

"Damn it! He was supposed to wake me up," she muttered, throwing her legs over the side of the bed. The full-sized bed nearly filled the whole cabin, leaving room for only a built-in desk and a chair. She grabbed her old jeans from the duffel bag and tugged them on. Since she'd slept in a T-shirt, she only needed to pull on her hiking boots and she was ready to confront Captain Tough Guy. The jerk!

She stormed up the ladder to the wheelhouse. "I guess you forgot we're supposed be a team," she snapped.

Glancing over his shoulder, he smiled a lazy smile. Morning whiskers darkened his cheeks, making him look more pirate than Army Ranger. "When I checked on you, you were so knocked out I didn't want to wake you."

"You should have." She crossed her arms over her chest, somehow both embarrassed and aroused to know he'd watched her while she slept.

"How 'bout stirring up that breakfast we talked about, then I'll hit the sack. You can take the next watch."

"Humph. Hope you're ready for burned eggs." That was an idle threat. Though she wasn't the greatest cook in the world, she could handle eggs just fine. To her father, her meager accomplishments in the culinary world had been a disappointment. *Italian women cook,* he'd told her.

"I'm hungry enough to eat 'em raw."

"Don't tempt me."

He laughed out loud, his voice gravelly and warm, a wonderful sound, all the more so because his laughter was so rare.

"By the way," he said, "I found the marine radio frequency for weather. Chilean National Weather Service reports a storm coming up from the south. We'll probably hit the front in a couple of hours. The swells are already starting to increase."

The voice of the weather announcer droned from a speaker mounted above the electronics console. For a moment, Taylor concentrated on news of the deteriorating weather.

"Should we head for a safe harbor?" she asked.

"This old tub should ride it out all right. Since we aren't that many miles from Valparaíso yet, I'd just as soon stick it out."

"Fine by me." Since the sky was still clear, Taylor thought it best to release the little brown bird now while there was still a chance she could make it safely to shore. She peeked into the box.

"How's your bird?" Rafe asked.

"Seems pretty alert. I'll take her outside and see how she feels about flying home."

The stiff wind caught Taylor the moment she stepped outside. Definitely stronger and cooler than the prior evening, a cold front was moving up the coast.

She opened the box. The bird eyed her for a moment, hopped to the rim of the box, then took off. The breeze whipped the little bird toward the back of the boat before she could pick up any headway. Finally, she turned into the wind, steadied herself and veered off toward the distant shore. Taylor sighed with admiration for the little bird's courage.

Taylor wasn't exactly a deep-water sailor, but she'd experienced rough seas on a sailing yacht a time or two. She'd get her sea legs, much as the bird had found its wings, and would see the storm through.

Going below, she started a fresh pot of coffee. Rafe had apparently drained the last pot during the night. Then she scrambled some eggs, made toast and found some applesauce for a side dish.

They ate in the wheelhouse again. The changing sea was obvious, the wind catching the tips of whitecaps and tossing them in the air as spray, showering salt water on the main deck.

Rafe ate quickly, then went below to catch a catnap, and Taylor took the helm. She suspected he wouldn't be gone long. The sea was turning pretty rough. He wouldn't stand for being belowdecks when he could play hero topside.

Rafe, feeling refreshed, was back in the wheelhouse in less than an hour.

"That didn't take long," Taylor commented.

"I understand Ben Franklin recommended naps over eight hours of sleep."

"Is this where I tell you to go fly a kite?" she asked sweetly.

His lips twitched into a half smile as he took a quick survey of the situation. The sea had grown much rougher since he'd gone below, the waves now washing over the deck. The windshield wipers flicked back and forth trying to clear a combination of rain and spray from the windows with only momentary success. Visibility was less than a mile and closing fast.

"Looks like the weather service may have underestimated the storm," he said. "Come starboard five degrees. We'll head into the waves."

"Five degrees starboard, aye."

He smiled at her nautical vernacular as well as her calm confidence and quick wit. Not a bad combination to have in a partner, even if she did question his every order. She'd shoved aside the captain's chair and stood at the helm, legs spread apart for balance, her hands firmly on the wheel. A competent sailor. One helluva woman, too.

He'd found a couple of yellow slickers in a locker belowdecks, and the life vests. He hung a slicker on a hook behind Taylor and shrugged into the other one. The life vests he piled on the floor beneath the slicker.

"I'm going to go check on our life raft," he said.

She turned quickly, her green eyes wide. "Are we sinking?"

"Not that I know of. The owner said the life raft was fitted out with food and water for six people for six days. I didn't have time to check it last night. Thought it

156

would be good to know if we actually have a way off this tub, or if we'd have to go down with the ship."

"That's an inspiring thought."

He chuckled, tugging on a matching yellow rain hat. "I'll be right back."

"Shouldn't you have a life vest on?"

"I don't plan to get that wet."

She gave him a disapproving eye roll as he pulled open the hatch and stepped outside. The wind caught him broadside and nearly blew him down the gangway. Rain and saltwater stung his face. Grabbing the ladder, he pulled himself up rung by rung to the flying bridge.

The wind was stronger here but there was less spray; the height above the deck, however, magnified the pitch and roll of the old boat, making for a roller-coaster ride. No doubt the *Reina de la Mar* had survived rougher seas than this and stayed afloat to tell about it. Rafe had to assume she would do the same this time.

A surplus military life raft was securely lashed to the deck and appeared to be in good shape, although it was barely large enough to hold two, not six. Any additional passengers would have to stay in the water and hang onto the straps. Fortunately, they were only a crew of two.

The compartments that held food were full, but Rafe was reluctant to check the expiration dates. He hoped they wouldn't have to deal with that problem.

A sharp pitch of the boat staggered him as he made his way back to the ladder and down to the wheelhouse.

"How you doing down here?" he asked after he yanked the hatch shut. Rainwater dripped onto the deck around his feet.

Taylor glanced over her shoulder, the color high on her cheeks, and quickly returned her attention to the compass and the oncoming sea. "It's hard to keep on course."

"Just stay headed into the waves as best you can." Taking off his hat, he slapped it against his thigh to shake off the water, hung it on a nearby hook and un-snapped his rain slicker. "We'll be fine."

"I'll take your word for it." She didn't sound convinced.

Rafe could understand that. A Sunday sailor puttering around the San Francisco Bay wouldn't encounter a storm like this. But despite her apprehension, she was holding her own. He gave her points for that.

Gripping an overhead pipe to steady himself, he watched the waves wash over the bow railing and slap against the windshield. With every wave, the shallow draft boat yawed off to the side, putting them in danger of broaching, finally righting itself in the trough, only to roll off again at the top.

This was some bitchin' summer storm. If he'd known how rough it was going to get, he might have thought twice about his grand plan to get Taylor away from the mafia goons.

"What's the latest weather report?" he asked, having to shout over the incessant roar of the storm.

"Not good. They're reporting winds up to fifty knots along with heavy squalls."

The boat crawled up the front of another wave, then banged down hard on the other side, slewing sideways. At that very moment, the engine sputtered, gave one last cough and quit dead, leaving only the pounding of the waves to shake the boat.

"Shit! This ol' bucket of—"

"Rafe! The engine—"

"I know. Keep her into the wind as best you can. I'll go below, see what the problem is."

In one leap, he shot down the ladder to the galley and scrambled, lurching back and forth with the waves, to the engine room. He opened the hatch to the stink of diesel fuel and a foot of saltwater flooding the compartment.

"Son of a bitch!"

It didn't take him long to discover the air intake was flooded. The old rubber tube had cracked wide open. Rafe figured it served him right, being in this mess, buying the damn boat sight unseen.

It would take a while to jerry-rig a fix. Meanwhile, he had to get rid of the water in the engine room. He switched on the bilge pump. The subtle hum of the electric pump told him it was working. For the moment. But the wildly oscillating motion of the boat was going to get them sunk if he didn't do something quickly.

In the forecastle at the bow of the boat, he found a rolled up canvas sea anchor along with some line. He raced back up the ladder to the wheelhouse.

"I'm going put out the sea anchor," he told Taylor. "See if that will give us a little more control until I can get the engine fixed."

Without taking her eyes off the oncoming waves, she warned, "Don't you go out there again without a life vest and a safety line. I have no intention of trying to ride out this storm by myself. And I sure as hell can't turn this bathtub around to search for you if you go overboard."

"Aye, aye, mate. Whatever you say." He wasn't entirely a fool, and knew this time she was right. Safety came first. For both of them. "When I get the anchor rigged, I'll signal you to bring the rudder amidships."

"Understood. Amidships." Her voice quavered a little.

Seconds later, he was struggling against the surge of waves across the bow, the wallowing of the boat, and feeling damn lucky he was attached to the boat by a safety line.

Despite the Queen's apparent lack of maintenance, the cleats and stainless steel swivel on the bow looked solid. He rigged the sea anchor, dropped it over the windward side of the boat and waited while the nylon line played out. When he felt the boat trying to turn into the wind, he waved his hand over his head to signal Taylor.

Grabbing the railing, he started back toward the wheelhouse, the fifty-knot wind blowing him along.

From her position at the helm, Taylor fought against both the wildly pitching boat and the fear that churned in her stomach. She'd never seen the ocean this chaotic, the curl of the waves so high. So angry. None of her boating experiences had prepared her for this.

She gasped as a rogue wave twenty feet higher than the main deck crashed over the bow. The ocean slammed against the wheelhouse like an angry monster determined to devour everything in its path and blotted out her view. Her heart was in her throat as the wave receded, revealing a wave-washed, empty deck.

"Rafe!" Oh, God, what had happened? Panic whipped through her. He couldn't have gone overboard. He couldn't! He had on a safety line. She'd seen it.

Abject terror coursed through her as she raced from one side of the wheelhouse to the other, peering down to the deck. Looking for Rafe. Praying.

"Where the hell did you go?" she screamed, knowing full well, wherever he was, he couldn't hear her over the pounding sound of the sea. Tears burned in her eyes, but she wouldn't let them fall. She had to be calm. *Think*. For both their sakes.

Finally she spotted him, or at least one of his hands, clinging precariously to the gunwale on the port side.

"Dear God . . . ," she sobbed.

Without hesitation, she grabbed a life vest, pulled it on and hooked the safety straps, then went out into the storm. The sea anchor was doing its job, steadying the boat, but the pitch and yaw and the waves washing over the bow still made the deck a dangerous place to be.

Bent into the wind, fighting it every step of the way, she clung to the safety line, following it to the port side of the bow where Rafe was hanging on, his knuckles white. She braced herself against the railing and leaned over. With the sea churning below her, she extended her hand toward Rafe.

"Grab my hand!" she ordered.

He looked up, the strain of his effort to hold on obvious in his face, the taut muscles in his neck corded like steel. "What are you doing? You'll be washed over—"

"Grab my damn hand, Rafe, before I yank you up here by the short hairs."

"I can do it myself. I just need to wait—"

"Now, Rafe! Now!"

"Go back inside. I'm okay."

"I'll go inside when you do."

He grimaced and shook his head, but she didn't budge.

"Give it up, Rafe. I'm as tough as you are."

He seemed to concede that was true. Then, with an enormous effort, he swung himself up far enough to wrap his big hand around her wrist. The weight of him shocked her, but she managed to hold steady. Then she began to pull. Seawater tasting of salt lashed cold and fierce at her face, and soaked her clothes through to the

161

skin. She strained with all her might, so hard she was afraid her right arm would pop out of the shoulder socket. He was one hundred and eighty pounds of dead weight being dragged away from her by the wind and waves. Impossible to budge no matter how hard she tried.

Their eyes met. She saw determination in his dark eyes. Years of struggle. Battles won and painful defeats. The will to succeed. To survive.

Adrenaline surged through her. Together they'd survive this test, this contest between the power of the sea and their resolve. Their lives depended upon it.

Digging deep for strength, using her legs for leverage, she hauled him up little by little until finally he could risk letting go of the gunwale in order to gain a solid grip higher on the railing. With a final lunge, a renewed surge of strength, he came up and over the railing, crashing down on top of her. They were both breathing hard. Spray and mist pelted them. The deck tipped, threatening to eject them into the sea. This time for keeps.

Somehow they held on. To each other and the deck.

"Let's get inside," he finally said, his ability to speak recovering faster than hers.

"You go first." She sucked in a lungful of air. "I can't move."

"Sure you can." He rolled to his feet as though what they'd experienced had been just another stroll in the park, then pulled her up beside him. He looped his arm firmly around her waist. "See? Steady as a rock."

"My hero," she said, wheezing and coughing.

"At this point, I'd say you're the one who gets today's gold star for heroism. Also for being as crazy as a fruitcake for risking your neck to save me."

"You can complain later, okay?" Secretly pleased he

had acknowledged her heroism, she staggered with him across the deck and up the ladder to the wheelhouse. Once inside, she began to shiver both from shock and the freezing cold water.

"Get below," he ordered. "Get out of those wet clothes and into something warm. I'm going to see to the engine."

"You're s-shivering, too. You should—"

"I'm used to it. Go!" He all but shoved her down the companionway to the galley below, following quickly on her heels. "After you're dressed, if you can make some coffee, that would help."

Without waiting for a reply, he hurried aft to the engine compartment.

So cold that her skin was blue, Taylor changed out of her sopping wet clothes and put on dry ones and the heavy jacket she'd bought. Starting a pot of coffee wasn't easy as the boat continued to pitch and roll with the rough sea. Her hands shook like she had palsy. Finally, with a mug of dark black coffee, she went up to the wheelhouse again, although there was little she could do but watch the waves pound against the trawler as if it were no more than an insignificant toy.

The radar showed they were still well off the coast of Chile; the global positioning system indicated they were holding steady. But if this storm kept up much longer and they couldn't restart the engine, Taylor imagined they'd be blown back to Valparaíso by nightfall.

Time and the seascape blurred, marking only the sweep of two matching windshield wipers that were hopelessly outmatched by the rain and waves battering them.

And then, amazingly, she felt rather than heard the diesel engine start. The rhythmic throb rose up through her feet and brought with it a sense of enormous relief.

"Thank God," she said with a sigh. They weren't out of danger yet, but at least they had a means of propulsion.

A few minutes later, Rafe appeared in the wheelhouse carrying a mug of coffee. His hair was still wet, his eyes bloodshot from the saltwater, but he'd changed clothes and was no longer shivering.

He cocked her a half smile. "You did good out there, Legs."

She felt warm under his steady gaze. "So did you, Rafe."

"Looks like we make a pretty good team."

"That's what I tried to tell you. We're a team." She tried not to consider that they could be more than that. He'd made it clear he wasn't interested in promises. She'd have to take his word for that. But she knew in that desperate moment on deck when she feared she'd lose him, that he'd become the most important person in her life. More important than her father. Even more important than her brother, who had always meant the world to her. For now, she'd keep that realization to herself.

Over the next few hours, both the storm and the day waned. Rafe fixed them some cold sliced-beef sandwiches to eat before sending Taylor below to get some rest. He took the early watch and woke her when it was her turn at the helm. By then, the autopilot had been engaged and they were plowing through gentle seas on their original course, south-southeast to Puntas Arenas.

Taylor was about an hour into her watch when she heard Rafe shouting.

"Get down! Spread out! The bastards! Stop them! Stop them!"

Shocked and puzzled by his outburst, Taylor hurried down the ladder to the crew's quarters, a cabin no larger than the captain's that held three sets of bunk beds with paper-thin mattresses. Rafe was lying on a lower bunk, his legs entangled in an old Army blanket, his khaki T-shirt dark with sweat, his arms flailing as though he were trying to drive off a swarm of bees.

"Don't shoot her! Run, Lizbeth! Run! Please run!"

Sitting down on the edge of the bunk, Taylor gently rubbed his arm to wake him. "Rafe. It's okay. You're dreaming."

"Gotta get Katy. She needs me."

"Shh, Rafe. It's all over. It's just a bad—"

He grabbed her wrist with one hand. The other closed around her throat and squeezed tightly. Although his eyes were open she knew he didn't see her. It was some other vision he was attacking.

"Rafe!" she gasped. The air stalled in her lungs with nowhere to go. Blood pounded behind her eyes, and she began to see stars. She struggled to get free, hitting at his arms, chopping down on his wrist with the side of her hand. Almost too late, her karate training kicked in. She rammed her hands up and out between his arms, breaking his grip on her. Then she spun away.

"Wake up, Rafe! Wake up."

Suddenly, his eyes focused on her. In a split second, recognition set in.

"What the hell?" he muttered. Clearly disoriented, he looked around, not yet able to make sense of what had happened.

Coughing, she drew oxygen into her starved lungs. Blood pulsed through her veins again. She staggered back, collapsing on a bunk on the opposite side of the small cabin.

"You were dreaming." The words rasped against her larynx.

"I hurt you." He shook his head, apparently still not entirely in the present. "I'm sorry."

"It's okay." Rubbing her throat, she coughed again. There'd be bruise marks tomorrow, she was sure of it.

He sat on the edge of the bunk spearing his fingers through his hair. "Those flashbacks don't happen very often."

"Thank God. I wouldn't want to relive that scene every day." His anger, his agitation, had frightened her. And yet, he had her sympathy, too. She was sure the nightmare had to do with his military experiences. And the wife he had lost. "You want to tell me about it?"

"Not particularly."

"It might help."

He lifted his head. "What? In your spare time you're a shrink?"

She felt him lashing out at her emotionally and decided to ignore it. "I'm a good listener."

"Only because I didn't quite kill you."

"No, because I . . ." She held the thought. "Talk to me, Rafe. Tell me about Lizbeth. And Katy."

He leaned back, almost as if she'd struck him. "You don't want to know."

"Yes, I do. Furthermore . . ." She rubbed her throat. "I think you owe me an explanation."

CHAPTER TWENTY-THREE

In an exclusive residential area of Santiago, the lights in Aquilar Mendoza's home burned brightly. Servants dressed in white circulated through the crowd of wealthy and influential guests, offering fine Chilean wines, champagne, aperitifs and dainty canapés. From a balcony overlooking the great hall, a string quartet played classical music. Following dinner, they would be replaced by a livelier band suitable for an evening of dancing.

All of the important people of Chile were present, or would be by the time *el presidente* arrived. No one had the political will to refuse an invitation from Aquilar Mendoza for a black-tie affair. He was that powerful. He'd seen to that through well-placed bribes and well-timed threats to disclose the dark secrets of those who would rule his country. Soon he alone would be the undisputed leader of Chile.

His cell phone chimed. Excusing himself, he stepped away from the wife of the minister of agriculture, a woman with as much charm as a fat cow. He flipped open the phone.

"*¿Que?*" What? He answered brusquely.

"The sport fishing boat was a decoy," the man on the other end of the line announced without preamble. "The pair we were looking for were never on board."

Mendoza nodded and grimaced a smile at a passing financier, then turned away to continue his phone call. "Where are they?"

"We don't know. The trail has gone cold."

Had he been alone, he would have cursed at the incompetence of his underling. "Then you have failed in your duty. Return to Santiago at once. I will have to rely on my people in Punta Arenas to stop that woman and her companion. And you had best hope they are successful, or you will suffer the consequences for bungling such a simple task."

He disconnected before the caller could respond, an angry pulse throbbing at his temple. *How hard is it to find and halt one woman's futile search for her brother?* he thought with disgust. If he had the time, he'd have done the job himself and been finished with it. But he had to remain in Santiago. When the moment came, he had to be in position to assume his proper place in the new government. There could be no delays, no opportunity for others to reorganize and snatch control of the country away from him.

It was his destiny! At the age of eleven a fortune teller had told him so. He'd been poor, going to bed hungry more nights than he cared to remember. But he would become *el presidente*, she had told him. All through the years, the cards had turned in his favor. The time had arrived to make that prediction come true.

He would not fail.

CHAPTER TWENTY-FOUR

A pair of dolphins leaped in unison beside the trawler, bringing a smile to Taylor's face. The two sleek black-and-white animals had been escorting the *Reina de la Mar* for the last several miles as they approached Punta Arenas, cavorting in the boat's wake or leading the parade. They seemed to be saying, "Watch me! Watch me!"

Protected by dozens of islands from the worst of the weather, the Strait of Magellan and the peninsula where Punta Arenas was located could still be whipped by gusty winds. Today, whitecaps in the bay tossed spray into the air beneath a bright blue sky.

Taylor and Rafe had been at sea for almost a week. Now they could spot wrecks of nineteenth-century sailing vessels stranded on a long sandy beach and the robust city of more than a hundred-thousand people stretching back from the shoreline. Buildings as tall as eight stories dotted the landscape of the largest city in the Patagonia region and its capital. This had been Terry's initial destination in southern Chile, according to his last phone call with Taylor.

The daunting task of finding her brother in this sprawling town seemed suddenly impossible. She didn't know where to begin. Rafe joined her on the flying bridge where she'd been handling the helm for the past couple of hours while he napped. The corners of his Navy peacoat fluttered in the breeze.

"Pretty country," he commented.

"*Big* country," she countered. "With lots of people. How on earth are we going to find Terry or figure out where he went from here?" When she'd arrived in Santiago, she had believed finding her brother would be a relative snap. It had not proved that easy.

"Don't worry. We'll think of something."

Standing behind her, he began to knead the tension from her shoulders and neck. He had wonderful hands. Long, strong fingers that could also be gentle.

Since that night when he'd told her about the death of his wife and child—and his guilt over not being there with them—Taylor had known she couldn't fight the ghost of the woman he had loved so deeply. But she and Rafe had formed a relationship that was both caring and supportive. She'd call it more than friendship but less than lovers. A bond shaped by the storm they had survived together and the emotional turmoil Rafe had relived in the aftermath.

Taylor might want more than he was willing to give, but she accepted that part of him that he was ready to share.

"I reached the harbor master by radio," Rafe said. "There's no pleasure-boat marina here. It's too cold, I guess, for year-round boating. And the fishing fleet is based up north. Except for the Chilean Navy Base, where we wouldn't be welcome unless we were an official U.S. Navy vessel paying a courtesy visit, the only dock is the one the cruise lines use." He pointed toward a huge eight-stories-tall Norwegian liner where crewmen were loading supplies for the ship's next cruise to Antarctica. "With our shallow draft, we can tie up in front of that baby."

"Good grief. Their lifeboats look bigger than our *Queen of the Sea*."

"That's okay. We'll show all those rich folks what real sailors look like."

"I'm sure they'll be thrilled."

"Maybe later we can slip onboard and join the passengers for dinner. I'm guessing they've got a great chef."

"With your week-old beard, they'd think you're a pirate and have us both walking the plank before we got through the soup course."

He chuckled and gave her shoulders one last massage. "You think you can dock her, or you want me to take over?"

Eyeing the gigantic ship and the limited space in front of its bow, she said, "You're not one of those guys who believes a woman can't park a car at the curb, are you?"

"Not me. Equal opportunity dinged fenders, is my motto."

"Good. Because I like a challenge." Smugly, she grinned at him. "You play deckhand and toss the line to the guys on the dock. I'll bring her in smooth as silk."

"Terrific. Meanwhile, I'll hang as many fenders as I can over the side to protect our hull from getting scraped bare of what little paint she's still got."

Laughing, she threw a mock punch at his shoulder, which he easily dodged.

As he hustled down the ladder to the main deck, she considered that she hadn't met many men like Rafe. Despite the pain he'd experienced, and his losses, he had a great, if subtle, sense of humor. He could cope with almost any circumstance or threat. He was, in her view, a natural hero.

And it was just a damn waste of good male libido that he still suffered from post traumatic stress and was hung up on his deceased wife.

Not that there was anything she could do about it.

A few minutes later, she winced as she bumped the dock far harder than she intended. So she wasn't a perfect pilot yet. No great harm done. Except the arrogant *I-told-you-so* smirk on Rafe's face.

After they tied up at the dock, Taylor having maneuvered the trawler with considerable precision into place after the first bump, she changed into the skirt and sweater Rafe had purchased for her. She had to admit she was getting used to the ease of caring for short hair that barely reached her collar, although whenever she glanced in a mirror the brown color still surprised her.

Securing the hatches, they disembarked and went in search of a cab.

"You still have your brother's picture?" Rafe asked.

She patted her waistpack. "Right here."

"We could check with the police first, see if there have been any reports about Terry."

"Given my recent and seriously unpleasant experiences with the *policia,* let's leave that as a last choice," she said.

"Roger that." He signaled to a taxi that was dropping off passengers for the cruise liner. "We'll start with hotels then. See if we can find anyone who recognizes your brother." It occurred to Taylor that her adventure had started with a visit to a hotel and gone wrong from there—except for meeting Rafe, of course.

They asked the cab driver to recommend moderately priced, non-chain hotels, which were the type Terry preferred to patronize. For the next two hours, they had what amounted to a tour of downtown Punta Arenas. A useless tour, as it turned out, but lucrative for their cab driver. Not a single hotel clerk or manager remembered seeing Taylor's brother.

Paying off the taxi, Rafe said, "Let's get something to eat and rethink our strategy."

"Some strategy," Taylor mumbled, both discouraged and worried about her brother. "People don't just vanish from the face of the earth. Not in this day and age."

With his hand warming the small of her back, Rafe ushered her across the street to a cluster of sunny tables outside a small restaurant. The afternoon was comfortably warm, in the low seventies, and several people were enjoying a few moments of relaxation, drinking beer or eating a light meal. Rafe held out a chair for her.

"You want beer or wine?"

"How 'bout a double whiskey, neat?" She forced a weak smile and sat down.

"Sit tight. I'll be right back."

He went inside, presumably to order their drinks, while Taylor did a little people-watching. The pace here seemed slower than Santiago, the pedestrians not so rushed, cars traveling at a less frantic speed. Mothers with young children in strollers made their way along the sidewalk next to businessmen in suits who seemed to be in no particular hurry.

As she observed the peaceful scene, she noticed a black sedan with tinted windows cruising toward her. She tensed, ready to leap out of its path if it accelerated in her direction. But it crawled on by in the slow moving stream of traffic, the driver apparently uninterested in her.

She exhaled in relief. Clearly, she'd developed a bad case of paranoia over the past ten days or so.

Rafe reappeared with a beer and a glass of wine. "The bartender tells me this is Chile's best homegrown sauvignon. If you don't like it, he'll give you a free beer."

"Who could resist a deal like that?" She took a sip, enjoying the fruity bouquet and the slightly dry flavor, then put the glass down again. "You know me too well, Rafe Maguire. I'll take a good wine over a beer any day."

"Figures, the way you've been pampering those vine clippings the whole way down here."

She shrugged. "I don't want them to dry out."

When the waiter arrived, Taylor ordered a tuna salad sandwich with a small salad on the side; Rafe ordered a burger and fries. Guy food.

He'd consumed about half of his beer when he pulled some brochures out of his coat pocket. "I picked these up at the last hotel. They're ads for guided trips through Patagonia and Tierra del Fuego. Thought Terry might have hired somebody to take him there, and we could track him down that way."

"My, God, you're a genius, Rafe! Why didn't I think of that?"

"You would have. Eventually."

His smile was a bit smug, but she let it go. After all, he had come up with the idea. And it *could* work. She had to give credit where credit was due.

He pulled his cell phone from his pocket and began dialing. Several times en route to Punta Arenas, he'd tried his cell but couldn't get a connection. Much of the sparsely populated area of southern Chile had no cellular service or even landlines. Only here in a reasonably well-developed city was cell service available.

Their sandwiches arrived. Craving fresh vegetables, Taylor ate her salad with gusto.

Between phone calls, Rafe consumed his burger and fries, and ordered another beer. But he had no more luck in locating Terry with the guide services than they'd had at the hotels. Taylor tried not to feel discouraged. Keeping up her spirits—and her hope—wasn't easy.

Two well-dressed men in sport jackets and slacks approached their table.

"Señorita Travini?" one of the men inquired.

She froze and slipped into Spanish. "Do I know you, señor?"

"No, señorita. I have not had that pleasure." Bowing slightly, he showed her an official-looking badge. "We believe you are looking for Terrence Travini, your brother. Is that correct?"

Her heart gave a leap, and the air in her lungs tangled with both hope and trepidation. She cut a quick look at Rafe, who seemed to be as on edge by the arrival of these gentlemen as she. Chilean police were not on her good-guys list these days.

"Who are you?" Rafe asked, standing and taking a defensive posture.

"Our pardon, señor. We're with the Punta Arenas police department. I am Detective Halpern," the older of the two men said. "This is my partner, Detective Bosno. I'm afraid we have some bad news for Señorita Travini. If you would both come with us . . ."

Wary of subterfuge, Taylor didn't want to go. She'd been harassed enough by cops lately, and by men who claimed to be cops but weren't.

But she sensed these two were telling the truth. They

had some knowledge of her brother. It was an aura she could sense. The same aura, she suspected, military chaplains projected when they visited family members to announce a loved one had been killed in action: on some level, they wanted to share her grief.

Not Terry! Please God, not Terry!

CHAPTER TWENTY-FIVE

It took all of Taylor's strength and willpower to get up from the table. She felt lightheaded, her knees as rubbery as if she'd consumed far more than one glass of wine. A breeze fluttered the hem of her skirt, and she felt shaky on her feet.

With a light touch, Rafe cupped her elbow, steadying her. In a low whisper, he said, "We don't have to go with them, Legs. We can get somebody else to check out what they know. They won't make a scene in the middle of the day on a busy street."

Taylor wasn't sure that was true, but she shook her head. "I need to know."

"This way, please." Detective Halpern indicated an unmarked steel-gray Toyota parked at the curb two doors down, then turned to lead the way. He didn't look back. Apparently he was confident Taylor would follow him.

She did. Numbly. Terrified to think about what she might learn, what the detective knew, she followed him down the sidewalk to his car.

Rafe walked beside her, so close his denim work shirt

brushed against her bare arm. He curled his fingers around her hand and squeezed lightly. Fighting the urge to cry, she swallowed a sob. *Terry!*

With little leg room in the backseat of the Toyota, she had to cock her legs sideways. So did Rafe, and their knees butted. His thighs looked rock hard beneath the taut fabric of his jeans.

Where are you, Terry? Don't die on me.

Detective Bosno had slid in behind the wheel. Looking over his shoulder from the passenger seat, Halpern rested his arm on the back of the driver's side. "Police headquarters isn't far. A few blocks, near the central park."

Taylor remembered walking through that square earlier, its centerpiece a twenty-foot-tall bronze statue of Ferdinand Magellan celebrating his discovery of a safe passage through the straits that were named for him. Four bronze supplicants occupied the corners of the statue's base. Custom had it that if you kissed the bare toe of one of these peasants, you would return to Chile again. Both Rafe and Taylor had opted to skip the gesture.

Taylor shivered. She feared in the future even the mention of Chile would give her nightmares. But you could bet your last peso, if kissing that absurd toe would make her brother magically appear, she'd do it in a nanosecond.

They passed a road sign directing visitors to the Chilean Navy Base but turned inland instead. Taylor, battling hysteria, had to repress a nervous giggle wondering what sort of an armada Chile might raise if they went to war—and whom they would battle.

As promised, within minutes they arrived at the police station, an imposing four-story building constructed with an eye toward function and not architectural style.

The two detectives escorted them to the fourth floor, where they were admitted to Chief Antonio Pelegrosa's office.

A large picture of the president of Chile hung on the wall behind his mahogany desk. That was flanked by photos of Chief Pelegrosa shaking hands with assorted other individuals, whom Taylor could only assume were the leaders and politicos of the country, or at least the elite in Punta Arenas. Added to the wall collage were plaques giving praise to the chief for his contributions to his community. And in the corner of the room stood the flag of Chile with its single star and bold stripes of red, white and green.

The one thing Taylor didn't want to look at was the square cardboard box about the size of a half-gallon of ice cream that sat on top of the chief's otherwise pristine desk. She wanted the contents to remain a mystery— contents that would not concern her.

The chief rose from his chair. "Señorita Travini, thank you for coming." Walking around his desk, he extended his hand. "I regret the situation is not a more pleasant one."

"How did you know Señorita Travini had arrived in Punta Arenas?" Rafe asked.

A tall, stately man with graying hair at his temples, the chief lifted a single brow. "The questions you and the young lady were asking around town were hardly designed to keep your presence a secret. And seldom is our modest community honored by a visit from a decorated war hero and U.S. Army Ranger, Señor Maguire."

"Former Ranger," Rafe corrected.

Shrugging, the chief said, "As you wish. Please be seated." He gestured to the chairs in front of his desk, then returned to his place with the desk a barrier between them. "As I indicated, the situation is difficult. I fear the news about your brother, señorita, is not good."

Despite the fact her throat was tight with grief, Taylor said, "Tell me."

The police chief opened his desk drawer and withdrew a watch, which he placed on the desk, pushing it toward Taylor.

"I believe this belonged to the brother you are seeking."

Her fingers shook as she drew the watch toward her. Swiss Army brand. Stainless steel. Shock resistant. Water proof. It provided time, date, compass direction and a dozen other features only an astronaut could fully utilize. But Terry loved it and swore he'd never take it off. Carefully, she turned the watch over to examine the back. To her dismay, the engraving provided the evidence she wanted to deny: *From T to T with Love.*

A sob escaped her throat.

Rafe's hand covered hers. "Easy, Legs."

Easy? Nothing was easy. Not when her brother was dead. Her twin! How could he haved died and she not have known? Not sensed that he was gone?

"How did you know that watch belonged to her brother?" Rafe asked.

"The picture you showed at several of our hotels was similar to the one we circulated when we were trying to, um, identify the deceased. One of the hotel security men recognized the resemblance and phoned us." The chief carefully folded his hands on the desk. "It was then that I sent my men in search of you."

Rafe nodded. "Can you tell us how he died?"

Chief Pelegrosa cleared his throat. "It was one of those unfortunate things. A bar fight. Too many drunks. Sometimes they get out of hand."

Taylor's head snapped up. "Terry never fought. He would walk away before he'd throw a punch."

"I am sorry, señorita. If you would like, I can provide you with a copy of the police report."

"I'm sure she'd appreciate that," Rafe said.

With the tilt of his chin, the chief ordered Detective Halpern, who had remained in the room, to fetch the report. They all waited. A clock on the credenza behind Pelegrosa's desk ticked so loudy it sounded like a sledgehammer pounding inside Taylor's skull. She could barely draw a breath. Her chest felt so tight she imagined her heart might never again beat with the same strength as it had only minutes or hours ago.

"How long . . ." Her question caught in her throat and she had to try again. "When did my brother die?"

Pelegrosa drew his fingertips over a nonexistent beard. "I believe it was two weeks ago. Perhaps more."

Before she'd left California. From the beginning, her search for Terry had been futile.

Halpern returned and handed the report to Rafe.

"Why wasn't my father contacted?" Taylor asked. "Surely you found my brother's identificaton."

"Regretfully, no." Pelegrosa hung his head as though filled with remorse. "Before the police were called, his wallet was stolen. We only presumed, from his attire, that he was a *norteamericano*, but we had no idea of his name until you arrived searching for him. Then my officers connected our John Doe—as you in America call unidentified people—and the watch to our unknown victim." He lifted his shoulders in a helpless apology.

"My father . . ." Her voice stalled, and she was unable to express either her grief or her anger at her brother's senseless death. Terry had been so full of life. So looking forward to the future. Their father would never under-stand why or how his only son had died.

The chief finally touched the ugly cardboard box on his desk. "If you would like, we can arrange for your brother's remains to be buried here in Punta Arenas. Naturally, when we did not know how to reach your brother's next of kin, cremation was our only recourse. But you will find our cemetery is quite nice. I am sure—"

"No!" The word burst from Taylor like a gunshot. Her face flushed. "I'm sorry. I have to—our father is ex-pecting me to bring Terry home." *But not in a box. Never in a box.*

She realized Rafe was reaching for the abomination. The world's cheapest urn, government-issue for a John Doe. *Terry's remains!*

She blocked Rafe's move. "I'll take care of him." Her vision blurring, she took the box into her arms and held it as tenderly as she would a baby. She'd always taken care of her brother. Been there when he needed her. Ex-cept this time.

"My men will see you back to your boat," the chief said. "I assume you will be returning to the States now."

Rafe said, "We'll do whatever the lady wants."

She wanted this to be a terrible nightmare; she wanted to wake up.

Accompanied by Detective Bosno, they rode the eleva-tor down to the first floor and walked outside to where he had parked the gray Toyota. Vaguely, Taylor was aware of uniformed officers coming and going, a stray dog sniffing at the tires on police cars in the parking lot, and the laughter of two dark-haired women smoking cigarettes and flirting with a policeman.

In her head, the anvil of grief pounded out the words *Terry is dead* over and over again, and still she couldn't believe it. In an effort to mute that persistent voice, she turned to Rafe, who had remained close to her side. "How could this have happened to—"

"Later," he interrupted. He opened the car door, helped her in, then walked around to the opposite side to slide in beside her. With a subtle tip of his head, he indicated he didn't want the driver to hear their conversation. "We'll talk back at the boat."

The drive to the harbor seemed interminable, though Taylor knew they needed to travel only a few miles. Taylor's eyes were so dry they hurt. The ache in her throat promised tears would come the moment she let herself go. But she'd never been one to cry in front of others. She'd been tough since that day in first grade when Shaun Peterson, a third grader and the school bully, had pushed her down on the playground, bloodying her knees and cutting her lip. She hadn't wanted him to know how badly he'd hurt her. So instead of crying, she'd turned on him, throwing wild punches, connecting with a few, and finally chasing him into the boys' bathroom. He'd never picked on her again, or on any of her friends. Only later, at home alone in her room, had she cried.

Here in Punta Arenas, clutching the container of her brother's ashes in her lap, her tears were even harder to hold back. She had no one to fight.

The solicitous way Rafe touched her, resting his arm on the back of the seat behind her, showing that he cared, wasn't helping her self-control, either. For reasons she couldn't quite understand, she didn't want to lose it in front of him. He was the toughest guy she'd ever met.

The dectective dropped them off at the foot of the pier. "Have a good journey," he said before driving away, leaving them to find their own way to the trawler.

The Norwegian cruise liner tied to the dock in back of the *Reina de la Mar* was boarding passengers. Busloads of laughing, excited tourists streamed down the pier; piles of suitcases festooned with identifying colored ribbons were arranged alongside the ship in neat rows like cemetery grave markers decorated for a holiday remembrance.

Taylor wanted to scream at these people. Didn't they know her brother was dead? How could they be so happy when every molecule in her body, felt the loss of her twin so painfully?

Rafe stepped onto *Reina*'s gangplank and held out a hand for Taylor. He'd never liked weepy women. Didn't know what to do or how to act in the face of tears. But Taylor was even scarier. She was hurting; he knew that from the rigid way she held herself. The stubborn set of her jaw. The bleakness in her eyes. But she hadn't shed a single tear.

That much courage, that kind of determination, got him right in the gut.

"Let me help you," he said.

"I can manage."

"I know." But when he cupped her elbow, she didn't argue. She was that far out of touch with herself and reality.

He steadied her across the gangplank, then up the ladder to the wheelhouse. He took hold of the hatch to open it and froze.

Someone had been here. The tell he'd left by habit was gone.

Carefully, he eased open the hatch a half-inch and felt around the edge for a trip wire. The goons who'd been after Taylor—and killed Igor—wouldn't be above setting a booby trap that would blow him, Taylor and the *Reina de la Mar* sky high. But the hatch was clear.

184

And now that Taylor was basically on her way back to the States, Rafe didn't know why they'd still be pursuing her. Hell, he hadn't figured that out in the first place. Except now her brother was dead.

And Chief Pelegrosa had known who Rafe was! Since Santiago, he'd been traveling incognito. Paying cash for everything. The only way the head cop or anyone else could have known Rafe's identity was because they'd talked with the guys who had tortured Igor.

Damn! Something was still going on, but the what and why continued to elude him.

He stepped into the wheelhouse, quickly scanning the area for any disturbance as Taylor followed him inside.

"I think I'll go lie down," she said.

"Hang on a second."

Surprised, she hesitated at the top of the ladder to the galley. When he touched his finger to his lips, asking for silence, she frowned. He gestured for her to be patient.

Doing a quick search of the wheelhouse, he said, "I'm really sorry about your brother." It took him no more than a minute to find what he was looking for, a tiny microphone no bigger than the tip of a pencil eraser, stuck under the control panel. Amateurs! That had been too easy to find.

He held it up for Taylor to see.

"What is—"

He jerked his head, silencing her whisper and returned the bug to where he'd found it. "I'm sorry I never had a chance to meet Terry."

"You would have liked him," she said tentively.

Nodding his approval, he dropped down to the galley. A cursory search turned up another bug under the table. He pointed it out to Taylor.

"What's going on?" she mouthed.

Finding pencil and paper in a drawer, he wrote: *Some-one bugged us.*

Her eyes widened as she realized what he meant, then anger turned the irises dark green. In a fury, she put the container with her brother's ashes on the counter and planted her fists on her hips. "Why, those sons-of—"

He clamped his hand over her mouth and brought his lips close to her ear. "We don't want to let them know we've found the bugs just yet. We may want to play with the dudes who planted them first."

"I want to strangle them," she hissed. "They have no right—"

In Rafe's experience, the best way to silence a woman was to kiss her. So that's what he did—slowly and gently at first, just enough to get her mind off the bugs and who-ever had planted them. The kiss was sweet and uncertain, her taste somehow tinged with the salty flavor of the tears that had threatened since she'd been told of her brother's death. Although Rafe knew it wasn't possible, he wanted to erase that memory. To alter reality.

And if he couldn't change reality, he wanted to com-fort her, to take away the desperate sadness he'd seen in her eyes. The raw pain that radiated from her with every breath she took.

For a moment, she didn't respond. Then with a sigh, she sought the comfort he offered, the escape he could provide, however briefly. Her lips parted and her arms locked around him.

A tidal wave of heat surged through him. What had started as a way to silence Taylor, to expunge the truth of her grief, had turned into a tsunami of raw need Rafe wasn't sure he could control. It roiled over him as he plunged his tongue into the sensual warmth of her

186

mouth. She met and matched him stroke for stroke, an equal partner in the growing storm.

At some level he realized she was vulnerable in a way she'd never been before. He didn't want to take advantage of her or the situation.

But his body had taken on a life of its own, disengaged from any rational thought. He was as hard as a rock, aching like he was a damn seventeen-year-old about to get laid for the first time.

He didn't have anything to offer Taylor, not for the long run. Here and now, he could give her his protection, maybe help ease her grief. But their worlds were too far apart for there to be a future. All they had was a brief past and whatever existed in the present.

For a moment, he played with her hair, feeling the silken threads. "I knew I'd be sorry I cut your hair." So short it barely covered her neck, when long, luscious and blonde was what he wanted. Not the mousy brown she'd dyed it.

"I'm kind of liking it this way. Easy to . . ." She lost her thought in their kiss.

For a week, they'd been building to this moment. Their flight from her pursuers. Their kiss at the airport, another in the vineyard. The weather they had survived at sea when he'd nearly gone overboard and she'd risked herself to save him. Only by steering a strict course had they avoided turning a single casual touch into a tempest of carnal lust before this.

Now Rafe didn't think he could stop. He knew damn well he didn't want to.

Moaning, she broke away. Her lips were slick from his kiss, her eyes dark and filled with elemental hunger.

"Rafe, make love to me," she whispered.

"We can't. Not now. The bugs." His protest was a lie. One last effort to remain honorable. To give her a way out. To save her from her own emotional turmoil.

"Now, Rafe," she pleaded. "I need to feel alive."

Confronted with her need, no man could have refused her. Rafe stopped trying.

CHAPTER TWENTY-SIX

Taylor had never begged for sex. Ever. But she needed to now, needed to reaffirm that she was a living, breathing woman. That the death of her brother, however devastating, did not affect her existence. She need not die, even metaphorically, with him.

"I'll never ask anything else of you," she whispered, not wanting the people who had bugged the boat to listen to her intimate conversation with Rafe. "I promise."

Rafe framed her face with his large, capable hands, and she melted into his kiss again. She'd never known more provocative lips, a man more skilled at kissing. He was like the difference between table grapes and those meant to become fine wine. He took her away from herself as their tongues tangled. He captured and stole her off to another plane. Her breathing was labored but her heart soared as though no longer tethered to the earth.

When his lips left hers, she tilted her head to give him access to her neck. His hand, so competent, cupped her breast, and she shuddered as his thumb passed over the nipple. How could a man trained to kill, an exquisite specimen of a fighting man, be so gentle, she wondered as his mouth covered her breast. Even through layers of her sweater and bra, she felt his heat. Relished it.

With his tongue, he toyed with the pendant that hung in the hollow between her breasts. "Nice necklace," he murmured, rolling it back and forth.

She moaned at the erotic friction of stone, tongue and flesh together. "My father gave it to me."

"He probably didn't mean for a guy to do this." His words were barely a whisper, as was the touch of his tongue.

No other man had found that erogenous zone or tormented it so successfully. Her body was on fire. "He probably didn't have it in mind, but I'm glad you discovered such an original"—she moaned—"use for the necklace."

"The captain's cabin," he said, his voice hot and needy and filled with the same wanting that pulsed through her veins.

"Good idea."

"I'll check for bugs."

She hesitated, stunned back to reality for a moment, then decided she didn't care. If the creatures who were listening could get off on hearing her make love to Rafe, let them. She wanted Rafe. Now. No one, nothing, mattered as much as loving him. The rest of the world be damned!

He walked her backwards into the captain's cabin, kissing her lips, her eyes, her neck. Her legs trembled. She was breathless, drowning in the most potent wine she could ever imagine, unable to stay afloat.

"Wait here," he ordered when the back of her knees met the narrow captain's bed.

With swift, economical movements, he checked under

the edge of the bed, beneath the mattress, around the circumference of the portal. Finally, he plucked a tiny, round disc from the frame of the metal opening.

"Why don't you take a shower," he said aloud. "It might make you feel better."

"Sure." A shower was the last thing she wanted, but she went along.

"I'll turn on the water for you. Warm it up."

She was about as hot as she could be. Still, she smiled as he returned to the galley, put the bug into the sink and turned on the water. Whoever was listening was getting an earful, and Taylor loved it.

Rafe returned to the captain's cabin and studied her with his deep, dark eyes. "Are you sure?"

"Never more so."

"Thank God."

Spearing her fingers through his hair, she brought his mouth to hers. He pulled her closer, so that their bodies molded together from lips to thigh. The solid press of his arousal against her pelvis, his moan of pleasure, made her feel terrifyingly, wondrously female.

His heat became hers; his need multiplied hers. Passion as she had never known it altered the act of making love from shadowy gray to vivid shades of wine red and the verdant greens of spring. Hope and excitement appeared where only despair and melancholy had been.

With skillful hands, he removed her sweater and bra. Her skirt dropped away to puddle at her feet, and he studied her with undisguised hunger and the approval of a connoisseur.

"Very nice." His husky words spread over her like a fine, warm mist.

"I'd like the same privilege of seeing you."

"I'm a battered old soldier."

"It doesn't matter." She remembered his nightmares, the screams of pain that had awakened him on the boat. A wounded hero, both inside and out. "I want to touch you."

Crossing his arms, he pulled his shirt off over his head, revealing a muscular chest with a cross of dark hair arrowing down to his belt. But it was the jagged scars that drew her attention, one on his shoulder and another at his waist. In a swell of emotion that twisted in her chest, his pain became hers.

"Don't," he warned. "I don't want your sympathy."

Tentatively, she ran her fingertips over the raised rope of flesh on his shoulder. "That's not what I'm feeling." The emotion she experienced as she caressed his scar was far more complex than sympathy; it was a combination of anger at those who had hurt him and love for a man who had withstood so much.

He didn't let her lingering exploration last long before pulling her into his arms again. His kisses became greedy, more carnal than before and more electrifying. He was in complete control. But she was not a victim. She was a willing participant in a wanton assault on his senses and hers. The salty flavor of skin. The scent of sex mixed with the sea air. Callused hands caressing smooth skin, soft hands stroking warm flesh.

Somehow he had toed off his boots, rid himself of his pants. Both naked, they rolled around on the bed, tangling sheets and blankets. Touching. Feeling. Learning intimate secrets. Arousing each other to frantic desire.

"Rafe! Please."

He answered her plea by retrieving a foil packet from his trouser pocket. He'd known this moment would come, she realized, and was grateful for his forethought, if a little chagrined that she hadn't taken precautions, too. Actually, she hadn't considered the consequences at all. A foolish oversight on her part.

Returning to her, he said, "Are you okay?"

"I will be as long as you don't quit on me now."

His lips hitched into a wicked smile. "Not much chance of that, Legs."

Her responding smile evaporated as he tested her readiness, then filled her with a determined thrust. She gasped with surprise and pleasure. He waited, looking down into her eyes, until she adjusted to his size and moved against him. Slowly he began stroking her until she could no longer think, could only feel the spiraling tension within her. When it reached the peak, she went over the top, floating briefly on a cloud of satisfaction before descending to earth, Rafe's weight keeping her grounded.

For a time they both dozed as the rising tide gently rocked the trawler. The engines of the nearby cruise ship hummed a low-pitched sound, blocking other noises on the dock that might have disturbed them. But nothing could block the thoughts that crept back into Taylor's awareness, and she gently touched the aquamarine birthstone that was both hers and her brother's.

Terry is dead. In a barroom brawl. Two weeks ago.

Why hadn't he called home before that? Kept in better touch? He should have been farther south by then, taking pictures of penguins, exploring the islands and glaciers of Tierra del Fuego, not fighting in a bar. It made no sense.

She glanced at Rafe, who was sleeping soundly, his arm thrown across her bare midriff. She'd never had a better lover. Not that she was all that experienced, of course. But she was confident everything Rafe did, including making love, was in the top one percent. He was simply that perfect.

With a sigh of pleasure mixed with regret, she slipped from under his arm and picked up his pants, searching his pockets.

"You lookin' for something?" he asked.

"Sorry if I woke you. I wanted to read the police report."

She found it just as he said, "Right back pocket."

He'd folded the papers into a square. With some trepidation, she opened the document.

"There's no picture of Terry here." In some ways that was a relief.

"Maybe they didn't want you to see it. Looking at a picture of someone you love when he's dead can be pretty brutal."

"*Hmm,*" she said noncommittally as she focused on the report. Typed in Spanish, it provided the bare essentials—time, date, location and description of the fatal incident. A list of witnesses. The nature of the injuries and cause of death—massive head trauma.

Blinking, Taylor looked away. Why hadn't someone been arrested for murder? Or at least manslaughter? No suspect was even named.

She reached a decision. "I want to see where my brother was killed." And find out why he'd been at the bar and not in Tierra del Fuego.

Rafe had pulled a sheet up, covering himself to his waist, and lay with his arm tucked behind his head propping him up on the pillow. "That may not be such a good idea."

"Why not? Maybe I can understand why he died. My father will have questions. I need to be able to answer them." Both for him and her own peace of mind.

"If it's a place that has regular bar fights, it's not going to be exactly a five-star restaurant. They might not like you snooping around."

"So what? It's the only way I'll get the answers I need. I can take care of myself."

"Yeah. I know." He tossed the sheet aside and rolled out of bed, magnificently naked. "You don't mind if I come along? Just in case you need a little backup?"

For a moment, she considered jumping his bones again and putting off her visit to the place where Terry died. But in this case, her brother had to come first. Maybe later . . .

"I'd be glad for your company," she said.

She dug her jeans and a T-shirt out of the miniscule closet in the captain's cabin, while Rafe picked up the clothes she'd helped him remove earlier, and they both dressed. Although the day had been comfortably warm, they both grabbed their jackets against the cooler evening air. For the benefit of those listening, just before they left the trawler, Rafe announced they were going out to get something to eat.

They hailed a cab at the foot of the pier. Rafe gave only vague instructions, asking the driver to take them downtown.

As they drove toward the exit of the parking lot, he kept an eye on a dark sedan that had been parked near the pier with a driver inside and no passengers. The guy started his engine and fell in behind the cab as they turned onto the boulevard.

"Make a left at the next corner," Rafe asked the cabby.

Since the corner didn't have a signal, the driver had to wait for a break in traffic. The sedan pulled up right behind the taxi, the driver now talking on his cell phone.

The world's dumbest undercover cop, Rafe thought.

"What's going on?" Taylor whispered.

"I think we picked up a tail." He had the cabby make a couple of more turns before he said, "Take us to the Duty Free shopping center." As a way to encourage people to stay in this rugged, southern region of Chile, the government provided some extra perks, like low-cost cars and other high-ticket items.

"You should have told me sooner, señor," the driver complained. "This is the long way to get there."

"No problem. We'll pay the extra fare." Rafe leaned back comfortably in the cab.

The driver shrugged, no doubt figuring his passengers were either very rich or just plain suckers.

Taylor's eyes questioned Rafe. His lips hitched into a half smile. "A shopping mall is a good place to lose a tail," he said under his breath.

"Ah." She nodded in understanding.

Five minutes later, the cab dropped them off at one of the main mall entrances, Rafe paid the fare, and they strolled inside at a leisurely pace. It was a two-story mall that filled an entire block, brightly lit and looked much like one you'd find anywhere in the States. The shop windows displayed both American- and European-made merchandise.

"The prices look pretty good," Taylor commented, glancing in the windows as they walked unhurriedly along. In a clothing store, the manikins wore the latest styles at prices she wouldn't mind paying. A toy store, although not as big as a Toys-R-Us, seemed to carry a lot of the same merchandise, including fancy-dressed Barbies and Tonka dump trucks. As a kid, she'd always preferred the dump trucks.

Taking her hand, Rafe kept her from lingering. "Another day, Legs. If we're going to lose our tail, we've gotta pick up a taxi on the other side of the mall before he calls in reinforcements to follow us on foot."

"And if our buddy figures out what we're doing and spots us again?"

"Then we'll think of something else."

They ducked out another entrance and hastily climbed into a different taxi. Using the same procedure, Rafe had the driver make several turns to be sure they weren't being followed before giving him the address that was on the police report. But the driver wouldn't take them all the way there. Instead, he dropped them off about a block from where the bar was supposed to be.

"That place is no good," he said. "*Muy malo.*" Very bad.

He drove off, leaving them in a neighborhood of rundown buildings with graffiti on the walls, boarded-up stores and few signs of life.

"I can't say much for your brother's taste in neighborhoods," Rafe commented.

"He was never into posh, but this does seem a little extreme." Worrisome, too. Taylor couldn't imagine what had brought him to this part of town.

The late twilight of summer meant they didn't have to rely on streetlights to find their way, which was fortunate since most of them were broken. In some spots, shattered glass covered the uneven sidewalk. Debris filled the gutters, and all around them was the stink of decay.

Two dogs trotted by, their ribs visible beneath their motley coats. One dog sniffed at a discarded plastic bag and moved on, apparently deciding the contents weren't worth his trouble.

Rafe stopped and looked up at a boarded-up building. Above the arched doorway were the words LA FUENTE in faded paint streaked with soot, and the number 1757. The location and name—The Fountain—were the same as on the police report.

"I don't understand," Taylor said.

"Maybe we weren't meant to come here."

"Why would they put a phony address on the report?"

"I'm not sure." He looked around and spotted an old woman shuffling down what passed as a sidewalk in this part of town. Dressed all in black, her back was hunched and her hair streaked with gray. "*Señora, un momento, por favor.*" She turned back the way she had come, and he hurried after her. "Don't be afraid, señora. I'm not here to hurt you. We just need some information. I have pesos."

That brought her to a halt, though she still looked at him with suspicion. "*¿Cuantos?*" How much?

"It depends," he told her.

Shaking off her paralysis, Taylor caught up with them. "Please, señora. The police tell me my brother died at *La Fuente* two weeks ago in a bar fight. Is that possible?"

The old woman made a hacking sound that could have been a cough or a laugh. "Three, four years ago, maybe. That place had a bad crowd. But two weeks ago?" She shook her head. "That is not possible."

"Why not?" Taylor asked.

"There was a fire. Many people died. That was three years ago. Maybe more. Since then, there is no *La Fuente.*"

"Thank you, señora. You have been very helpful." From his pocket, Rafe pulled out a clip of hundred-peso bills and handed her enough to make the old woman's eyes light with gratitude.

"No police come to this street anymore," the woman

added, as though she felt she'd been overpaid for her information and needed to balance the scales. "It is too dangerous for them. Only drug people." She spat on the ground to emphasize the point and her disapproval.

Both Rafe and Taylor thanked her again, then watched as she walked off in the direction she had begun.

Rafe looped his arm around Taylor's shoulders, offering comfort. "The mystery gets stranger and stranger."

Her brain clicked through what she knew—and what she didn't—and found few of the puzzle pieces fit together.

"Could your brother have gotten involved with drug dealers?" Rafe suggested.

"Not on purpose. More likely those aren't Terry's ashes they gave me." But how would she ever know?

"Whatever the answer is, I'd say the conspiracy that had the goons chasing you around Santiago goes much deeper than I imagined, and in some way Terry is involved."

She nodded. "I want to go south, to Tierra del Fuego. Terry may still be alive somewhere. I need to find him."

"It's a big island," he warned. "And there are a whole lot of little ones that aren't even named. There's not much chance we'd land on the right one."

"He was interested in penguins. We'll start with places that are penguin hatcheries. If we don't find him that way, we'll go to Puerto Williams."

Rafe suspected hers was a hopeless dream constructed of wishful thinking. But he couldn't deny Taylor the chance to follow that dream.

And there sure as hell was something going on that he couldn't explain.

"We'll leave on the tide in the morning, make it look like we're heading north then cut back to the south, dumping those nasty little bugs overboard somewhere along the way. We want whoever is behind this charade to think we're going to Valparaíso, and that you're planning to go back to the States."

They walked several deserted blocks before they came upon a street vendor selling soft pretzels and corn dogs from a cart. Hungry, Rafe ordered a corn dog and squirted a line of yellow mustard down the length of it; Taylor settled for a soft pretzel.

Eating as they walked, they finally spotted a taxi to take them to the docks. When they arrived, they found the cruise ship had departed, leaving *Reina de la Mar* tied up alone.

In the galley, Taylor placed her hands on the cardboard box and closed her eyes. She was hoping for some psychic connection to Terry, some feeling he was alive elsewhere. Or that, God help her, these were his remains. There had been other times when she'd known he was in trouble. In sixth grade he'd fallen off his bike and rolled down a hillside, hurting his ankle. She'd been at home practicing her jump shot when she sensed he needed her. There was no explaining it. She simply got on her own bike, pedaling as fast as she could to the exact spot where he'd gone off the road.

That was what it meant to be a twin, at least for her. But not this time.

"Did you get enough to eat?" Rafe asked.

She nodded. "I'm fine."

"Then let's get some sleep. We'll be leaving early in the morning."

Relinquishing her hold on the box, she allowed Rafe to lead her to the captain's cabin. He made love to her again, slowly and tenderly. When she woke crying in the night, he soothed her as she had him after his nightmare. Then when she fell back to sleep in his arms, she rested peacefully until the night sky turned gray with dawn.

Dressing warmly against the cool morning air, Taylor took the wheel while Rafe cast off. She backed the trawler away from the dock until she could turn it around with the bow pointing out into the Strait of Magellan.

While Punta Arenas was still in sight, Rafe dropped the bugs over the side, then pulled out his cell phone. The number he punched in rang twice before it was answered.

"Landry," his friend barked.

"Hey, Hacker, how's it going?"

"Rafe? Where the hell are you?"

"Just offshore of Punta Arenas heading down to Tierra del Fuego."

There was a long pause before Donovan said, "Can I assume you're not on a pleasure cruise?"

"Too true." Succinctly, Rafe briefed his buddy on what had happened since Valparaíso when they had last talked. "I don't know what's going on or if Taylor's brother could still be alive, but whatever it is, somebody thinks it's worth killing people for."

"I'll alert the authorities."

"No. Don't do that. As nearly as I can tell the police are involved. Just keep your eyes and ears open. This could be about drug smuggling or something similar. I'll just have to see how it plays out."

"It could be dangerous, Mac."

"Yeah. I know that." He wasn't worried for himself; only Taylor. "I got one stubborn, determined lady on my hands, and she's not going to let this go until she gets some answers. I figure I'd better stick with her."

"I hope she's worth it."

Rafe thought about last night and believed she was. "I'll keep you posted as best I can."

"Watch your back, buddy."

Rafe intended to.

Later, as he and Taylor reached Cabo Froward, the point where they should have turned north and instead navigated south around Isla Dawson, Rafe noticed a two-engine plane circling overhead. He got an uneasy feeling at the base of his skull.

Except for that one time when he'd led his men into an ambush, his instincts and hunches had served him well. At the moment, he was feeling like a butterfly pinned to a board by a bully who wanted nothing more than to see him and Taylor wiggling to get loose.

Rafe's job was to figure out how to do just that.

In the wheelhouse, he pulled out the charts for Tierra del Fuego and studied them while Taylor was at the helm.

"What's up?" she asked.

"We're going to have to play hide-and-seek before we check out your brother's penguins."

She looked over her shoulder at him, her expression etched with concern. "Is someone following us?"

"Keeping track of us by air. But I think we can lose him. A lot of these passages between islands are narrow. There'll be some cover where we can hide and wait him out. Eventually, he'll run out of gas." At least, that's what Rafe hoped.

CHAPTER TWENTY-SEVEN

Minister of the Interior Aguilar Mendoza got the phone call in his Santiago office at 3:02 P.M.

"My pilot sighted their trawler heading south past Isla Dawson," Chief Pelegrosa reported. "They are not returning to Valparaíso as expected."

"Didn't you give that woman her brother's remains? Why in the name of *Christo* didn't she go home?"

"I do not know, Minister Mendoza. I did all that you asked. Perhaps her companion convinced her to do otherwise. Or perhaps she opened the box and discovered only wood ashes."

Aguilar could all but hear Antonio Pelegrosa's sweat dripping onto his desk and smell the man's fear. Incompetent *bastardo!* Why hadn't he used some poor peasant's ashes instead of wood? No one would have been the wiser.

Pacing to his office window, which overlooked Plaza de la Constitutión, he stretched the phone cord to almost full length. At this point, he wished he could wrap the cord around the neck of the Travini woman. And hang her U.S. Ranger friend with it too!

He would not let those two Americanos defeat him. There were only days to go now. Al Faysal and his men were in place and ready. The Russian submarine was en route. Even if he had wanted to turn back, to attempt the coup another time, it was too late for that.

"Minister? Are you still there?" Pelegrosa asked.

A muscle jumped in Mendoza's jaw. "I am."

"What would you like me to do now?"

"Nothing, you fool. Nothing at all except count your blessings that I do not stand you before a firing squad because of your stupidity." Mendoza hung up before Pelegrosa had a chance to respond.

Within fifteen minutes, Hamid Al Faysal had been given word via radio that the Travini woman and her associate were still on her brother's trail. They had to be stopped before they discovered Faysal's island lair or notified the authorities of his presence.

Hamid Al Faysal gathered his men and gave the order. They were to find the whereabouts of the trawler *Reina de la Mar* and sink the boat before an S.O.S could be sent, and capture or kill the occupants. He would prefer to question the woman and her friend to determine what, if anything, they knew of his plan and if they had shared that knowledge with others. But if the infidels went down with their boat, Al Faysal would not shed a single tear.

In any event, he would not let the jihad fail. *Allah be praised!*

As was his custom, Aguilar Mendoza stayed late in his office. In the face of his incompetent associates, however, there was little he could do except wait and hope they somehow bungled their way through their assignments without destroying his plan or bringing him down due to their stupidity. He summoned his chauffeur to meet him in the underground parking area protected by security forces and rode the private elevator down, one that was used only by the highest government officials. The doors parted at the underground level, and he stepped out into the dimly lit garage.

"Minister?"

Alert, he turned at the sound of his name. In the shadows, the silhouette of a man dressed all in black appeared.

"I have told you never to come here," Mendoza snapped.

"I have come to warn you."

An icy cold wash of fear froze Mendoza where he stood. *Had his plan been discovered?* "What is it?"

"Federal intelligence agents have taken Captain Jaime Dulante into custody for questioning."

One of Mendoza's longtime friends and a co-conspirator. They'd grown up in the same neighborhood and both had gotten out—Mendoza through politics, Jaime into the police force where he had risen to be the superintendent of the jail. "What are they questioning him about?"

"They say it is about irregularities at the jail. I believe that is only an excuse."

Little beads of sweat formed above Mendoza's lip. "Will he talk?"

The man in the shadows shrugged. "One cannot be sure of another man's courage."

Mendoza agreed. With so little time left before the coup, he would have to protect himself. True leaders had no friends.

"Eliminate him," Mendoza ordered.

A faint flash of white teeth appeared in the shadows. "As you wish, Minister."

Mendoza experienced only the smallest twinge of remorse for his former friend as he entered the backseat of the limousine that pulled up beside him.

Destiny demands sacrifice from each of us.

CHAPTER TWENTY-EIGHT

Onboard the *Reina de la Mar*, the rotating radar beam painted the towering cliffs on both sides of the glacier-lined fjord, solid green shapes appearing on the monitor. Miles of packed ice that terminated in the fjord created uniquely local weather, forming clouds in a splotchy gray sky when only a few miles away the day was sunny. Sea lions rested at the base of granite walls the glaciers had not been able to wear away, seals played tag in wind-chopped waves and an albatross soared above the water in search of food or a resting place.

Rafe throttled back, bringing the ship's port side close to shore where they'd be hard to spot from the air. Assuming the two-engine Cessna was still out looking for them.

"This is incredible." Taylor was like a kid at Christmas, going from window to window in the wheelhouse to get a different view of the scenery. "I've seen pictures of glaciers, but this is so, well, awesome." She shrugged as though she knew the word was inadequate but couldn't think of a better one. "I should have come here with Terry."

"Actually, I'm glad you're here with me." Among other things, she was alive, and Rafe's best guess was that Terry wasn't. Had Taylor traveled with her brother, likely she would be dead, too. That possibility rankled more now than Rafe would have expected a couple of weeks ago.

She flashed him a quick smile. "Thanks. For a cruise director, you're not too bad yourself."

"You may not think that after you check our larder. We should have taken time to get more supplies in Punta Arenas."

Her expression shifted into a frown. "We'll shop in Puerto Williams."

"Sure. No problem." Except, with a plane tracking them and a conspiracy that had cost at least one man his life, Rafe couldn't be positive they'd make it to Puerto Williams.

Across the fjord, a glacier calved a big chunk of ice. Even inside the wheelhouse, the sound was like a cannon going off as the huge piece broke free, leaving a sheer wall of clear blue ice behind. The newly born iceberg splashed into the water, sank and wobbled back up, in the process sending a wave out across the fjord.

"Mother Nature is one tough lady," Rafe commented as their boat rocked in the wave.

"She has to be. A lot of folks are out to do her in."

Rafe didn't disagree. But as a soldier he had other priorities. To him, protecting people was more important than trees or sandy beaches, buildings or institutions. Damaging the environment sometimes came with the territory, whether he liked it or not. He mostly hoped the damage wouldn't be permanent.

He checked his watch. It had been several hours since he'd spotted the plane overhead. By now, the pilot had either given up the search or run out of fuel. In either case, it seemed reasonable they could get back on course to find *los penquinos* and, hopefully, Taylor's brother.

He turned the wheel to starboard and shoved the throttle forward, coming about one hundred-eighty degrees to go back the way they'd come. With luck they could slip out of this dead end fjord and find their way back to the main shipping lane. If Terry had made it this far south, maybe he'd left a few footprints. The only hope left would be to find his tracks. Which might take more than a little magic.

Rafe made a mental note that the fjord was alive with birds and mammals that apparently fed upon a robust population of fish, but there was no sign of human habitation. Not a single wisp of smoke from a chimney or even an abandoned cabin. And they were well out of range of any cell phone connection. Which meant if they got into trouble, there was no one to call for help. Even the boat's marine radio wasn't going to be much help this far back in the maze of islands and towering cliffs. He'd need an antenna planted on top of one of those mountain peaks to reach Santiago by radio.

"Look!" Excited, Taylor pointed ahead of them where the fjord widened. The late afternoon sun had caught a rain shower that refracted the light into ribbons of color, streaks of red, yellow and blue. "A double rainbow. That means we'll have good luck."

"I thought it meant we'll find a pot of gold."

She grinned at him. "Better yet, maybe it means we'll find Terry at the end."

"Come here, Legs." When she joined him at the wheel, Rafe slid his arm around her waist, pulling her close. Despite having had sex with her twice in the past twenty-four hours, he was still as randy as an adolescent. The way her eyes lit with eagerness at the sight of the rainbow only fed his desire.

"What do you say we drop anchor, hang out here for a while?" he asked.

She leaned her head on his shoulder where the fruity scent of her shampoo teased his senses. "Hmm. That's a tempting idea, Ranger Maguire. Any other time, I'd jump at the chance to spend a leisurely few hours in your company."

"But my timing's off, huh?"

She sighed, and he thought the sound was one of regret.

"I think we should keep going, don't you? If Terry's out there somewhere—"

"Yeah, I know." What the heck was he doing, thinking with his body instead of getting on with the mission? Even if they did find her brother, which Rafe sure as hell doubted, what was he gonna do? Invite her to hang around his scuzzy apartment in Santiago while he trained Chilean army forces? Not likely. She had a vineyard to get home to and a father whom she loved more than the man deserved.

He brushed a kiss to her temple.

"Hey, you can do better than that." With the ease of familiarity, she kissed him long and seductively, a sensual assault on what little good sense he had left.

"You want to reconsider that layover I mentioned?" he teased when she finally gave him a little breathing room. "Pun intended."

Her husky laugh as she danced away nearly had him chasing after her, her brother be damned! And the mafiosa or whoever the hell was after her.

"Sail on, Maguire. We'll have plenty of chances later."

The wicked glint in her green eyes promised at least as much as he could handle, maybe more.

He hoped to God she was right.

"In that case, Ms. Travini, how 'bout you rounding up some chow? With any luck, I'll be needing my strength later."

"Aye, captain. I'll see what I can find."

With another laugh, she ducked down the ladder to the galley.

As he motored out of the fjord, the sea grew choppier, the rainbow vanished and twilight began to fall. Rafe kept one eye on the radar and the other on Taylor. Despite her worries about her brother, she was enjoying herself. She'd become quite a sailor, and was more courageous than any woman he'd met—Lizbeth included, he realized.

They rounded a point of land and the stern caught the wind from the open ocean, pushing them forward. Whatever Taylor thought, Rafe knew they needed to find a safe anchorage for the night. No way could they spot penguins or any sign of her brother after dark.

Looking down, he studied the chart for a suitable cove where they could lay up for the night. When he glanced back at the radar, he cursed. A boat that rode low in the water, one that was neither a fishing vessel nor patrol boat belonging to the Chilean navy, was approaching at about fifteen knots. Faster than safety dictated in these waters. Running without lights, he never would have spotted them without radar.

That was a chilling thought.

"Taylor! We've got company," he warned.

Suddenly the *Reina de la Mar* was flooded by a spotlight, blinding Rafe so he couldn't make out the size or type of the approaching boat, or its registry.

211

A loudspeaker annouced, "Ahoy, *Reina*! Come about and prepare for boarding."

Rafe had only enough time to think that that wasn't a good idea before the boat rained 50-caliber machine gun fire down upon the *Reina*'s deck. Debris flew in all directions.

"Rafe?"

"Get your life vest on, Legs. Now!"

When outgunned and outmanned there were only a couple of choices—retreat or attack. Under the circumstances, retreat wasn't an option. These guys were not friendlies. Retreat wouldn't get Rafe and Taylor anywhere, and surrender would get them sunk. So Rafe opened up the throttle and turned the *Reina* toward the oncoming boat. Bow-to-bow would make the *Reina* the smallest target possible. Given the breadth of the old fishing trawler, that wasn't saying much. But maybe the maneuver would surprise the other boat long enough to give Rafe some small advantage.

The diesel engines that powered the old boat labored to pick up speed. Another round of .50-caliber fire strafed the wheelhouse, shattering the windows, splintering wood and barely missing Rafe.

Taylor came up the ladder halfway so only her head appeared. "What the hell is—"

"Bad guys. Stay down."

She slid his life vest across the wheelhouse. "Put yours on, too."

"Thanks." Crouching, he grabbed for the vest and hunched into the straps. He figured they were less than thirty seconds from ramming the attacking boat, assuming it didn't give ground. And he suspected it was far more maneuverable than the aging *Reina*.

Sliding him his gun, which he'd been fool enough to stow in the cabin, Taylor said, "Use it if you have to."

Grabbing the Sig Sauer, he came to his feet and leaned out the window the automatic fire had shattered. One shot and the spotlight exploded. Everything went dark. He held his breath as his eyes adjusted to what little light existed.

What he saw was a boat out of World War II, a PT boat with a sharp hull and more weapon power than he had ever imagined. It swerved to avoid a collision with the *Reina* and to gain a better angle.

Shit!

He ducked down just as the boat launched what could only be an old torpedo. "Hang on!" he yelled to Taylor.

The explosion deafened him. The *Reina* lifted out of the water, hesitating momentarily in the air, then dropped like a stone. Almost immediately it began to list to the starboard side. Without seeing it, Rafe knew there was a hole in the hull below the waterline that would take them down.

"Come on, babe. We gotta get out of here."

"Wait! I have to get Terry's ashes."

He dived down the ladder to the galley, grabbed her by the arm and yanked her back up to the wheelhouse. "There's no time." He wasn't even sure he could get them to the life raft lashed to the upper deck. Going into the icy cold water, barely above freezing, meant they had little chance of survival.

Likely, that was what the attackers wanted—both Rafe and Taylor dead.

He could feel the old trawler struggling to stay upright. But it was a lost cause, as water rushed in belowdecks.

He took Taylor's hand. "We're going over the side.

213

Make for land as best you can. And whatever else you do, keep moving."

"Rafe! I'm scared."

So was he. For her. Whatever sins he had committed in the past, whatever foibles her brother had, she didn't deserve to die.

He shoved open the hatch and pulled her outside. The wind whipped across his face; the water below him was as dark as a black cat on Halloween and far more threatening. He thought about the life raft lashed to the flying bridge, but water was already washing over the deck. There wasn't time.

Taking Taylor with him, Rafe jumped over the side into the sea. The cold sucked the air from him; stole his strength. His fingers went numb, and he lost his grip on Taylor. Saltwater filled his lungs.

Inside his head, he screamed, *Taylor!* But there was no answer. Only silence, the dark of night and the icy cold of the grave.

CHAPTER TWENTY-NINE

Taylor ached from the top of her head to the soles of her feet. Her body felt like it had been wrenched into the shape of a corkscrew. She couldn't stop shivering. If it hadn't been for the uneven floor with a sharp lump pressing into the small of her back, she wouldn't have known up from down. Dark as it was, she could be in a cave. Or a tomb.

Another shiver racked her body as she rolled to her side, and she groaned. "Rafe?"

For a moment, she felt woozy and couldn't remember what had happened. They'd been on the boat. She'd heated a can of soup. . . .

The memory of exploding gunfire came careening back to her in quick flashes. Loud and frightening. The boat listing dangerously to starboard. Rafe's hand holding hers as they jumped into the water. The rush of cold that numbed both her mind and her body. So painful it made her teeth hurt.

"Rafe! Where are you?"

Pushing herself to a sitting position, despite her vigorously protesting body, she felt around her. A dirt floor that was damp to the touch. Air almost as cold as the sea she'd leapt into. And silence.

"Hello!" Wherever she was, the darkness absorbed her voice and gave back nothing in return. No echo. No acknowledging sound. Not even a moan.

Panic twisted and tightened in her chest. Nausea, from fear and the intake of too much saltwater, churned in her stomach. She didn't remember being taken out of the water, and her head hurt like hell, so she must have been knocked unconscious. For minutes? Hours? And who had pulled her out?

If it wasn't Rafe who had rescued her, then it had to be the people who had shot at them. And who had sunk the *Reina*.

"Oh, God . . ."

Struggling, she got to her knees. Like a blind person, she held one hand in front of her and crawled around in an ever increasing circle. "Rafe! Please be here." *Please be alive*. The thought that he was dead was more painful than when she'd believed her brother had died. Instantly, she rejected the possibility that Rafe had succumbed to their dunking in the ocean. He was too strong, too wonderfully stubborn to give into the forces of nature, no matter how cold the water had been.

But even Rafe could be beaten by a bullet.

Her hand brushed against something metal. Smooth and round. Larger than a scrub bucket but smaller than a wine barrel. Next to that there was another one the same size and shape. The top of the second felt slightly oily. She brought her fingertips to her nose. Diesel fuel.

Was it fuel for the boat that had attacked them? Very likely. Except, now she could hear the low hum of what sounded like a generator. Wherever she was, and whoever had captured or rescued her, they had a source of power. Maybe they also had a way to call for help, if she could get out of here and find it.

From the corner of her eye, she realized she was seeing a narrow strip of gray, a shade or two lighter than the pitch black she'd been staring at. Cautiously, she shifted her gaze to the crack of light she'd seen. The faint outline of a door appeared.

She almost laughed aloud when she realized the light was dawn creeping in to relieve the impenetrable darkness of night. "Thank God!" Maybe she could find her way out now.

A quick examination of the door revealed it was either locked or barred from the outside, and as the dawn inched its pale light inside, she discovered she was in a ten-by-twelve-foot metal storage shed. The slanted roof was about ten feet high at the apex. It looked just like any one of a number of sheds at Travini Vineyards, probably ordered directly from Tuff Sheds or Home Depot, she thought, suppressing a nearly hysterical laugh.

Dear Lord, how she'd love to be home now. Home, with her brother safe, her father taking a sip of a new Travini blend and smiling at them both.

But where would Rafe be? Not in Sonoma, she knew. His life was that of a soldier of fortune. A mercenary. A soldier hired to train other men to fight.

Tears of anxiety stung at the backs of her eyes. This whole trip to Chile had gone terribly wrong from the beginning. And still she didn't know why. Who were these people that pursued her? And what made her life, and that of her brother, a threat to them? If she knew the answers to those questions, maybe she'd know what to do next. Assuming she could get out of here.

Investigating the shed more closely, she found a hand

pump and hose for the diesel fuel, containers of oil and axle grease, an empty trash can and a partial roll of heavy, black, trash-bag plastic that could be used to cover or hide large objects. Even a boat, if there were enough of it. Or a structure like the shed.

Unfortunately, she found nothing that resembled a weapon or anything that would help her escape.

Still cold, she paced back and forth in what little floor space she had available. Her shirt and jeans were damp, her feet wet inside her boots. As she rubbed her arms to keep her circulation going, she wished desperately that she had the warm jacket she'd purchased in Valparaíso.

No such luck, since she hadn't been wearing it when she went overboard with Rafe. Furthermore, whoever had brought her here had taken her life vest away.

The door rattled as though someone was about to open it.

In two quick steps, she flattened herself against the wall beside the door. Poised for action, she took a deep breath and readied for what needed to be done. She focused her thoughts on her would-be opponent, picturing her strategy. Kick to the kneecap. Fingers to the eyes. Fist to the back of the head. And run like hell!

But run to where?

The door opened. A man appeared in silhouette against the brighter daylight. Taylor's muscles tensed. She had just begun to raise her foot to strike the first blow when the figure staggered in front of her and fell to the ground. She had a fleeting impression of dark hair cut short and a strong, familiar profile as a plastic bottle of water was tossed inside. Then the door slammed shut behind the man, throwing the shed into the dim light of dawn again.

"Rafe!" Taylor fell to her knees as the door lock dropped into place behind her.

Gingerly, she stroked Rafe's head, felt his back, arms and legs looking for broken bones. Then she carefully rolled him over. He moaned.

"Come on, Ranger. You're a tough guy. Stick with me, sweetheart." From what she could see, he had cuts and bruises on his face. She suspected his body had taken a beating, too. Reaching for the bottle of water, she poured a little on the corner of her shirt and dabbed at the cuts on his face.

"I'm getting too old for this," he muttered, but it sounded more like "I'm gettin' 'oo old 'or this," because of the cut on his lip.

She held the bottle to his mouth, and he took a swallow. That seemed to revive him enough that he could focus on her.

"You okay, Legs?"

"Peachy-dandy." Assuming she didn't count the fact that she was half frozen and her body had its own share of bruises. But nothing like Rafe's.

When he struggled to sit up, she helped him. "Why did they beat you?"

"Wanted to know who knows we're here."

"I don't think anyone does. I didn't even call my father." Because she hadn't wanted to tell him that his precious son was likely dead.

"I know that, and you know that, but they can't be sure."

Which was why they'd beaten him. "Oh, Rafe, I'm so sorry. I never should have—"

"Not your fault. One of the guys wanted to shoot us and get it over with, but the head honcho said he'd check with his boss first."

Trembling, she wrapped her arms around him, holding Rafe, resting her head against his. Despite his injuries, he felt strong and capable, the same man she had learned to trust and depend upon.

The man she had learned to love.

"Why are they doing this to us?" she asked. "What's going on?"

Rubbing his hand along her spine, he said, "I don't have all the answers, but I do know there are at least ten bad guys here. The leader is an Arab—and not a friendly sort."

"An Arab? Here? Why?"

He shook his head. "Don't know. But whatever they're up to involves some pretty high-tech communication gear."

"Who do they want to communicate with?"

"That I haven't figured out yet. But you can bet it isn't Santa Claus or the Tooth Fairy." Considering the battering he'd taken, he got to his feet with amazing ease and rolled his head from side to side as though trying to work out the kinks. "What's the layout here?"

"Metal shed. One door, no windows. I couldn't find anything to use as a weapon." In retrospect, she might have been wiser to attack the man who'd brought Rafe. Disable him with her karate skills. But then what would she have done, given that Rafe had been nearly unconscious? She couldn't have carried him even five feet, much less to safety.

"I'll take a look around." Rafe scanned the room looking for a weak spot, any exit that could be squirmed through or around, something the Arab, who called himself Hamid, hadn't anticipated. Rafe was pretty damn sure he and Taylor had fallen into a nest of terrorists. What he didn't know was why they'd picked any part of Chile for a target, let alone this desolate southern tip of the country.

"What else do you know about Tierra del Fuego, besides it has penguins and glaciers?" he asked as he tested a barrel of fuel to see how full it was.

"Not a whole lot. Terry was the expert. I do know it's a bird-watcher's paradise and it's the closest land to the South Pole. The country has tried to encourage people to move here by creating economic benefits like duty-free zones, but beyond a few sheep ranches—*estancías*—I'm not sure how successful they've been."

Picking up the hand pump for the diesel fuel, Rafe decided it had the potential to become a weapon—or a tool to dig them out of there; so did the nozzle on the hose. Anything metal offered a possibility, which apparently Hamid hadn't considered. Or the Arab had figured Rafe would be dead before he could put a makeshift weapon or tool to any use.

"From what little I could see," he said, "we're either on an island or a peninsula of some sort. If it's an island, we're about a half-mile from the nearest land."

"Which could be another island," she pointed out.

"Not in this case. There's a glacier that has retreated from the opposite shoreline, leaving a forested area, then granite cliffs." He continued to ponder the resources at hand that might help them escape. Diesel fuel was flammable, but it took a lot of heat or pressure to set it off. Rafe didn't have a source of either.

He tried to recall the navigation charts he'd been using on the *Reina*. This terrorist base must be close to the fjord where Rafe and Taylor had been hiding out. But the only boat around belonged to Hamid and his men. Rafe had seen for himself that it was well guarded. Without a gun, plus a helluva lot of luck and surprise, he wouldn't be able to overpower the guards.

If Rafe was going to get them out of here, they'd have

to go north, which meant crossing a half-mile of frigid water, then make their way to some semblance of civilization over rough terrain. Their best chance might be a sheep farm. From there he could contact the Chilean military authorities—and Donovan.

But how much time did Rafe have left to warn them? Hamid had seemed damn agitated, as though his scheme was about to come to fruition. Did that mean the kick-off would happen within days? Hours?

Inside an empty trash can Rafe found a partial roll of duct tape—another item that could be useful.

"Have they brought you any food?" he asked.

"When they dumped you in here was the first time I'd seen anyone."

By nightfall, they'd both be pretty damn hungry. He was used to going without food for a couple of days. Taylor wasn't. All they had was one sixteen-ounce bottle of water between them. They'd have to live off the land.

"I noticed they didn't have a guard on the door," he said. "Must have figured there was no way for you to get out."

"They figured right."

"Hmm. Maybe not." He'd lost his 45 when he went into the water. Later, one of Hamid's men had taken his knife from his boot, but they hadn't removed his belt or the garrote wire hidden inside, and a plan began to form in his mind. "How good a swimmer are you?"

"I can do laps in a pool, but you're crazy if you think we can swim more than ten feet in the water around here. We'd die of hypothermia within minutes."

"The original Fuegian natives managed. In fact, they didn't wear any clothes at all, in or out of the water."

"You're kidding," she gasped.

He grinned at her and shook his head. "My visit to the national museum in Santiago was very enlightening."

"It's nice to know you're well-informed. But if you're planning on us escaping, shouldn't we try to steal their boat? Whatever the natives did, getting wet once was one time too many for me."

"Sorry. The boat's too well guarded to attempt a takeover."

She didn't look pleased with his response, but he was more aware than Taylor of the difficulty of winning a battle when you're outnumbered two against ten or more heavily armed men. It didn't take long to lose the advantage of surprise, and then you were dead meat. If he got killed, Taylor wouldn't have any chance to survive.

Knowing what he had to do, he made a careful inspection of the perimeter of the shed to look for a spot where the soil was the softest and there weren't any large rocks. After a few minutes of searching, he found what he needed, an area where the dirt appeared recently disturbed. Then he pulled the wire from his belt and used it to cut the nozzle from the hose.

"What are you doing, Rafe?"

"In the tradition of all great prison escapes, we're going to dig our way out of here, Legs. Then we're going for a swim, the two of us buck naked."

She muttered something about him being crazy, and he laughed as he worked the handle free on the hand pump. After he moved a barrel of diesel fuel away from the wall to give them some room to work, they both squatted on the ground and began to dig.

"If you hear anyone come to the door, you dive for the far side of the shed. I'll roll the barrel back into place to cover up our efforts."

"Got it."

It didn't take long before a trace of sunlight appeared under the wall, making it easier for them to see what they were doing.

Taylor sat back on her haunches while Rafe poked away at the dirt with his primitive tool, loosening the soil so she could scoop it out of the way.

"Rafe?" Her voice quavered, and she pointed to the wall near where they were digging. "Look at this."

Frowning, he made out an inscribed T-T, followed by a date roughly etched into the metal with a sharp object or maybe a rock. A little Chilean graffiti.

"Terry was here," she whispered.

"Huh? What makes you think—"

"Those are his initials, the way he always signed them. And look at the date. Four weeks ago!" She turned to Rafe, tears streaming down her cheeks despite the hope in her eyes. "He was alive four weeks ago. Now we know for sure those people in Punta Arenas lied to us. Those ashes weren't Terry's remains."

Rafe nodded. "You're probably right. He sure as hell didn't die in a bar fight." Chances were good Terry had stumbled onto the terrorist camp in his search for penguins, been captured and paid the ultimate price because—in addition to his initials—there was a streak of blood on the wall. Rafe was reluctant to point that out to Taylor, suspecting the watch they had been shown in Punta Arenas had been filched from Terry right here. Very likely from his dead body.

Pushing herself to her feet, she rushed to the door and began pounding on it. "What did you do with my brother?" she screamed. "Where is he?"

Rafe went after her and wrapped his arms around her. "Don't do this, babe. It's no good."

She struggled against him, as strong as most men and twice as determined. "They have to tell me what happened to Terry."

"Shh. It doesn't make any difference."

"He's here somewhere. They could still have him. He could still be alive."

"There's blood, Taylor. Terry's blood."

Suddenly, her body went slack. "No." Her moan denied the possibility.

"Right next to where you found his initials."

Wrenching away from his grasp, she raced back to the hole they were digging and fell to her knees. Her fingers trembled as she touched the reddish-brown streak on the wall; then she looked up at Rafe.

"He could have cut himself. Or had a nosebleed. He used to get those a lot when we were little."

A knot formed in Rafe's throat. He didn't want her to lose hope. She'd already been through so much, had tried so hard to find and rescue her brother, even if it was from his own foolhardiness. Traveling alone in an unfamiliar country wasn't always a smart thing to do.

"Maybe so," he said. "But I don't think Terry is here on the island." Unless the terrorists had buried his body here, which would be a waste of energy when they could have easily dumped him into the sea with a rock tied to his ankle. No one would be the wiser.

"Maybe he escaped." Her hope momentarily restored, she picked up the nozzle to resume digging. "He was always a good swimmer. He even beat me sometimes when we raced. If he got off the island, then we have to break out of here, too, and find him."

Rafe gave her credit for resilience, if not a lot of objectivity. It seemed to him that Terry wouldn't have had much of a chance to avoid being recaptured by the terrorists, assuming he managed to get away in the first place. But then Rafe's plan of escape wasn't exactly foolproof, either.

He only knew if they stayed put, they'd both end up dead. These terrorists weren't about to leave witnesses to whatever they had up their respective sleeves.

Digging with such awkward tools made for slow going, particularly when Rafe hit a large rock only a few inches under the loose soil, and he had to start over again in a different spot.

About mid-afternoon, Rafe made Taylor drink half the remaining water in the bottle to avoid dehydration. The morning had passed with no one arriving with a tray of bacon and eggs; noon came and went without the delivery a hearty sandwich. Feeding the prisoners didn't appear to be on the terrorists to-do list, although periodically they heard men shouting back and forth in a language neither Rafe nor Taylor understood. Not that Rafe was a great linguist, but he had learned a little Russian and knew that wasn't what they were speaking. Ergo, his best guess was Arabic.

Al Qaeda? he wondered. Possibly, except only Hamid had looked Arab. The rest of his men appeared more like European Muslims sporting shaggy beards. Definitely Islamic terrorists.

But why here? he asked himself again and again. Chile didn't have atomic weapons to steal. Or buildings more than twelve stories high. Another revolution? To put the followers of Pinochet back in power? Possible, but a real stretch.

"You've turned quiet on me," Taylor said, sitting back against the wall to take a break. She flexed the fingers of her hand as though they had cramped.

"Thinking."

"About what?"

"Mostly about a big, thick, juicy steak."

"I don't believe you."

He leaned over and planted a kiss on her lips. "You know me that well already?"

"A guy who thinks gourmet is putting a few drops of Merlot in the stew isn't all that serious about steak."

He chuckled. "I may have to rethink my image."

Her lips lifted into a smile no less seductive because of the streaks of dirt on her face. "Your image is just fine with me."

"Tell you what, Legs. Let's you and me cuddle up for a while and take a little nap."

"Nap?" She laughed, a suggestive twinkle in her eyes despite the circumstances.

"Once it's dark, we're breaking out of here, babe. I want us both well-rested."

"You mean it, don't you? About sleeping?"

"I'll take a rain check on the other option and cash it in later when we have more comfortable accommodations." He hoped like hell they both got that chance.

Her expression serious, she nodded.

Standing, he rotated the drum of diesel fuel into place to hide the hole they'd dug. The depression was just big enough for him to snake through. Then he could unlock the door so they could both escape with what they needed to survive a half-mile swim in frigid water.

He could only hope his half-ass plan would work, and wished like hell he wasn't putting Taylor at risk. But there was no way he'd leave her behind.

And he suspected time was growing shorter by the minute for the terrorists to act. If he was to send up the alarm, he had to do it in a hurry.

CHAPTER THIRTY

"Okay, Legs, it's time to strip."

Taylor looked at Rafe as if he'd lost his mind. After an hour of cuddling together, she'd finally gotten warm. Now he wanted her to take off her clothes? The man was friggin' crazy!

Except he'd already pulled off his denim shirt and rolled it into a tight ball, placing it in the middle of a big sheet of black plastic that he had cut off the roll with the jagged edge of the nozzle. His T-shirt went next, and then he started to unsnap his jeans.

"If this is how you treat all your girlfriends, I'd say you need some work on your seduction technique." Shrugging out of her shirt, she tossed it to him. The shed was almost completely dark, and the chill night air raised gooseflesh across her back.

"I haven't had any complaints so far."

She unlaced one boot, then the other, and pulled both of them off while he did the same. "That's probably because you—and your weapon of choice—intimidate the women you date."

"I don't intimidate you."

"I happen to be quite fond of your weapon," she teased suggestively, although her nerves were jumping and tangling together. She couldn't imagine how they'd survive a half-mile swim in water so cold it made her teeth numb. Being naked wasn't going to help.

When they were both standing as bare as models in a life art class—except for the belt that Rafe had hooked around his bare waist—he wrapped their clothes in more plastic, then put them in the trash can along with their digging tools and the bottle of water. He used the duct tape to seal the lid in place and attached strips of plastic to the handles.

"Okay, here comes the fun part." Picking up a smaller can, he dipped his hand inside, pulling out a glob of axle grease. "This is going to give new meaning to finger painting. Come here, Legs."

"You're not going to—"

He slapped the grease onto her chest and rubbed it around, over and under her breasts, leaving it thick and gooey. "Man, if they'd let me do this in kindergarten, I would have gotten straight A's in art."

"You're sick, Maguire. Definitely sick." Although, under other circumstances—and with a nice warm body lotion—she would have enjoyed the experience.

"Think of this as returning to nature."

She shuddered, both because of his gentle, almost sensual touch, and the realization that he was covering her with greasy goo. "Remember, my turn next."

"I'm looking forward to it." His smile was a quick flash of white teeth in the deepening darkness.

When she began lathering him with grease, she said, "Are you sure this is going to work as well for us as it did for the local natives?"

"No. They used seal blubber, but I didn't happen to have any handy."

She rolled her eyes, but kept up her tactile exploration of his body, learning more intimately than ever the shape of muscle and sinew, the power of his masculinity, the roughened ridges of his scars. If they got out of this place alive, she was definitely going to jump his bones—as soon as they could wash this gunk off.

The greasy task accomplished, Rafe went to the door and listened. He tapped lightly. No one responded.

"The shed is barred but there's no lock," he said.

"How do you know that?"

"I wasn't quite as far out of it when they dragged me in here as they thought." Crossing the shed to where they'd dug the hole, he pushed the diesel barrel aside. "I'm going to crawl out the hole, come around to the front and open the door for you. Then we'll make a dash for the water with our favorite trash can."

She looked at the hole skeptically. Suddenly it seemed small and inadequate. "You can't get through there. Your shoulders are too broad. I should be the one to—"

"What are you going to do if I'm wrong and there is a guard on the door?"

"I'm not helpless, Rafe."

"Thank God for that. But I'm the one trained in special ops. So I'm the one who goes. We don't have many hours of darkness when we can safely make our getaway."

She couldn't very well argue with his logic, but she hated to simply sit and wait while he took all the risk. "We could both go?"

He kissed her, a slippery, sliding kind of smooch that could have made her laugh but didn't.

"Be careful," she urged him.

"Survival is job one."

Before she could say anything more, he was flat on his back and slithering head first into the hole, pushing and jockeying with his legs and hips.

The top half of his head vanished, leaving his mouth and chin visible, then he stopped. She held her breath, hoping to God he wasn't looking straight up into the business end of a shotgun.

Finally, without making a sound, he started moving again, inch-by-inch. He had to raise one shoulder and somehow snake an arm through the hole to make it to the other side. His chest was a tight squeeze. By the time his slim waist and hips were exiting the shed, he was moving much faster.

Taylor gave up watching. She hurried to the trash can containing their clothes and tools, carried it to the door and waited.

Her breathing sounded loud to her own ears. Despite the cool air and her naked body, she started to sweat. Where the hell was he? Why hadn't he opened the door? As far as she could tell, there wasn't a single living thing within a mile of the shed, including the men who had captured her. For all she knew, the bad guys had already left to accomplish whatever evil deed they had in mind.

The door rattled. Taylor stepped to the side. It had to be Rafe. It *had* to be.

When the door opened, she exhaled the breath she'd been holding. "What took you so long?"

"A little reconnoitering." He hoisted the trash can by the handle. "There's no guard posted by the shore, but the ones on the boat are awake and alert. Let's go."

He took off at an easy jog. Taylor followed. A sliver of moon provided enough light to make out the faint trace of a rocky path, and with each step she felt the sharp stab of stones on the bottom of her feet. During summer months when she was young, she'd gone barefoot so much that the soles of her feet had gotten tough. They weren't now.

Branches of stunted southern beech trees encroached on the trail, forcing Rafe to push them aside or leave the path and jog through muddy ground where ferns and moss grew. A glance over her shoulder told Taylor the shed where they'd been held captive was already invisible. Nor was there any sign of the boat that had attacked them.

They reached the rocky shoreline. The still, black water reflected a faint trail of moon glow, and on the far side of the water, the face of a glacier glinted in the pale light. From where she stood, the distant shore looked miles away.

She shivered and whispered, "Rafe, I'm not sure I can swim that far."

"You don't have to." Using the strips of plastic he'd cut, he tied the trash can securely to his belt. "All you have to do is hang on. The trash can will float and keep your head above water. I'll pull you."

"My God, Rafe, you can't swim all that way with me hanging on."

"I can and I will. The subject is not up for discussion. If you can kick, that'll help. But don't let go of your flotation device. Got it?"

She lifted her chin. "I'll swim on my own as far as I can. *Then* I'll let you pull me, if I have to. But I'm not going to hold you back any more than necessary."

"You are one stubborn woman, Legs."

"And your point is?"

He exhaled a long breath. "Let's get the hell out of Dodge while we can." He stepped off the shore into water waist-deep, and cursed under his breath. "Man, that's cold."

Even knowing what was coming, the icy water shocked her. She gritted her teeth. She'd swim, damn it! She wasn't going to be a burden to Rafe.

Filling her lungs, she shoved off as though she were doing laps in the U.C.-Davis swimming pool. When she'd attended the university, she'd loved the feel of warm water enveloping her body, the way her muscles stretched and responded with each stroke she took, the ease with which she covered the distance from end to end and back again.

But this was different. The cold drained her strength. Her muscles balked at doing their job, and every stroke was a battle of will. The trash can floated beside her, a temptation she fought to resist. It would be so easy to give in, to let Rafe carry her along with his strong, confident assault on the sea.

Or simply to sink to the bottom of the channel and give up altogether.

Despite the numbness that invaded her body, she concentrated on matching Rafe stroke for stroke, and thought about Terry. If there was any chance at all he'd escaped the terrorists, she had to find him. His initials carved into the wall of the shed were a message to her. He'd known she would come.

Her arms and legs grew heavy, concentration difficult. Sleep was an invitation she could no longer resist.

Rafe saw Taylor's head go under the water. In one stroke, he was there, diving for her, pulling her back up to the surface. He flipped her onto her back.

"Breathe, damn it!" Treading water, he slapped her cheek hard enough that her eyes blinked open, though

233

they remained unfocused. She was so damn stubborn, so determined to do things on her own. Hadn't anyone ever taken care of her? It was high time someone did. And he was damn well elected. "Talk to me, babe."

"I don't like to be called babe," she mumbled.

"Tough."

Awkwardly, his arms and legs resisting the orders his brain sent to his muscles, he hefted her halfway onto the trash can. It was already riding low in the water, apparently leaking, and with her added weight it sank even lower. Holding her in place, he began kicking with all of his remaining strength. They weren't far from shore. She'd done a helluva job to keep going at all, given the conditions. He'd take her the rest of the way.

He fought against the grinding chill in his bones until his feet touched ground. Lifting Taylor, he half-dragged, half-carried her onto the sandy shore, the trash can bouncing along behind him. His lungs were exploding, his body convulsing with shivers. But he couldn't stop there. Before the sun rose, he had to get them out of sight, hidden behind the line of beech trees that were twenty feet away.

Stumbling, he fell to his knees, Taylor falling onto the sand with him. With shaking fingers, he untied the trash can from his belt and struggled to get to his feet again. His sluggish brain barely functioned. He could make the trees with Taylor, then come back for the can. They had to have dry clothes. Soon. He'd have to cover their tracks. The terrorists must not know they'd made it this far.

But the loudest sound he heard was Taylor whispering, "I love you."

Her words stunned him. He didn't want that, didn't want the complication, he told himself. Couldn't handle the emotion and all it implied.

In truth, he didn't know if she had actually spoken the words or if he had imagined them in his frozen, water-soaked brain, but they energized him in a way nothing else could have. He couldn't, *wouldn't* fail her. Not this time.

With a grunt of determination, he picked up Taylor, hoisted her over his shoulder and headed for the tree line.

Taylor groaned, rudely brought back to awareness by the jarring ride on Rafe's shoulder. When he finally put her down, none too gently, she began to shake.

"Cold," her voice croaked.

"I know. Hang on."

She knew he was shivering, too, but it didn't stop him from jogging off and leaving her alone. She yanked a handful of leaves from a low shrub and began to dry herself off. She hadn't made much progress by the time he returned with the trash can. It seemed his whole body was trembling as he worked the lid free and dumped the contents, including a gallon or two of sea water, onto the ground. Then he ripped open the package containing their clothes.

He handed her his T-shirt. "Use this to dry yourself."

Gratefully, she did just that, drying her hair first, grateful that she'd cut it short. In contrast to her chilled-to-the-bone skin, the soft cotton material felt almost warm. It seemed as though she was simply shoving the axle grease around, not wiping it away, and when she finished her teeth kept on chattering.

"We made it, huh?" she said, her voice trembling. She handed him the T-shirt to use, although he'd already pulled his jeans and denim shirt on. After wiping his chest, he tucked the tail of the wet T-shirt in his hip pocket, letting it hang loose.

"You deserve an Olympic medal."

Somehow she doubted that was the case. But they were both alive and had escaped the terrorists. For now, that was enough.

By the time she'd put on her clothes, she'd warmed enough to stop shaking and the sun had risen, just peeking over the top of the sheer granite cliff behind them. Rafe was dressed, too.

"Wait here," he said. "I'm going to get us some food, then we've gotta move out."

Move out? After their ordeal, it would take a crane to get Taylor to her feet. But he didn't wait around to hear her complain. As swiftly and silently as a bird in flight, he was gone. To where, she didn't know. A nearby grocery store seemed unlikely. But the growling of her stomach made her wish food would be that easy to find.

Within an amazingly short amount of time, he returned and squatted down beside her.

"Fish and berries for breakfast." He unfolded a piece of plastic to reveal two small fish about six-inches long and a handful of small, dark blue berries. "We'll get more berries later, and I'll try to snare a rabbit or a bird once we're farther inland."

She plucked a berry from his cache of goodies and found it sweet on her tongue. "In case you hadn't noticed, there's a glacier and some really high cliffs between us and inland."

Picking up a fish, he bit off the tail and chewed with what appeared to be relish. "We're going up and over. Eat. You'll need your strength."

Her stomach threatened to rebel as he took another bite of fish, and she pondered the impossibility of climbing the sheer walls of the canyon they were in.

"Think of it as survival sushi," he urged her when

she hesitated. "Real gourmet fare when it's all that's available."

Gingerly, she plucked the other fish from his ersatz serving dish, closed her eyes and ate. It was salty and chewy. The ocean equivalent of a granola bar, she tried to tell herself, but she knew the sushi treat would never make it into Mama Mia's favorite cookbook, not even with a nice red sauce.

"Listen!" Rafe said.

Opening her eyes, she looked around. A few minutes ago she'd heard a bird singing, but now . . .

"A diesel engine," he provided. "Come on! We've got to get out of sight." Grabbing her hand, he pulled her at a run deeper into the forest. They jumped over a fallen tree, and he pushed her down flat on the ground where it was wet and muddy and smelled of decay. "Keep your head down."

She had no trouble obeying his order.

Suddenly, gunfire erupted. Bullets ripped through tree branches and thudded into the mud. Frightened, a flock of seagulls took flight. Taylor covered her head, which did little to halt the fear that rose in her throat.

The gunfire stopped as quickly as it had begun. The only sound Taylor could hear was her own breathing and the rumble of the diesel engine.

Keeping her head down and speaking as softly as she could, Taylor asked, "What are they shooting at? They can't see us."

"Probably trying to impress their boss that they're doing their job."

"If they come ashore, they'll see our tracks," she whispered.

"Nope. Not unless they're experienced trackers. I

took the time to wipe out our tracks. A little trick I learned in Survival 101."

"I sure hope you got an A in the class."

She felt the reassuring pressure of his hand on her shoulder. If she had to be captured and shot at by terrorists, Rafe was the man to be with.

But climbing up the face of the mountain to reach safety would make them easy targets if the terrorist boat stayed put. Remaining where they were didn't seem like a good option either, in case the bad guys decided to explore more deeply into the forest.

Taylor hoped Rafe had an alternate plan in his pocket along with his soggy T-shirt.

CHAPTER THIRTY-ONE

Hamid al Faysal waited impatiently on the shore of his island hideaway as the boat pulled into the natural cove where it was protected from sight by a rock overhang and screened by a thick shield of trees. If his idiot freedom fighters had guarded the man and woman as he had ordered, his plan to hijack the Russian submarine would not be at risk. Through the laziness of two men, his scheme to force the world powers to their knees and restore morality to the people was now in jeopardy. Had they learned nothing when that weakling birdwatcher slipped away? At least they had shot and killed him, although they had been too lazy to retrieve his body. Or too incompetent.

As the crewmen secured the boat, the captain jumped down to the stone ledge where Hamid stood.

"Did you find them?" he asked in Arabic.

"There was no sign of the two Americans. The water is ten degrees celsius. No one could have survived long in water that cold."

"I heard shots being fired."

"A precaution only. If they reached the opposite shore, which I do not believe is possible, they are dead now."

"Then you found their bodies?"

"My men went ashore to search. There was no sign anyone had landed there."

Hamid doubted his Chechen associates were as thorough as they should be, so this time he would teach them a lesson they would not soon forget. With less than four days until the submarine entered local waters, he could not afford any further mistakes.

"Bring me the two men who were ordered to guard the Americans."

With a fearful look in his eyes, the captain did as he was told. Minutes later two men were brought to Hamid. From the holster on his hip, he drew his Glock. It felt powerful in his hand, a tool well-used in the name of Allah.

"There is a penalty for disobeying orders," he said loudly enough that all the members of the crew could hear. "Kneel and pray that Allah will forgive you."

One man knelt, as ordered, but the other had to be forced down. He sobbed like a child.

As a reward, Hamid first shot the man who had bravely accepted his fate in the back of his head. The second man screamed, begging to be forgiven, pleading that he had a wife and children. Hamid took his time, dragging out the moment that death would silence his cries.

Finally tiring of the game, he executed the man in the same manner as his friend.

"Allah be praised," he said.

No one on the small island spoke. This time the lesson had been well learned.

* * *

Back in Santiago, Donovan Landry returned to his quarters following a terminally boring meeting with the Chilean Army authorities, who were coordinating the upcoming joint exercises. He'd thought the U.S. military was good at paper-pushing. That was before he'd met General Tilio. *Shit!* Landry could have fucking run all of World War II with less paperwork than Tilio wanted for what amounted to a small training operation.

Still worried about Rafe, he unhitched his cell phone from his belt and tapped in his buddy's number. He didn't like that his friend had been incommunicado for so long. Particularly since there was a woman involved.

Or maybe that was a good sign, he thought as the number responded. It was high time Big Mac started to live again.

"The party you have called is either out of range or the phone is turned off," a sexy female voice announced.

Donovan snapped his phone closed. Knowing his neighbor had been tortured and killed should have sent Rafe running back to Santiago. Unless he figured there was a bigger problem out there. Something humongous that had taken Rafe and his lady friend to Punta Arenas.

"Where are you, Big Mac?" Landry said under his breath. "And what kind of mess have you gotten yourself into this time?"

CHAPTER THIRTY-TWO

Rafe kept Taylor pinned to the ground behind the fallen tree long after she heard the growl of the boat's diesel engines departing. A damp chill crept into her body, not that she had yet gotten entirely warm since their swim in arctic-cold water. Here in the woods, with scrawny trees, dwarf shrubs and bog-like ground, there wasn't a sound. No flies pestered them. No mosquitoes or black gnats swarmed around their faces. Nothing enticed a bird to perch on a tree in search of a meal. The land was devoid of life usually found in a forest; it was eerie.

And the lingering smell of axle grease on both her own body and Rafe's was an offense against the cleaner scent of nature.

"Can we get up now?" she whispered.

"I want to make sure they're really gone and didn't leave a man behind to catch us by surprise."

"Maybe if they left a man on shore, you could over-power him and get his jacket. I'm really cold."

"Good idea." He rose to his knees to peer through the trees.

"I didn't really mean that. If they left someone behind, he'll have a gun. I don't want you to—"

"Wait here and stay out of sight."

As silent as the empty woods, he was up and running in a crouch before she could stop him. She exhaled a disgusted breath. Rafe Maguire was making a habit of playing macho man and leaving her behind. She wasn't one of those helpless females. He should know that by now.

Cautiously, she sat up and looked around. There wasn't a sign of any other living soul. From what she could see, Rafe hadn't even left footprints on the mossy ground. Considering he weighed in at a hundred-eighty-pounds, she wondered how he did that.

With one last glance toward the beach, she stood and walked toward the cliff that towered above the forested area. Rafe wasn't the only one who could do a little foraging. On hiking excursions with her brother, they had often supplemented their packaged rations with edible roots and herbs.

Walking through the forest was no easy task. Trees had fallen in a Pick-up Sticks pattern, their trunks crisscrossing, branches entwined. The same cold climate that kept flies and mosquitoes at bay apparently discouraged the process of decomposition as well. When wind or snow caused a tree to keel over, it simply lay there waiting for the next ice age to arrive.

Standing in a triangle of downed tree trunks, she spotted a knee-high bush bearing the dark blue berries Rafe had found, and she smiled. She knelt to pluck a few and quickly realized she'd need something to carry them in. If she hadn't been so cold—the morning air was about forty-five degrees—she would have taken off her shirt to make into a knapsack. Instead, she cupped the hem of her top to carry what she gathered.

She had picked a handful of berries when she noticed a cluster of mushrooms growing in a particularly damp and shady spot. She'd had some experience telling the difference between those that were poisonous and those that weren't, and she hoped her earlier lessons held true here in Tierra del Fuego. Within a few minutes she had the equivalent of a small bowl of berries and mushrooms.

Then she recognized a parasite clinging to the trunk of a beech tree. White and pasty-looking, she'd heard it called Indian bread. As she plucked a clump, she hoped it tasted like its name.

"I believe I've found a Patagonia wood nymph."

She whirled at the sound of Rafe's voice and almost dropped the berries and mushrooms she'd collected.

"Lord, Rafe! Don't sneak up on me like that."

He shrugged. "I thought I told you to stay put."

"In case you've forgotten, I don't take orders very well. And I don't like sitting around waiting to be saved by some man. I can take care of myself." Considering he'd saved her ass more than once lately, she knew she was being bitchy. "Look, I'm tired and hungry and it's been a helluva day. But I don't like being treated like a dumb blonde—particularly when I'm temporarily a brunette. All my life people have misjudged me and underrated my abilities, including my own father. I'm not going to let that happen anymore."

He eyed her speculatively. "I don't underestimate you, Taylor." He spoke so softly, with such sincerity, it was like he had wrapped her in a warm blanket. "I've never met any woman, and damn few men, who are stronger or more determined than you. Or more stubborn. I admit I'm used to taking care of people, worrying about their safety. It's part of the job description for a Ranger.

I messed up once. If I seem overly protective, it's because I don't want to mess up with you."

To her surprise, her anger dissipated like a morning mist, and she felt herself step toward him. "You'd never mess up. It's not in your character. What happened in Afghanistan—and in South Carolina—wasn't your fault. Sometimes bad things happen to good people. No one can prevent that."

"It was my job."

"You're not God, Rafe. I wouldn't want you to be."

They stood inches apart. The air was cool on her bare midriff but the warmth in his gray eyes touched her deep inside, sparking a flame that had nothing to do with the temperature. The dark bruise on his cheekbone marked him as a hero willing to take a beating for the good of the cause.

Lifting his hand, he ran his knuckles down her cheek. His lips curved ever so slightly. "How can you be so tough and so soft at the same time?"

She smiled. "That information is classified."

"Need-to-know basis?"

"Something like that."

Closing the gap between them, he pressed a swift kiss to her lips. "When we've got more time, I expect I'll want to know all your secrets. But right now we've gotta get moving."

"Timing is everything, isn't it?"

"Yeah." He checked the small hoard of food she'd gathered and helped himself to a mushroom, testing it beneath his tongue before chewing. "You did good, Legs. I bet you're great in a kitchen."

"Not likely, to my Italian mother's everlasting dismay."

"Then she underestimated you, too." He took a mo-

245

ment to shift the stockpile of food to his black plastic carryall, tying it to his belt. "Of course, she might not have approved of you running through the woods gathering berries for a strange man."

"You're no stranger, Rafe, and my guess is that you like it just fine."

"You got that damn straight." Laughing, he headed off through the tangle of downed trees toward the sheer cliff face.

She followed, thinking Rafe might well have a savior complex for good reason. He'd spent his whole adult life saving people he cared about. With any luck, this time she'd show him how they could save each other.

By late afternoon they reached the summit and collapsed onto ground covered with moss and low-growing vegetation. What trees there were at this elevation and southern latitude were stunted, most of them no taller than five feet.

Taylor's breath sawed through her lungs. Her hands were bloody from climbing over razor-sharp rocks. The muscles in her calves and arms quivered from exhaustion. If Rafe hadn't roped her to him with entwined lengths of plastic strips, she would have fallen more times than she cared to remember.

"Here. Drink some water."

He handed her the bottle that he had twice filled with glacier runoff while she had rested on a ledge midway up the cliff. They'd eaten the mushrooms and Indian bread she'd found, then he filled the water bottle again, carrying it along with what few tools and supplies they had hooked to his belt since they'd left the garbage can behind.

Gratefully, she gulped down half the water and gave

246

the bottle back to him. His endurance amazed her. Nothing seemed to faze him. After a rugged climb of more than five hundred feet, he was barely breathing hard. The man was a damn mountain goat.

"It's really not fair." She brushed her sweat-dampened hair back from her face. "Until you came along, I thought I was in pretty good shape. I can't hold a candle to you."

"As far as I'm concerned, your shape is perfect. You're terrific, Legs. With any luck, the hard part is over."

"I don't see how you can say that." From her perspective, all she could see was the great expanse of a glacier ice field lined on either side with jagged peaks carved ten thousand years ago, in the last ice age. Periodically during their climb, huge chunks of ice had splintered off the face of the glacier, dropping into the milky-white water below. Her palms had turned sweaty at the thought of slipping from the rock face and joining the iceberg at the bottom of the fjord. In this forbidding environment, Taylor thought, they were more likely to come across a wooly mammoth than a human habitation where someone could help them.

He pointed across the rim of the glacier-filled basin. "To the north there's a low saddle through the peaks. If I'm remembering the charts on the *Reina* right, there's a plateau on the other side. I'm guessing that would be a good spot for a sheep ranch."

"But you're only guessing."

"Yep. I'm open to other ideas, if you have any."

Hardly. They couldn't go back to the terrorist camp. Going forward was the only choice; knowing which direction was forward was the hard part.

"How far do you think it is across the glacier?"

Squinting, he looked to the far range of peaks. "It's narrow here, two or three clicks. Not far."

"Easy for you to say."

He chuckled. "You rest. My turn to do a little foraging, see if I can fill our larder."

"Steak and fries for me this time, the greasier the better."

"With a nice red wine, I assume." Kneeling, he pressed a warm kiss to her lips, lingering as his fingers ran through her hair in a gentle caress. "We'll make it out of here, Legs. Trust me."

"I do," she whispered. She palmed his whisker-roughened cheek. Deep down, she knew no man was more trustworthy than Rafe. To get her to safety, he'd give his life. She didn't know if he would as willingly give her his heart, and that hurt at some basic feminine level she hadn't known existed within her. Still, from the beginning she'd told him no promises were necessary. It was too late to change the rules now.

When he jogged off to find something for them to eat, she lay back and tried to relax. Under different circumstances, the dramatic scenery would have made her heart soar. Now the lifeless glacier, the cold, dry air and craggy mountain peaks frightened her. From this vantage point, it seemed impossible they'd find help any time soon. Yet, because of the terrorists, they needed to press on. Time could well be getting short.

The depth of quiet was uncanny. Not a bird chirped, no babbling brook could be heard. Finally, well overhead, a jet plane silently crossed the sky at too great an altitude for the pilot to notice any signal she might send up. Closing her eyes, she tried the only things that were left—ESP and prayer.

"Dinner's ready!"

Taylor started awake at the sound of Rafe's voice, and

her heart thudded against her ribs. "Good grief! You scared me to death again. You've got to stop sneaking up on me."

Grinning, he spread his black-plastic bundle of goodies on the ground like Santa Claus emerging from the chimney. "High-class vegetarian fare tonight. Some roots that taste like onions, which would be great if we were making stew. A few greens that aren't too bitter. And more of your favorite berries for dessert."

"What happened to the rabbit you promised?" she teased as she tentatively bit into a root. The flavor tingled her tongue, but she was hungry enough not to care.

"That'll have to wait for another time."

Divvying up his harvest, he settled down beside her to enjoy their brief picnic; then they washed the meal down with more water. If Taylor's stomach wasn't full, at least it wasn't complaining so loudly now. And after her nap she felt refreshed.

"Are we going to try to make it across the glacier while it's still light?" she asked.

"We'll be on our way just as soon as we put together some snowshoes."

"My, you're a regular Boy Scout. How'd you happen to have snowshoes in your back pocket?"

"The school I went to taught an advanced class in resourcefulness."

Once again Rafe proved he was an A student as he cut and bent beech branches, tying them together with duct tape and strips of plastic, then strapping them onto their boots.

"These won't be perfect," he admitted as he stood and tested the imitation snowshoes. "But if you're up to it, we'll give it a try."

249

Shrugging, she let him help her to her feet. "Is this where I'm supposed to say 'I'll follow you to the ends of the earth?'"

"Look around, babe. I think we're there."

The ice field wasn't as smooth going as Rafe had hoped, and they sure as hell weren't dressed for traversing a glacier. Wind had blown snow ridges across the glacier, and the sun had melted the top layer, which meant with every step he sank ankle deep despite the snowshoes. So did Taylor, whom he'd roped to him again.

The glacier was a living, moving creature. That meant there were wrinkles hidden beneath the snow cover, some of them hundreds of feet deep. He had no desire for either of them to end up at the bottom of a crevasse, not even together. That's why he'd found a long branch to use as a walking stick. Before each step, he shoved the stick into the snow, testing to make sure there was something solid there.

So far, so good, but damn slow going.

Earlier, he'd spotted a jet fighter overhead and had waved his shirt but got no reaction. He wished Donovan had had the sense to send out a search patrol when Rafe had gone so long without contact. In fact, maybe Donovan had. Not that he'd have any idea where to look.

Behind him, Rafe heard Taylor's heavy breathing. That she had come this far was nothing short of heroic. An amazing woman. Sexy as hell, too. The kind of woman a man could rely on to be there for him, no matter what.

Suddenly, his walking stick sank more deeply into the snow than usual. Then, in a slow crumble, the snow bridge that had hidden a deep crevasse fell away. Made awkward by his snowshoes, Rafe scrambled back from the precipice. Without his walking stick, he would have fallen in—and taken Taylor with him.

"What's wrong?" She half caught him before he landed on his butt.

"A crevasse. Looks like we'll have to take a detour." They'd been hiking for a couple of hours and were past the midway point. No telling how far the abyss split the glacier, or how far they'd have to walk to get around it. "Let's take a break."

He sat down on the snow and pulled Taylor onto his lap so she wouldn't get chilled. "How you doing, Legs?"

"I've had less strenuous hikes that were more fun."

"Yeah, me too." When she rested her head on his shoulder, he looped his arm around her back. The residual smell of axle grease clung to them both and reminded Rafe of her courage, a surprisingly arousing scent. "Me and some buddies climbed Mount Whitney in California for kicks one time. We talked about trying Everest someday. I think I'll skip that gig."

"Getting too old, huh?"

"Naw. Not too old. Just a lot smarter than I used to be."

He sensed she was smiling but too tired to laugh at his weak effort to make a joke.

"What are you going to do when you get back to California?" he asked.

She was silent a full minute before she responded. "Have a talk with my dad, I think. If he doesn't want to make me an equal partner in the vineyard, I'll buy some land of my own. I still have money in a trust fund my grandmother left me."

"You mean, all this time I've been hanging out with a wealthy woman and I didn't know it?"

"I told you I'd pay my own way."

"Yeah, but I didn't believe you."

"I was keeping a list of our expenses. Of course, it went down with the *Reina*, so we'll have to agree on the estimated cost."

Cupping her chin, he smiled. "I can think of an alternate repayment plan that we can both live with."

Slowly, he lowered his mouth to hers. The crisp, dry air had chapped her lips, and he soothed them with his tongue. As she opened for him, sweetly and eagerly, enough heat radiated through his body to melt a dozen glaciers. He'd never reacted so fast to a woman, never went so hard with such a painful ache that had as much to do with his heart as his crotch.

Not even with Lizbeth.

That thought lingered in his head as he continued to taste Taylor on his tongue. He hadn't thought of his wife in days. Now when she came to mind, it was without guilt. Only distant memories of Lizbeth and little Katy.

When had the change happened? he wondered. On the *Reina*, when Taylor tried to save him? Or when Taylor had struggled so courageously in the freezing cold water?

More likely this new reality had sneaked up on him from the moment he'd seen her at the bar and taken her home to save her. Now it seemed she had found a way to save *him* from the guilt that filled him for three long years.

As he eased back from their kiss, he became aware of a new sound on the glacier. At first he thought it was ice breaking loose.

"Rafe? Do you hear dogs barking?"

He scanned the horizon. If there were dogs, chances were good there were people nearby. He thought the distant barking was coming from beyond the notch in the razor-tooth peaks he'd spotted.

"Up and at 'em, Legs. If we get going, I'm guessing we'll have mutton stew tonight."

She struggled to her feet. "What makes you so sure whoever owns those dogs will help us? Maybe the terrorists have tracked us down."

"Not likely. We know they didn't follow us up the cliff, and we'd be able to see them if they were crossing the glacier behind us." He looked back across the wide expanse they had already traveled, then to the notch in the nearer range of peaks. "My money is on the dogs belonging to friendlies."

She shrugged. "I hope you're right."

Hours later, with the light beginning to fade, Taylor staggered off the glacier onto solid ground. She was so tired, her legs wobbled. Despite the food they'd found earlier, she was so hungry her stomach felt hollow.

"We're almost there," Rafe said. "Smell the smoke?"

She sniffed at the bouquet of chill air and low-growing vegetation and caught a hint of wood smoke. *A fire!* Somewhere to warm her hands and feet. *Thank God!*

The land sloped downward. Rafe took her arm, steadying her over the rocky terrain until they reached a grassy plain not unlike the steppes of northern Europe or Argentina. Off in the deepening shadows, a baby sheep bleated for its mother, and Taylor smiled despite her fatigue. Mutton stew sounded just fine to her.

The dogs started barking again. From out of the gloom, two border collies appeared at a run. Sheep scattered, confused by the dogs' behavior.

"Anita! Ollie!" The man's shout was followed by two

253

shrill whistles that brought the dogs to a halt and had them circling around each other, their tails wagging like black-and-white semaphore flags. As their owner approached, he lifted an oil lantern and called out. *"¿Quien esta allí?"* Who is there? In his free hand he held a shotgun.

"Amigos," Rafe replied. "We need your help."

The stranger approached cautiously. Taylor saw that he was an old man, hunched with age, his dark skin weathered by time to the texture of leather. Ignoring Rafe, he walked up to Taylor and held his lantern as high as he could.

"Señorita Taylor?"

Hearing her name stunned Taylor. "Sí. How did you know?"

"Your brother, he said you would come."

CHAPTER THIRTY-THREE

Taylor's heart soared. In her excitement she nearly lunged at the stranger, wanting to hug him. *"¿Terry esta aquí?"* Terry's here? "Where? Is he all right? Was he hurt?"

"Please, señorita. You must come with me."

"Did you hear that, Rafe? Terry's here. He's not dead."

"Easy, Taylor. That's not exactly what he said."

The man whistled for his dogs, and they came running.

"But he knew my name," Taylor insisted. "Terry told him I'd come looking for him." She was grateful now that her father had insisted she search for her brother. She hated the thought that she might have failed Terry, that he might have waited for her and she hadn't come.

"I have a cabin," the old man said. "It is not far."

"What is your name, old man?" Rafe asked.

"I am Hector Lillo." He straightened in a show of pride. "I have cared for these sheep here on their summer range since I was a boy of eleven."

Introducing himself, Rafe extended his hand. "We would be honored to visit your cabin."

Eyeing Rafe with caution, Hector shook his hand. "The brother of the señorita did not say she would come with a friend."

"It was a last minute decision."

"It is perhaps good you are with her."

Impatient with their polite exchange, Taylor resisted the urge to roll her eyes. "I'm really anxious to see my brother. Could we go now?"

For a moment, Hector gazed at her somberly, then nodded. "He is this way."

An uneasy feeling twisted in Taylor's stomach as Hector turned away and began walking across the grassy field, his lantern held high. She followed him, aware of the incessant bleating of sheep all around her as though they had some tragic story to tell her. The grass brushing against her jeans made a whispering sound as though the earth itself knew the story, too. Even Rafe seemed unnaturally subdued considering they had escaped the terrorists and should be celebrating.

"There's something wrong, isn't there?" she asked.

"I haven't been giving your brother enough credit. He must have gotten here on his own. That's quite an accomplishment."

"I told you he was an experienced traveler. And adaptable."

"Yeah, you did."

"You don't think this Lillo guy is in cahoots with the terrorists, do you?"

"Nope."

His terse responses did nothing to ease Taylor's anxiety, but all she could do was doggedly follow the shepherd and his energetic border collies.

She was glad when the shadow of a small cabin appeared in the moonlight, and she made out the silhouette of a wooden caravan of the type gypsies often used—or shepherds when they moved their flock. But there was no light in the cabin window, no sign of her brother.

Hector veered off to the right of the cabin, walked a few paces and came to a halt beside a mound of freshly disturbed dirt. A simple wooden cross was planted at one end of the mound.

A cry rose in Taylor's throat. "No. Please, no." She would have known if Terry had died! She'd been so sure—

"Lo siento, señorita." I am sorry. "Your brother was a very brave man."

"Rafe? This is not real. It can't be. It's part of the same conspiracy. Terry can't be—" He wrapped her up in his arms, and she buried her face in his shoulder, smothering her sob.

"Can you tell us what happened, Hector?" Rafe asked the old man.

"Sí. Come inside. I will give you something to eat and will tell you what Señor Terry told me. Perhaps there is still time for you to stop this terrible thing that will happen."

While Hector heated a pot of stew on a two-burner stove in the small cabin, Rafe got Taylor settled in a straight-back chair at the table. He knew she had to be numb with grief. This time Terry's death was no lie. The old man had shown them Terry's Nikon camera—with a roll of film still in it—a gold neck chain that Taylor was able to identify, and her brother's passport. There was no doubt in Rafe's mind that Terry's body lay under that mound of dirt outside Hector's cabin.

He was just amazed Terry had escaped the terrorists and made it here.

Hector brought two shallow bowls filled with stew to the table, then poured glasses of what appeared to be homemade beer for them all.

"Please, you eat and drink now. I will tell you of your brave brother."

Picking up a spoon, Rafe took his first bite of stew. His stomach acknowledged the gift of food and drink with a loud growl as he washed the stew down with a sip of beer.

"It's not bad," he said. "Eat up, Legs. You need your strength."

She shook her head, but tasted the stew anyway, or at least put a bite in her mouth and chewed. Rafe doubted she was aware of the spicy flavor. Only the salty tears of her grief.

Compared to her stoic reaction in Puenta Arenas when she'd been told of Terry's death, the raw pain of her loss wrenched at Rafe's heart. She'd been so strong. Now he saw the depth of her vulnerability and couldn't help but want to give her his strength and take away her pain.

Standing across from them in the narrow kitchen, his back to the stove, Hector assumed the pose of a storyteller. He tilted his head to one side as though that would help him remember the words and his eyes were slightly unfocused so he could see the past in clear detail.

"It was rainy that night," he began quietly. "That was almost four weeks ago now. The dogs began barking as they did again this night. We do not have wolves here. Only a fox now and then. But sometimes the wild guanacos—something like your llamas or vacunas—disturb the sheep. My dogs run them off. But that night Anita and Ollie kept barking.

"I put on my coat and took my shotgun outside. The moon was hidden behind clouds so it was hard to see. I

258

whistled for my dogs, but they did not come. They are good dogs and do not often disobey me. I followed the sound of their barking to where I found them circling an object on the ground I did not recognize."

Rafe decided the old shepherd rarely had an audience for his stories, and that this was going to be a long night.

"As I came closer, I saw it was a man on the ground. At first I was afraid. Bad men had come here to my camp earlier, at the beginning of the summer season when I brought the sheep to the plateau."

"Bad men?" Rafe questioned.

Nodding, the old man took a sip of beer and smiled sadly. "I will get to that later. First the señorita wants to know about her brother."

If one of Rafe's troops had dragged out his action report this long, he would have had the man up on charges. In this case, he didn't have much choice but to be patient, although that meant grinding his teeth to keep from yelling at the guy.

"Okay, but let's keep it moving," he said.

"Sí, of course. When the man seemed unable to move, I rolled him over. He was unconscious but breathing. He had been shot, two times, I think."

Taylor gasped, and Rafe reached across the small table to cover her hand.

"He was a big man," Hector continued, "though not as big as you, señor. I tried to pick him up but it was not possible. I am old and not as strong as I used to be. So I returned to my cabin. I have a sled made of wood that I use to move heavy things like supplies. I dragged that out to where the man had collapsed and rolled him onto it. It was not an easy thing to do."

"Thank you." Taylor's voice was hoarse and barely above a whisper.

Hector smiled at her gratitude. "I pulled him back here and brought him inside out of the rain. He woke enough that, with my help, I got him onto my bed." Looking pleased with himself, he gestured toward the cot that stood against the opposite wall. "It seemed to me he had a fever. I washed his wounds as best I could and tried to cool him. He slept awhile, then awoke."

"He didn't die right away?" Taylor questioned.

"No. But he was very weak and had lost much blood. If I had medicines . . . A doctor. Perhaps . . ." He shrugged. "He was here for two days and then . . . I buried him. It is a nice view from that spot."

Grief filled Taylor's eyes, and she covered her face with her hand.

"Did Terry tell you what had happened to him?" Rafe asked.

"Sí. He told me the story. Señor Terry had been taking pictures of penguins and other birds. He had hired a guide to show him the good places for pictures, and they were on a small boat when they were attacked. Some bad men killed the guide, but they captured Señor Terry and took him to a small island. There Señor Terry discovered the men were terrorists—Arabs and Chechens, he said."

"Chechens! Damn, I didn't think of that," Rafe said.

"Señor Terry overhead conversations."

"He picked up some Arabic when he visited Saudi." Taylor kept her head down, her apparent focus on her dish of stew. "He is . . . *was* very good at languages. Better than I am."

Hector nodded sympathetically. "With the help of a traitorous sailor on board, these terrorists are going to hijack a Russian submarine."

"They're going to hijack a sub with the help of only one sailor?" Rafe asked, astonished.

"Sí. That is what señor Terry overheard. They will take it to Antarctica where they will use the submarine's nuclear power and maybe atomic missiles to melt the ice cap. When the ice melts, many coastal towns in Chile and other countries will be flooded. Even those in America."

Taylor's head snapped up. "Oh, my God! Melt the ice cap?"

"That is what your brother heard them say."

"How could they possibly do that?"

He shrugged. "I do not know, señorita."

Rafe realized Hector's story made sense. An atomic explosion would generate a huge amount of heat as well as radiation. Enough to melt plenty of ice. There was a Chilean submarine base in Puntas Arenas. A lot of countries sent their subs there on friendship visits. A diplomatic spit-and-polish event. Hijacking a sub didn't seem all that impossible if they had an inside man.

Letting an atomic weapon get into the hands of terrorists was the nightmare scenario the United States most feared.

"Shit!" he muttered. "Did Terry know who the traitor was onboard the ship?"

"No, I do not think so."

"What do the terrorists hope to gain with their stunt?"

"The brother of the señorita did not know. But he did want me to contact the authorities."

"Did you?"

The old man shrugged. "It was not possible. Those bad men who came here six weeks ago broke my radio. They used a hammer, and I was grateful they did not use

261

the hammer on me. I have no other way to reach the authorities until Fall when I move the flock back to lower pastures. On my own I cannot walk that far."

Rafe came to his feet. "Where's your radio? Maybe there is some way to fix the damn thing."

"I do not think so, Señor Maguire." Walking to the back of the cabin, Hector pulled aside a drape that revealed a jumble of glass and electronic parts on a waist-high counter. "They also broke my antenna."

Rafe cursed again. Now that he knew what the terrorists were up to, he had to reach someone, warn them. Donovan seemed the best bet. But besides smoke signals, how the hell could he contact anyone from this remote location?

"How far is it to where someone has a radio or a phone we could use?" Rafe asked.

"It is a long way. Coming here in the Spring, it takes five days to move the flock. A man walking very fast could reach the main *estancía* in perhaps three days."

"Did Terry tell you when this hijacking scheme was going to happen?" Rafe asked.

"He was not entirely sure," Hector said. "He tried to count the days. If he was right, the submarine will arrive at Punta Arenas maybe tomorrow or the next day, I think. They plan to hijack the boat before it reaches its destination."

Rafe picked up a circuit board that had been broken in half, the soldered parts ripped off and tossed away. It was impossible to repair in a reasonable time, and maybe not at all. "We have to find a way to warn the authorities. Or stop the terrorists ourselves."

"The *murderers,* you mean." Grief had turned to fury in Taylor's eyes, and blood revenge.

"If their plan works, they'll be killing hundreds of

thousands of people," Rafe agreed. He paced, considering the implications of the Arab's scheme. "The devastation would be worse than any tsunami the world has ever experienced. The economic impact would be enormous. Whole countries would fail. The industrialized world would be thrown back a hundred years. Maybe more. It's madness."

"All criminals are just a little mad," Hector commented. "This has always been so."

"Maybe that's true, but we're going to stop these killers, or damn well try." Animated by her anger and need to do something constructive, Taylor shoved her bowl of stew aside and stood. "I saw a jet plane fly over the glacier. We can set a signal fire. Lay out an S.O.S. on the ground. They'll notice. They'll have to."

Nodding thoughtfully, Rafe agreed. "We can set it up, and when you spot a plane, you and Hector can light the fire. But I'm going back to the island. With all the communications gear I saw there, I'll be able to get on the military frequencies and can contact them directly."

"Those are very dangerous men," Hector warned.

"If you go back to the island, they'll kill you."

"I'll have surprise on my side this time, especially if Hector will loan me his shotgun and any other weapons he's got. It's the best chance we have."

"Whatever I have is yours, señor."

"That's your savior complex talking, Rafe. You can't do it all alone."

Ignoring Taylor's comment, Rafe turned to Hector. "I'll need your sled to use as a raft, and some rope. Have you got another gun?"

"An old flintlock pistol that was my grandfather's. I have not shot it for years."

"I'll take whatever I can get and hope it doesn't explode in my face. I'll need a gallon of gasoline, too. I'll start a fire to divert the terrorists."

"Sí, I have petrol. There is also some dynamite in the back shed, leftover from digging the well many years ago. But it may not be good after all this time. The terrorists did not want to touch it. Unstable, I think."

Probably. But Rafe would have to risk it. If nothing else, blowing up the terrorists' communication center would slow them down—assuming he could do that without blowing himself up. But his primary objective would be to warn the authorities, then neutralize the terrorists. "How about knives? Matches?"

"Sí. I have those."

"Warm jackets?" Taylor added.

Rafe shot her a glance. "Jackets, as in plural?"

"You didn't really think you could leave me behind, did you? Not when they are the ones who killed my brother."

He'd been too busy planning his strategy to realize Taylor would insist on coming with him. That's just how she was. No sense to argue about it now.

He looked out the window. A hint of sunrise had begun to gray the sky. He was bone-tired and knew Taylor had to be, too.

"We'll have to get a couple of hours of shut-eye," he said. "Then we'll gather up what equipment we can and leave. If we move fast, we should get to the island after sundown tonight."

"I'd happily trade a few minutes of sleep for a bath." Taylor wrinkled her nose. "I think the axle grease is turning rancid."

Hector smiled at her. "There is warm water from the tank on the roof that is heated by the sun, señorita. After your bath, you and your man can sleep here in the cabin.

I will sleep in my caravan. Later I will fix you food to take with you."

"You're very generous, Hector. Thank you. And thank you for taking care of my brother."

"I am only sorry I could not make him well again. But if you can stop these bad men, his courage will not have been wasted."

Hector showed Taylor a small room containing an old claw-foot tub. Given the grime and grease that covered her, this was five-star luxury. She thanked him, and when he left she started to run water into the tub. It wasn't exactly hot but she wasn't going to quibble about the temperature. She stripped and stepped into the tub.

"You're not the kind of woman who'd cop all the hot water, are you?"

Her nerves jumped and tangled, and arousal spiraled through her at the sight of Rafe standing in the doorway, beautifully naked and thoroughly masculine. In a strange way, her instant reaction to Rafe validated her existence. She needed his comfort, needed to be held, and needed the knowledge that the loss of her brother had not crippled her as a woman.

"Do you always walk in uninvited on a woman taking a bath?"

He moved into the room. "Not usually. But for you, I decided to make an exception."

"I'm the lucky girl, huh?"

"Unless you don't want me to scrub your back."

Despite her fatigue and her grief for her brother, delicious flutters of desire tumbled through her tummy. "Only if I get to scrub yours, too."

With the ease of a self-confident man, he stepped into the tub and picked up the bar of soap from the holder. "Back first, then we'll work on the front."

"Aye, captain."

When his soap-lathered hands caressed her shoulders, she shuddered with pleasure.

"I've been wanting to do this since you took a shower at my place that first night," he murmured, the stroke of his hands both gentle and arousing. "I shouldn't have waited so long."

Pine fragrance mixing with his musky male scent swirled around her, making her fatigued brain dizzy. Her muscles relaxed. The thought that Rafe was so utterly strong—powerful enough to literally climb mountains—and yet could be so gentle, challenged her womanhood. She wanted to match him in every way, his vitality and energy, his natural sensuality and carnal charm.

His hands skimmed over her buttocks, making her womb clench.

"You did a good job as first mate." His low whisper vibrated against her ear. "I'll miss the *Queen of the Sea*."

"So will I." If they survived the next twenty-four hours, their time together would be over. He'd go back to his soldiering, she to Travini Vineyard. That was a loss she didn't want to face. She battled the lump that filled her throat that made speaking impossible and swallowing a foreign concept.

Kneeling behind her, he washed her legs, his palms caressing her front and back, and then he slid his soapy hand slowly, smoothly between them.

She gasped. "Rafe?"

"Right here, Legs."

"Maybe I ought to take a turn. Wash—" her voice caught "—your back."

"No rush."

"The water will get cold."

"That's okay. I'm tough."

She wasn't. Her insides had all but turned to jelly. Warm, slippery jelly.

She turned. "Enough."

As he stood, she took the bar of soap from him, but that didn't slow his erotic assault on her senses. This time he lathered her breasts with his already soapy hands, shifting her necklace from side to side, swirling the soap around and down, across her midsection and then to the vee between her legs.

Her hands trembled as she mimicked his actions on his sculpted body. In contrast to his olive complexion, her skin looked pale and cream-colored. Tiny bubbles caught on the cross of dark hair on his chest, and the scent of pine filled her nostrils. The muscles across his ribbed stomach rippled under her fingertips. His breath was warm on her face, her breathing labored.

She grasped his penis, forming a soap-slickened circle around his erection with her hand. He was thick and hard and very big. Everything about him was potent male.

He groaned. "Time to rinse, sailor."

"I haven't done your back yet."

"I'll give you a second chance." He sat first and brought her down onto his lap facing him.

His erection pressed against her pubis as she sat straddling him. With infinite care, he slipped his finger into her. On a sharp intake of breath, she closed her eyes.

"Open your eyes. I want to watch you when you come."

The friction of his finger and thumb working together was excruciating, riding the fine line between pain and exquisite pleasure. She moaned. Wanted to look away but didn't. Instead, she felt the building pressure. Watched his eyes darken to the coal black of midnight as the pupils dilated. Her heart rate accelerated, pulsing in her throat, pounding at her temple. Nerves and muscles bunched, ready for release.

Rafe held her gaze as steady as a lifeline. "Now, Legs."

The power of her climax shocked her, both mentally and physically. He stayed with her through the repeated waves, each one taking her higher and higher until she peaked and crashed over the top. She gasped for breath. Her muscles gave way and she collapsed against him. Her heart thundered in her rib cage, threatening to break loose.

"Nice," Rafe whispered, brushing kisses to her temple. "We'll have to do that again."

Somehow she managed to shake her head. "Give me a minute, okay?"

"We've all the time in the world."

That wasn't true. They might have less than twenty-four hours to live. Taylor intended to make the most of them.

CHAPTER THIRTY-FOUR

Aboard the Russian Delta-IV class nuclear-powered submarine K-407 Novomoskovsk, seaman Aslan Barayev left the mess hall where he'd had his midday meal and took the ladder to his station in navigation control. The faint hiss of air moving through the vents and the hum of generators were familiar to him after three tours of duty on the sub. This, however, would be his final tour.

Stowed in his locker were three canisters of fentanyl, a gas derived from opiates. When the time to act came, Aslan would don a breathing mask from the forward escape trunk. Then, in the nearby fan room, he would release the opiate gas into the air ducts. Within ten minutes, everyone on board would be asleep—except Aslan.

During the half-hour the crew would remain asleep, he would close and bolt the hatch, trapping the crew members in the aft compartments and tie up those in the forward sections. Taking command of the boat, he would order a skeleton crew to raise the boat to periscope level. From there he could contact his associates by radio. If anyone disobeyed him, he would shoot them with the captain's gun. After that, other crew members would not challenge his authority.

Familiar with the navigation charts for this part of Chile and the narrow channels cutting through the area, he would divert the boat from its original destination of Punta Arenas and guide it to the island where his Chechen countrymen waited. Once he surfaced the boat and they took control of the Novomoskovsk, Chechnya would become a free and independent muslim country.

Allah be praised!

Aslan checked the boat's position with the global positioning device and then the chronometer. By this time tomorrow the world would know its fate was in the hands of Chechen rebels who were capable and willing to become martyrs. Those in Russia and America who had fostered the spread of morally corrupt western culture would no longer rule the world.

And when they realized that he, Aslan Barayev, was the one who had hijacked their precious submarine, his superiors would realize that he should not have been denied the promotions he deserved.

Allah be praised!

CHAPTER THIRTY-FIVE

Quietly, Taylor slipped out of the cabin. She and Rafe had had about two hours of sleep, sacrificing the rest they needed for a chance to make love one last time.

Her throat tightened at the thought, and she swallowed hard. She didn't have time to question what the future might hold for her and Rafe. Or if they had a future at all.

Now she had to say good-bye to Terry. Probably the most difficult thing she'd ever had to do.

Anita and Ollie, tails wagging, joined her on the short walk from the cabin to the barren mound of dirt with the cross planted in it. From this vantage point, the plateau gradually descended away from the cabin, providing a view of distant mountains cut by silver ribbons of glaciers on the Chilean mainland. Around her a light breeze rippled the tips of verdant grass, bringing with it both the scent of the earth and the sea. Overhead an Andean Condor flew by, its huge black wings moving slowly through the cool air as though inviting Terry to take one last picture.

Taylor sank to the ground next to her brother's grave and crossed her legs Indian-fashion. Her throat felt so tight she could barely draw a breath. Her chest ached.

"You've got a terrific view here. I hope you got to see it before you . . ." Her chin trembled, and she patted the mound of dirt with her hand. "I should have come with you and kept you out of trouble." Picking up a handful of dirt, she let it sift through her fingers. The breeze took the fine particles of dust and blew them away.

"Remember that time in high school when Stanley Burgermeister trapped you in the locker room and took your clothes away? I sure scared the tar out of him when I came marching in to get you. You should have seen his face." She laughed, a choked sound, as tears blurred her vision. "He was buck naked and blushing all over, and I mean *all* over."

With her fingertip, she drew Terry's initials in the lose soil, T-T, the same as hers, yet representing someone quite different. In his own way, he had been stronger than she, more determined to be himself.

"Dad's going to be devastated. I don't think he ever understood you, but he loved you with all his heart. Give him credit for that."

Somewhere in the distance, the condor screeched as though providing a mocking answer for her brother.

Resting her elbow on her knee, she put her head in her hand and closed her eyes. "I'll do my best to make up with Dad now that he's lost you, but it may not be enough. If I can't handle it, I'll have to make my own life. You'll understand that, won't you?"

Terry had always understood her, been her best friend, knew how much she'd wanted to please their father. Now that Terry was gone, Taylor felt her heart had been ripped in half and maybe the best part of her had been buried with him.

And she was prepared to give the remaining part of her heart to a man who might not want it.

She shook her head. "I'm going to have to leave now. I'm not sure I'll be able to come back. But maybe this is the place you'd like to stay. Here with your birds and this incredible view. Oh, Terry . . ."

She sobbed, and tears flooded her eyes. One of the dogs nudged her shoulder, and she wrapped her arms around his neck. "You'll watch over him for me, won't you?"

With his big tongue, he licked the tears from her cheek. She gave him a weepy smile. "Thanks, Ollie. Maybe I can mail Hector some doggy bones for you and Anita."

"Taylor." Calling softly to her, Rafe approached from the cabin. "You need to eat some breakfast so we can get going."

She nodded, scratched Ollie between his ears. Someday she'd go to her own grave with the knowledge that she'd been fortunate to have Terry in her life for thirty years. Meanwhile, she'd do her best to live life to the fullest for them both.

Carefully she undid the necklace from around her neck, the aquamarine pendant that was her birthstone and Terry's, the one gift that her father had given her. She kissed the stone, then draped the silver chain over the wooden cross. "Good-bye, Terry. I'll miss you."

Drawing a deep breath, she stood and turned to face her future.

Rafe waited for her only a few feet away, concern and sympathy etched across his forehead. The purple bruise on his cheek had begun to fade. "You gave Terry your necklace?" he asked.

Her throat still tight, she tried to explain. "I needed a part of me to always be with my brother. I'll take Terry's gold chain and his passport home to our father."

"And the unfinished roll of film from his camera?"

She patted her pocket, indicating Terry's treasures were safe with her. "Hector can keep the camera—as a thank-you of sorts."

"I think Terry was a very lucky guy to have you for a sister." Rafe hooked his arm around her shoulders, pulled her close, and they walked together back to Hector's cabin.

An hour later, when they reached the rim of the glacier, Rafe checked the ropes that lashed the dynamite and other supplies to the sled. While crossing the plateau, he'd half-expected the antiquated dynamite to blow every time the sled bounced on the uneven ground. That was why he'd insisted Taylor and Hector, with his dogs, keep a safe distance away.

Cutting across the glacier ice was a different matter. Taylor would have to stick close to him or risk falling into a crevasse he hadn't seen.

A cold wind was blowing down from the head of the glacier, and dark clouds were building to the west. They'd have rain within hours, which might make for good cover once they reached the fjord, but would also make traversing the glacier miserable and the climb down the cliff treacherous.

"Time to strap on your snowshoes, Taylor," he announced. "Unless you've come to your senses and have decided to stay with Hector."

"Fat chance, hotshot," Taylor responded. "I'm coming with you."

"Some women don't know when they're well-off. Anyone can tell Hector has the hots for you."

The old man laughed, and Taylor gave Hector a hug.

"Hector, there's one more thing I want you to do for us," Rafe said.

"Of course, señor. Whatever I can."

"I want you to watch for planes flying overhead, particularly anything that looks like military aircraft. Then I want you to light a signal fire. With luck . . ." Rafe rested his hand on Hector's shoulder. "Maybe they'll figure out what's going on and send help."

"I will do as you ask, señor. For you and this lovely señorita. *And* her brave brother."

Nodding, Rafe turned away from the old man.

Fortunately, for the trip back to the terrorists' camp they'd be better equipped than they had been for the escape. In addition to providing food, water, gasoline, weapons and dynamite, all of which Rafe had covered with a tarp on the sled, Hector had given them his snowshoes and a couple of old parkas with hoods. Rafe's jacket didn't fit worth a darn—the sleeves barely covered his elbows—and smelled of wet wool, but it provided more protection from the cold than denim shirtsleeves. If the weather didn't deteriorate too badly, they'd be able to make good time. And time was crucial.

As he had crossing the plateau, he used the two lines he'd tied at the sled's front corners, harnessing himself to the sled like a plow horse. "Let's move out. Thanks for your help, Hector."

"*Vaya con dios, mi amigos.*" Go with God, my friends.

"Wait for me." Taylor hurried after Rafe. "Let me help you pull the sled."

275

"I want you walking in the tracks the sled makes. We can't be sure where the crevasses are."

"Why don't we walk in our own tracks on the trail we made yesterday?"

Scowling, he glanced over his shoulder. "Soldiers in my command don't usually question my orders."

"You don't usually have sex with the soldiers in your command, do you?"

His lips twisted into a half-smile. "Not usually."

"Well, there you go." Catching up with him, she took one of the ropes and wrapped it around her waist, taking on half the weight of the sled. "This woman's army is a-changing."

Rafe knew he'd never be the same after this trip—assuming he and Taylor survived. Odds were they wouldn't make it back alive, but he'd been on virtual suicide missions before, in Afghanistan and Iraq, so he believed anything was possible. Otherwise he would have tied Taylor up at the cabin rather than risk her life. He wouldn't say having Taylor on his side evened the odds against the terrorists, but it sure as hell made him more determined to get them both out of there in one piece.

They made it to about the midpoint of the glacier before it began to rain—not just a light mist, but heavy drops that were close to being hail and stung like the devil when they hit him in the face. Visibility dropped to five feet. The top six inches of snow turned to slush. Taylor's pace had slowed, which made the sled drag sideways.

"Let's take a break," Rafe said, coming to a halt.

"I'm all right."

"You're exhausted."

"We can't stop out here in the middle of the glacier. We'll freeze."

That was more true than she knew. Even through their jackets, they were getting wet to the skin. Hypothermia was a real threat. If the snow were more firmly packed, he could dig them a snow tunnel to get them out of the rain and cold. But there wasn't anything he could do with this mushy stuff.

Noting the dark circles of fatigue beneath Taylor's eyes, he unwound the rope from her waist. "Get under the tarp."

"Rafe, you can't—"

"If you're exhausted when we reach the top of the cliff, you won't be of any use to me. I'll have to leave you there and go on alone."

"And what happens if you're the one who's exhausted?"

"I won't be."

Evidently he'd gotten through to her, or she'd realized he could be just as stubborn as she, because she lifted a corner of the tarp and worked her way underneath out of the weather. When he was sure she was settled, he turned and headed for the far side of the glacier.

He sloughed through the storm, taking one step at a time. His shoulders flexed against the weight of the sled. He leaned his back into the effort. For much of his adult life, he'd marched into danger. Saving people. Trying to prove himself worthy.

Worthy of whom? he wondered now.

Not Lizbeth and Katy. Long before he'd met his wife, he'd been putting his life on the line. She'd loved him in spite of his job, hated that he'd leave her and their baby to fight another battle.

His father, then. A man he remembered more as a photograph on the fireplace mantel than as a flesh-and-blood presence. A decorated Army Ranger with a chest full of medals that used to scrape Rafe's cheek when his Dad picked him up to say another good-bye. His last good-bye.

Taylor had it wrong, Rafe realized. It wasn't a savior complex that drove him. Or even guilt for his shortcomings. He'd been trying to prove himself worthy of a man who had died thirty-three years ago.

The stormclouds suddenly lifted, and he saw an outcropping of granite carved by the glacier but not entirely worn away. He'd made it to the other side. So had Taylor.

He came to a halt where the glacier met solid rock.

"Hey, Legs!"

She poked her head out from under the tarp. "Are you all right?"

"I will be as soon as I catch my breath. We made it, babe. We're across the worst of it."

Tilting the hood of her parka back, she frowned. "I thought we'd discussed this calling-me-babe business."

Grinning, he unharnessed himself. "Must have slipped my mind. Let's eat Hector's lunch, and then we'll carry our gear from here to the cliff."

"Can't think of a thing I'd enjoy more."

She scrambled out from under the tarp and stretched. Even dressed like a shepherd, she looked damn good. Those long legs of hers would give any man a hard-on just thinking about how they'd feel wrapped around his waist. But he knew. Knew, too, the little sounds she made as he pumped into her. The way her green eyes turned to a deep emerald. Her cry of pleasure when she erupted around him.

He'd also figured out she was damn stubborn, as physically strong as many men; a woman who didn't know the meaning of intimidation, nor was she willing to blindly follow his lead or anyone else's. A special woman who insisted on taking care of herself even when he pulled the savior number on her. A woman who challenged him at every turn.

And he loved her.

Shit! He hadn't meant for that to happen. But there it was. She'd cast a spell over him, and he hoped to God no one would break it.

They sat huddled behind a rock out of the wind to eat chunks of lamb and bread washed down with cool springwater. Then, piecemeal, they carried their gear and the sled to the spot where they had ascended the cliff hand-over-hand less than twenty-four hours before.

Rafe peered over the edge. "I hope you know how to rappel."

She eyed the bottom of the fjord, five-hundred feet below. "I've done it a time or two."

"Great. There's a ledge about two-hundred feet down." He pointed to a small outcropping of rock. "I'm going to belay you to that point, then send our gear down bit-by-bit."

"And I suppose you're going to free-climb down to me?"

"That's the plan." He cupped her cheek, her skin cool and smooth against his palm. "Of course, I could rappel down and wait for you there."

"Smart ass." She punched him in the midsection, though not hard, and laughed. "As if!"

He rigged the ropes, set his position, then nodded. "Off you go, love."

279

Smiling, she cocked a brow. "Love. I think I like that better than babe." A moment later, she stepped back off the cliff and dropped out of sight.

Rafe added courage to his list of Taylor's attributes. He could only hope her bravery would be rewarded with the total defeat of the men responsible for her brother's death.

He'd do whatever he could to make sure that happened.

CHAPTER THIRTY-SIX

Chilean Military Headquarters
Santiago, Chile

As liaison to the Chilean military, Lt. Col. Donovan Landry, U.S. Army, attended an incredible number of briefings and planning sessions. The fear of terrorists in Chile might not be as dominant as it was in the States, but they had begun to take precautions. He was there to give advice and coordinate efforts, when necessary, and cooperate in joint exercises; but mostly he sat and dreamed of having a house with a view of San Francisco Bay, his retirement and his new career in securing vital American shipping interests.

The men sitting with him at the long conference table wore enough medals and ribbons on their chests to sink a small ship. The generals and admirals outranked him, but he was backed by the U.S. government. That gave him a fair amount of clout, if he chose to use it. Which he rarely did.

A junior officer entered the conference room and

headed directly for General Ignacio Vidal, the military chief of staff for the armed forces. All conversation halted while the general and young officer consulted in hushed tones.

With a shake of his head, the general dismissed the messenger. "I am sorry for the interruption, gentlemen. A civilian plane en route to the scientific station at Mc-Murdo Sound reported a grass fire in a remote area of Tierra del Fuego. The pilot thought it might be a signal fire from a downed plane, but we have no reports of missing planes." He gestured toward the general who had been reporting on airport security. "Please continue—"

"Excuse me, General Vidal," Donovan said, alert now with concern. "We have a U.S. Ranger in that area on personal business who is overdue to report. He's one of the officers who has been training your men—Captain Maguire."

"I know this man of whom you speak," the general conceded with a nod. "What is his business there?"

"I'm not entirely sure. I do know he is traveling with a woman, and shortly after they left Santiago, Captain Maguire's neighbor was tortured and killed."

The officers around the table glanced at each other.

The general raised his bushy eyebrows. "A love triangle, as they say?"

"No, sir. Not at all. The woman was in some sort of trouble." And soft-touch Big Mac was trying to fix things, as usual. "I do know if Captain Maguire were in trouble, he would think of lighting a signal fire. If you have the manpower available, it might warrant closer investigation. Just in case, you understand."

Donovan watched as the general mentally processed the information and his choices. Apparently the weight of the U.S. government won out.

"Very well, Colonel Landry. I will order a low-level fly-by, and we will see what we can see."

"Thank you, General."

After issuing the order with little more than the flick of his hand, Vidal returned his attention to airport security.

Although Rafe had asked him not to contact the Santiago police, Donovan made a mental note to have the federal authorities check into the murder of Maguire's neighbor. He had a feeling the culprits would lead them to a larger crime, one that was tied into Rafe's lack of contact and to the trouble his lady friend was in.

CHAPTER THIRTY-SEVEN

In the last light of the setting sun, Rafe sketched his plan of attack in the sand. Outlining the shore of the island where the terrorists were holed up, he drew an oval shape on the left side. "The boat that shelled us is docked here where it can't be seen from the main hutch. There should be at least two men on board acting as guards. The shed they held us in is about here." He drew a square to represent what had been their temporary prison. "After we reach the island, we'll go there first. I'll spread the gasoline around and plant a few sticks of the dynamite so that when they blow, they'll take the diesel fuel with them and start a fire."

"That ought to make quite an explosion," Taylor commented. "But I don't know why you want to blow up the shed."

"A diversion is what we're after. The explosion and fire that follows should draw most of the terrorists to the shed area to find out what's going on. Meanwhile, we head for the main communications shack via a back route." This time he drew a circle, which made the three

points of the terrorists' camp into a triangle. "I'll go inside and take out whoever is left, then try to raise some
friendlies on the radio for help."

"You want me inside, too?"

"No. And this is the dangerous part. I want you at the
shack's entrance with Hector's shotgun. Your job is to
prevent anyone from getting to me before I'm finished
transmitting."

Taylor tried to lick her lips, but her mouth was so dry
she found she couldn't. Although she knew how to use a
gun, she'd never shot at anything other than a paper target. After going pheasant-hunting one time with her father, neither she nor Terry had ever gone again. The sight
of dead birds strung together had made them both sick to
their stomachs. Now, the thought of actually shooting a
man brought bile to her throat.

"Can you do it, Taylor? I need to know now if you
can't so I can change the plan."

She thought of Terry, of the loss of his life, his
courage, and stiffened her resolve. "I'll do it."

Rafe studied her in the waning light, finally nodding.
"I know you will."

Knowing he trusted her to do her part of the job gave
her a jolt of pride. For Rafe. For Terry. She'd do whatever she had to do.

"I don't mean to be picky or anything," she said, "but
do we have an exit strategy? Just in case this whole thing
goes south on us."

"Last thing I do is set the remaining dynamite to blow
up the communications system. Worst case, they won't
be able to contact their associate on the submarine.
Meanwhile, we head for their boat"—he tapped the oval
he'd drawn earlier—"take care of any remaining guards,
and get the hell out of Dodge."

He made the plan sound so simple. Almost foolproof. Taylor suspected it wouldn't be that easy.

Sitting cross-legged on the ground, they watched the movement of a faint light across the channel. A guard making his rounds, Taylor thought, or relieving himself. From the direction of the boat dock, someone coughed, the sound easily carrying across the half-mile of open water. Closer at hand, tiny wavelets brushed against the near shore, making a soft, sibilant sound.

Everything seemed so damned normal. With the major exception that Taylor's insides were quivering with a combination of fear and anticipation.

"Okay, let's move out."

Rising, Rafe took hold of the sled, which they had reloaded with their gear after they lowered it down the cliff to the valley floor. Taylor picked up the other end of the sled, and they carried it to the water's edge. Except for a few stars that had begun to shine, the darkness was complete—perfect to camouflage their clandestine activities, or so she hoped.

Rafe began to shed his clothes. "You get a free ride this time. On the raft, so you stay high and dry."

Taylor considered objecting, that she was perfectly capable of swimming at least part of the distance, but Rafe had on his game face. Tonight he was Captain Maguire, U.S. Army; she was his foot soldier and would obey orders.

He eased the sled far enough into the water so that it floated, and she stepped aboard. The makeshift raft sank an inch or two under her added weight.

"Move to the middle and stay low," he ordered. "If someone spots this thing, I want them to think it's either some sort of natural debris or a whale passing by."

She did as instructed, kneeling in the center of the raft as Rafe, in his rope harness once again, walked it into the fjord. Water seeped over the top of the wood, chilling Taylor's legs from the knees down, but the raft stayed afloat. Leaning forward, Rafe slid all the way into the water and began a slow, determined breaststroke toward the far shore. Only the faintest ripples appeared on the surface as the raft progressed, and barely a sound could be heard.

Taylor kept her eyes on the opposite bank, holding her breath and praying no one would spot them while they were in the open, defenseless.

After what seemed like an eternity in the frigid water, Rafe staggered onto the shore and fell to his knees. Damn, he was too friggin' old for this crap. Nearly forty, and getting more decrepit by the minute. He ought to be sleeping in a hammock and drinking tall ones in Tahiti, not trying to eliminate some damn terrorist cell that had a bug up its collective ass. To top it off, he'd probably get himself and the bravest, sexiest woman he'd ever known blown up in the process.

Said woman grabbed him under one arm and half-dragged him and the raft up the beach to the tree line.

"We have to get out of sight," she whispered.

"Yeah, yeah. Let me catch my breath."

While he concentrated on breathing, she began drying him off with Hector's old jacket, then tugged his T-shirt on over his head. He managed to stick his arms through the sleeves, and somehow avoided her putting on his briefs for him, handling that task for himself. After he got into the rest of his dry clothes, they carried the raft into the safety of the forest.

Sitting on his haunches, he checked the location where they had landed, and listened for any sign that they'd been detected. All clear, so far.

From the raft, he retrieved their weapons, what little ammunition they had, the can of gasoline and the dynamite, surprised it hadn't already blown them to bits and not one hundred percent confident it wouldn't simply fizzle out when he lit the fuses. But there was no turning back now.

He handed Taylor the shotgun and made sure she knew how to load it. "If you have to use this, make sure your target is no more than five feet away from you. Then give 'em both barrels."

"Got it. I don't shoot till I see the whites of their eyes."

With a shake of his head, he primed the old flintlock pistol and tucked it into his belt. Maybe he could scare somebody to death with the damn thing. Otherwise, he doubted it would do much damage unless the confrontation was up close and very personal.

He hooked a pair of sheep shears on his belt and slipped a butcher's knife into his boot. With all this low-tech weaponry, hand-to-hand combat ought to be unusually challenging. He carried the dynamite in a sling he'd made out of the black plastic that had made the journey to Hector's hut and back to the island again.

He took a deep breath. "Ready, Legs?"

"Ready."

He wanted to say something to her. Not the usual *Hoo-ya!* shouted when men drummed up their courage to enter battle. Something personal. But his own valor faltered in the face of her determination, and he wasn't able to form the words his heart hadn't allowed him to say in years.

He wondered if he'd have a second chance later.

"On my six, Legs. Let's go."

He started off at a jog, and he heard her fall into step behind him. If it were in his power, he'd give her a chest full of medals right now for toughness.

Although southern beech weren't big trees, they grew close together, and there was lots of fallen wood on the ground. He didn't want to be on the paths the terrorists had worn through the forest and rocky areas. Too much chance of being spotted, even though it was well after dark. So he kept a mental heading, wending his way through the uneven growth in the direction he knew would lead him to the shed where they'd been held captive. He would have been more confident with night goggles. Predictably, Hector hadn't had any of those stashed in his cabin.

Reaching the open area that had been cleared for the shed, he held out his arm to halt Taylor. He stood listening for a moment, then advanced cautiously.

As soundlessly as he could, he lifted the bar and opened the door to gain access to the shed. The interior still smelled of diesel fuel and dirt, and was darker than the night outside. When Taylor joined him, he closed the door and risked lighting a match. He smiled as he saw the barrel of diesel fuel was just as he'd left it forty-eight hours ago.

Together they tipped the barrel over, letting the black oily liquid spill out onto the ground and ooze out the door; then from the five-gallon can he spread gasoline around the rest of the shed. He set three of the dynamite sticks beneath the diesel barrel, looked around, then lit the fuse. The flare traveled about two inches, sputtered and went out.

"Shit!" he muttered.

Once again, kneeling, he lit a match. If this didn't work, he'd be hitting the terrorists over the head with these damn sticks of dynamite. Not an encouraging picture.

This time, the fuse seemed to take.

On his feet, he snared Taylor by the arm, hustled her out the door and shut it behind them. Holding her hand, he took a circular path toward the main communications shack. He didn't want to be in the way when the terrorists came bolting out of their beds trying to figure out what had happened.

He and Taylor got within ten feet of the communications center and the dynamite still hadn't exploded. Rafe cursed under his breath. "We're going to have to go to Plan B." That was a plan he hadn't yet come up with.

Just then, the silence of the island erupted in a huge explosion. Instinctively Rafe ducked, pulling Taylor down with him, as shards of the storage shed burst into the air. A moment later, fire licked up from the remains of the metal building.

A light appeared in the communications shack.

Rafe held his position, crouching in the trees, counting off the seconds to himself, *one-one-hundred, two-one-hundred, three one—*

The door to the communications shack flew open. Three guys came running out, AK-47s in their hands. A fourth guy appeared in the doorway. As he jogged after his men, Rafe recognized him as the Arab who had tried to beat information out of him.

Surprise! We're back! he thought.

Four men had exited the shack. At least two others guarded the PT boat, and one was patrolling the area, based on the light Rafe had seen from across the channel. If his original count of ten was correct, that left three unaccounted for. Not good odds.

He slid the butcher's knife from his boot. "See that boulder to the right of the door?"

Taylor nodded.

"Use that for cover. Don't expose yourself unless you have to."

Her eyes wide, she nodded again.

Ducking down, he ran to the front of the shack, halted long enough for Taylor to reach the boulder, then cautiously opened the door. The naked bulb in the ceiling revealed one guy sitting at the radio console. His back was to Rafe. Nobody else was in sight.

In three silent steps, Rafe was behind the terrorist at the radio, his arm around the man's chest, slitting his throat. He turned to confront any remaining terrorists and found he was alone.

Working as quickly as he could, he eased the terrorist to the floor, took time to close the shack's door, and sat down at the console. The radio rig was a vintage Russian Volna-k Navy-issue receiver and an Ersh-p marine transmitter.

Dividing his remaining dynamite, he placed the sticks where they would do the most damage to the communications setup, then he switched the transmitter to the international emergency frequency and adjusted the receiver. Outside he heard the terrorists yelling back and forth in confusion. It wouldn't take them long to discover blowing up the storage shed had been a diversion. He figured he had two minutes at the most to make contact, warn the authorities about the submarine and get out of the shack.

Pulling on the headphones, he flipped the switch to transmit. "Mayday, mayday." The needles on the yellow glowing dial responded to his voice. "This is Captain Rafe Maguire, U.S. Army Rangers, assigned to Chilean

Army combat training detail. Mayday, mayday. Do you copy?"

Outside the shack, crouched behind a boulder, Taylor heard the sound of running footsteps coming her way. She knew Rafe hadn't had time to contact the Chilean authorities yet, and she didn't want to alert the terrorists who had raced off to the burning storage shed by using her shotgun.

She also wasn't sure she could handle a terrorist in a frontal attack.

Surprise is your secret weapon, her karate teacher had said when he spoke of self-defense.

Keeping as low a profile as she could, she darted from her hiding spot to the stand of trees that surrounded the shack. Dark shadows disguised her movement. Breathless, she waited for the approaching runner to come into view.

He arrived, loping along the path toward the shack. When he was within a few feet of the door, Taylor stepped out of the shadows.

"Hey, *hombre*. Wanna get a little nookie?"

The man halted and whirled toward her as though she'd yanked him back on a short chain. His eyes grew wide as she sashayed toward him, her hips and breasts moving as seductively as she could manage—until she was within striking distance. Then, as hard as she could, she delivered a kick to his right knee and heard a gratifying pop. He cried out, bending over to grab the crushed appendage. She took advantage of the opening with a round kick that caught him solidly on the side of his head. He went down without a wimper.

Grimly, she thought her attack gave new meaning to Rafe's nickname for her.

Grabbing the unconscious terrorist under the arms, she dragged him back to the tree line and off the well-traveled path. With any luck, he'd be out cold long enough for Rafe to reach the authorities and for her and Rafe to make their escape.

One down, she thought, as she scurried back to her hiding place behind the boulder. But how many more were left?

The earphones hummed with static in Rafe's ears. *Come on! Be there!* "Mayday, mayday," he repeated into the mike. "Captain Rafe Maguire, U.S. Army Rangers."

"Mayday caller," came a response. *Finally!* "This is Chilean Air Force niner-five-zero. What is your emergency?"

Rafe switched back to transmit. "Niner-five-zero, we are located on an unnamed island in Tierra del Fuego and under attack. A group of terrorists plan to use this base to hijack a visiting Russian submarine. I repeat, they intend to hijack—" A shotgun blast sounded outside the shack's door. Rafe winced and his heart squeezed tight. "—a Russian sub now en route to Punta Arenas. Do you copy, niner-five-zero?"

The buzz of static filled the airwaves. "Affirmative on hijack of submarine. Will notify my command headquarters. What is your status?"

A shot erupted outside the shack's door. Taylor cried out in pain, and then Rafe heard another shotgun blast.

She'd been hit, damn it! But somehow she'd gotten her gun reloaded and used it. *Brave girl!*

Rafe pulled his flintlock from his belt. "We are under attack. Repeat, under attack. If we get out of here, we will be on—"

The door flew open and the Arab appeared, an automatic pistol in his hand.

Throwing his chair in the Arab's direction, Rafe hit the floor in a tucked position and rolled under the nearest bunkbed as bullets missed him and smacked into the transmitter. The set shorted out with a pop. Sparks flew.

"You won't get away this time!" the Arab shouted.

Knowing he had to be close to the Arab to have any chance of effectively using the flintlock, Rafe stomach-crawled under the bunks in the terrorist's direction. A bullet slammed into the mattress above him, penetrated the thin cotton and grazed his leg. He ignored the burning sensation and kept moving, slithering and weaving like he was on an obstacle course.

"You can't stop our plan. It is Allah's will!" The next bullet bounced off the metal bed frame.

Rafe didn't know how many bullets the Arab had left, but he was damn well running out of cover himself, and in a hurry. He rolled out from under the bunk, rotating twice, felt the impact of a bullet in his side. A glancing wound, he hoped; but it stung like hell. He raised his pistol, aimed at the Arab's face only feet away and pulled the trigger.

The explosion reverberated in the metal shack even more loudly than the rounds fired from the Arab's automatic. A black puff of gunpowder rose from Rafe's gun. The barrel had split in two.

Knife in hand, Rafe rose to his feet and charged the Arab, who stood unsteadily, half of his face turned to blood and broken flesh. Rafe rammed his knife between the Arab's ribs in a killing blow, then stepped away. The Arab crumpled to the floor.

Rafe wiped the knife on his jeans, then bent down to pick up the automatic and stuffed it into his belt. He knew their gun battle was sure to draw a crowd, but he had one last crucial task to perform before he left the shack.

Lighting a match, he touched it to the dynamite fuses, made sure they'd keep burning, and ran for the door. Based on the length of the fuses, he had about twenty seconds to find Taylor and get them both safely away.

Two terrorists lay on the ground in front of the shack, one dead, the other curled into a fetal position, groaning. Taylor had done her job well.

He found her on the ground behind the boulder, her head bleeding from something that looked like a graze, her pulse weak but still pumping.

"Don't you dare die on me, Legs." Stowing his knife in his boot again, he hefted Taylor over his shoulder and started off at a jog around the back of the shack. A mental clock kept ticking off the seconds—*twelve one-hundred, thirteen one-hundred, fourteen one-hundred*—

The Chechen rebels were crashing through the forest on their way back. With luck, they might be inside when the dynamite blew.

—fifteen one-hundred, sixteen one-hundred—

He broke into a faster run. Taylor moaned. His side ached, the wound on his leg burning. A rebel yelled something. Bullets splatted the ground beside him.

—seventeen one-hundred, eighteen—

He dived behind a downed tree, landing on his back in an effort to cushion Taylor's fall, then rolled over on top of her, covering her body with his. The wall of the communications shack blew out, and shrapnel exploded all around him. A rebel screamed.

Except for the frightened screech of a seagull and the lick of flames reaching toward the sky, the island went silent.

CHAPTER THIRTY-EIGHT

Quarters of Lt. Col. Donovan Landry
Santiago, Chile

A determined knocking on his door woke Landry from his sleep, interrupting a dream involving a long-legged blonde and a game of strip poker. He'd had her down to her red bra and matching lace panties; he himself had been wearing black silk briefs and had a hard-on.

"Damn," he muttered. "Can't a guy even finish a decent dream around here?" He glanced at the clock on the bed table—0235, a helluva time for company. Particularly if it wasn't the blonde he'd been dreaming about.

Rolling out of bed—the caller at the door was growing more insistent by the minute—he pulled on an old Crown Beer T-shirt and a pair of jeans, and padded to the door in his bare feet. Clearly, if he was having strip poker dreams, he'd been without a woman for too damn long.

Looking through the peephole, he saw Lt. Col. Jaime

Bitar, his counterpart liaison officer between Chilean and U.S. forces, standing in the hallway looking impatient.

Opening the door, Landry said, "This had better be good, Jaime. You interrupted a—"

"We've heard from your man Maguire," the Chilean announced.

Landry opened the door wider to let the colonel in. "Where is he? Was he the one who set that signal fire?"

Jaime walked across the sparely furnished living room and turned on a table lamp. "Apparently not. Our pilot, who was in the area checking out the grass fire, received an emergency radio transmission from a man who identified himself as Captain Maguire. The man claimed he was on an island being held by terrorists who planned to hijack a Russian submarine."

Landry whistled under his breath. Big Mac and his lady friend had stumbled onto something big.

"We are wondering if this could be some sort of a hoax," Jaime said. "You Americans are very good at pranks, sí?"

"I don't think so. Not this time." He tried to process the information Jaime had given him and what he knew of Rafe's activities. "Do you know if there is a Russian sub in the area?"

"We have confirmed that a sub is expected to arrive in Punta Arenas in the morning. A diplomatic mission."

"That's it then. Somebody is going to try to hijack that sub."

"On the surface, that seems impossible. How could they—"

"If Maguire hadn't believed it was not only possible but probable, he wouldn't have sent that message."

"So you think it is a credible warning?"

"I think you'd better dispatch ships to that area and notify the Russian authorities as soon as possible. If a group of terrorists pull this one off, your country is going to have mud on its face. There will be bigger repercussions than there were after nine-eleven. None of them will be good." And God only knew what the terrorists intended to do with a nuclear sub after they had it. It boggled the mind.

Jaime hesitated, his gaze glancing around Landry's apartment. While it wasn't exactly homey, the furnished apartment looked lived-in—the latest Clancy book on the coffee table next to an empty beer can, an unanswered letter from Donovan's father on the end table along with a couple of recent copies of *Aviation Week* magazine, stains on the carpet where he'd tracked in mud and the maid hadn't cleaned it up.

"Call the general," Landry urged. "Better to err on the side of caution than get caught with your neck in the wringer. They'll make you the scapegoat if you screw up." In every military unit in the world, the bosses were always looking for someone to blame. Chile was no exception. Nor was the good ol' U.S. of A. How many had learned that the hard way?

With a curt nod, Jaime pulled a cell phone from his pocket and tapped in a number. Moments later, he was speaking directly with General Vidal.

Returning to his bedroom, Landry picked up a secure phone that had been installed for just such a purpose and dialed the number of the Pentagon duty officer. As succinctly as possible, he explained the situation. Assured that the proper authorities would be notified, Landry hung up, grabbed his uniform from the closet and dressed.

He'd hitch a ride to Punta Arenas with the Chilean Air Force. With a little luck, he'd be on the scene when all hell broke loose.

It was just like the good old days with Big Mac.

CHAPTER THIRTY-NINE

Rafe reached the shelter of trees near the PT boat and laid Taylor on the ground. Limp, she was more like a rag doll than the feisty woman he'd come to adore.

"Come on, babe. You've come this far. Don't quit on me now."

"Not babe," she moaned. "My head."

Relief swept through him. "Shh. You'll be all right." The fact that she had come around was a very good sign. The fact that the two armed Chechens guarding the boat were still at their posts was not as encouraging.

He checked the clip in the automatic. Three shots left. Not a lot of room for error.

"I have a little business to finish," he whispered. "You stay here out of sight, Legs. I'll be back."

With her nod of acknowledgment, he took off through the woods. The early sunrise at the bottom of the earth was less than an hour away. He'd have to surprise and overpower the guards before they spotted him. The way they were both in protected positions suggested that wouldn't be easy. He sure couldn't walk across the gangplank in plain view to attack them. He had to find some other way.

Worse, there could be other unaccounted for terrorists who might show up.

This is what he'd trained for most of his adult life. Except this time Taylor's life was at stake, too. He had no illusions. If he didn't get her safely away from the island, she would be killed by whatever rebels survived. They weren't likely to be gentle.

The guards had their attention focused on the main camp where all the action had been, so he made his way to the port side. The boat had a shallow draft. Since the terrorists hadn't needed deep water for their mooring, this small, rocky inlet had served their purpose. Holding the automatic above his head, he eased into the chill, black water and waded toward the boat. Salt burned into his wounds, and the cold took his breath away. He'd spent more time in frigid water in the past couple of days than he had on all his military missions combined.

He reached the bow undetected and worked his way along the hull to the stern. From there he climbed on board, careful not to let his weight rock the boat.

He needed to eliminate one of the guards without attracting the attention of the second man. With hands so cold he could barely feel his fingers, he stowed his pistol in his waistband and removed the garrote from his belt. Using all the stealth he could muster, he crept up behind the nearest guard. The man turned, but it was already too late. Rafe had wrapped the wire around the terrorist's throat and pulled it tight, muffling his shout of warning that came with his last gasp of breath.

The second guard turned toward Rafe, raising his AK-47 to take aim.

Rafe dived behind a torpedo tube, drawing his pistol as he hit the deck. The terrorist's first shot missed him.

From the shore, Taylor shouted, "Hey, over here, ape nose!"

Cursing under his breath that Taylor would put herself at risk, Rafe took advantage of the terrorist's brief distraction. He rose to his feet, leveled his gun with two hands and pulled the trigger. The force of the bullet's impact knocked the man and his weapon over the side into the water. He should have known Taylor wouldn't sit around like a helpless woman, his orders be damned. Which meant she was the kind of partner a man could count on. The Rangers taught their men to show initiative, to back up their buddies. Taylor took it to an extreme, which was why Rafe was still breathing.

Rafe pushed the first guard overboard as well. "Taylor, can you cast off?"

"Right." She appeared out of the shadows, moving pretty fast for someone who'd been knocked unconscious less than a half hour ago. For someone so sexy, she had plenty of grit.

"Get aboard as soon as you can." He made for the bridge. When he hit the starter, the powerful rumble of the twin engines vibrated the deck. The moment Taylor was onboard and had pulled up the gangplank behind her, he shifted into reverse and applied the throttle.

He heard a shout from the island. At least one terrorist was still alive. Probably still armed and dangerous.

Taylor joined him on the bridge.

"Are you okay?" He backed the boat out into the main channel.

"I killed a man, didn't I?"

Her voice was so soft, so unsteady, he shot a glance in her direction. Except for the brown streak of dried blood at her hairline, her face looked like porcelain in the remaining starlight, pale enough that he thought she might be ready to faint.

He maneuvered the boat around and shifted into forward gear. "Sit down, Legs, before you fall down."

"He was coming right at me. I didn't have any choice. If I hadn't stopped him, he would have killed you." Reflexively, she brushed her hair back from her forehead with a trembling hand.

"You did good. Real good." He'd known a fair number of men who had frozen during their first combat experience. She'd done a helluva lot better than that, and probably saved his bacon because of her action.

A burst of AK-47 fire raked the deck. He shoved Taylor down to her knees where she'd be out of the line of fire.

"Oh, God . . ." She covered her head with her hands.

"We're okay, Legs. We'll be out of range in just a minute." Then he'd see to Taylor. However strong and determined she might be, her wealthy, protected life hadn't prepared her for the trauma of fighting in a war zone and killing another human being. She'd acquitted herself so damn well. He wouldn't blame her a bit if she fell apart now. Ninety percent of the population would, after what she'd been through. He just wished he could have protected her from the ugly side of reality.

As they motored through the fjord, the eastern sky turned a pearl gray and the sun began to work its way above the ridge of the jagged peaks. Once they were well-away from the terrorists' island, Rafe throttled back and let the boat drift with the gentle tide as the channel widened.

Kneeling, he pulled Taylor into his arms and found that she was shaking uncontrollably—the aftermath of too much adrenaline, he suspected, rather than a reaction to the bullet that had grazed her head. His adrenaline still pulsed through his veins, too, a natural high compounded by the woman in his arms.

When she relaxed a bit and rested her head on his shoulder, he felt such an enormous rush of protectiveness . . . of *love* . . . he could barely catch his breath.

"It's okay, Legs. Go ahead and cry. You've earned it."

"You're not"—she hiccupped—"crying."

If he wasn't crying, then why the hell was his vision blurred, he wondered. He'd held it all in when Lizbeth and Katy died. When he'd led his men into a trap and lost them, he'd been stoic. The price of war, he'd told himself. So why couldn't he focus now? And why were tears stinging the backs of his eyes?

"Hey, I'm the tough guy, remember?" He told the lie he'd told himself since he'd been a young boy, a child trying to live up to his father's expectations.

Tentatively, she touched his bloody shirt. "You're hurt, too."

"A flesh wound. I've been hurt worse shaving," he quipped.

Her own pain and fears forgotten, she eyed him skeptically. "There's got to be a first-aid kit on board somewhere. I'll see if I can—"

"Relax, love. There's no rush. I like having you right where you are now."

"I like it, too." A hesitant smile curled her lips, and she settled into his embrace. "I could do with a lot less getting shot at, though. I think it must be time I went home . . . back to the States."

He wanted to tell her no, that she ought to stay right here with him. But she had her life to lead. His was the life of a mercenary, a hired gun, not a life suited to being a family man or to a long-term commitment.

Unless he changed.

The thought had barely surfaced before he rejected the idea. No way could he spend his life raising grapes, and a vineyard was exactly where Taylor belonged. She'd been born and bred to that life. His breeding was all about fighting.

The boat rocked, and Rafe thought they'd reached the open sea. Maybe he could reach the military authorities again with the radio onboard, find out where the hell they were and what was taking them so long to get there.

A voice hailed the boat in a language he didn't understand. Definitely not Spanish.

Rafe frowned. Cautiously, he lifted his head and saw the superstructure of a submarine rising up out of the water, its black hull long and sleek, a bullet nose at the bow tapering toward the stern, seawater slipping like liquid glass off the deck. Two men stood in the cockpit. A Russian submarine, he realized from the markings. And the one man who had his hands raised wore the uniform of a captain.

Shit!

Somehow his warning hadn't reached the Russian naval authorities, or they hadn't been able to reach the submarine crew in time to alert them to the hijack attempt. In either event, there was only one thing Rafe could do.

Fake it!

Standing, he waved his arm as though he was the happiest man on earth to see a hijacked submarine. He had a slim hope that his days-old beard would lead the Chechen terrorist on the sub to believe he was a Koran-reading rebel. But he had little choice. If he didn't act, the ship would submerge. Tracking the sub once it was under water again would be all the more difficult. Preventing their scheme to melt the Antarctic ice cap might be impossible if he let the sub get away now.

"This time, for God's sake, stay down," he warned Taylor as he slowly pulled the automatic from his waistband.

Hector had said there was only one traitor onboard the sub. It had to be the guy standing next to the captain.

He hoped.

Shouting something unintelligible—which probably really meant "Your wife is a sweet potato" in Chechen—Rafe raised his gun, aimed and shot the man standing beside the sub's captain. Only belatedly did he realize that if the terrorist had switched uniforms with the captain, he might have accomplished exactly the opposite of his intent.

The boat's captain, or at least the guy in the officer's uniform, ducked out of sight.

"I am an American!" Rafe shouted, one of the few Russian phrases he'd learned while serving in Afghanistan. "Don't shoot!" He waited for the whole crew to come running on deck, either to cheer that they'd been rescued or to machine-gun him down.

Finally, another head appeared in the conning tower. "Identify yourself," the sailor ordered in accented English.

"Captain Rafe Maguire, U.S. Army, assigned to Chilean Special Forces Training. We have escaped a Chechen rebel camp. Do you have your hijacker under control?"

The sailor glanced toward his feet. "Thanks to you, sir. Our captain is once again in control of our boat."

Just then a pair of jet fighters with Chilean markings flew by at low altitude, their engines screaming. Better late than never.

"Taylor, get below. See if you can reach some friendlies on the radio." He gave her the frequency to use. "I don't want those fly-boys to start using us for target practice."

Less than an hour later, two Chilean Navy patrol boats arrived on the scene, and a helicopter lowered Donovan Landry onto the PT boat. Taylor was briefly introduced to Rafe's friend; then the two men and the ranking naval officer boarded the submarine.

After they were gone, Taylor sat on the boat deck while a Navy medic treated her head wound. The sailor looked to be about twenty, with a quick smile and flirting mocha eyes. In comparison, she felt like an old hag with weathered skin and lank hair that needed a good washing.

She winced when he dabbed her wound with antiseptic. "The man I was with, Captain Maguire, is hurt worse than I am. You should be treating him first."

"He told me to take care of you." The young man ripped opened a packet and applied the bandage to her forehead. "How does that feel now, señorita?"

"Like I have a very bad hangover."

"I could give you some pain medicine, if you wish."

"A couple of aspirin would help." Since she didn't like taking pills of any kind, the aspirin was a concession to the throbbing pain in her head.

"Sí, señorita." He rifled through his supplies. "The gentleman also said you were very brave."

"There's a fine line between bravery and stupidity." In terms of falling in love with a man who was unattainable, she'd easily crossed over the stupid line. It wasn't like her to fall so hard or so quickly for a man.

Although great sex had contributed to her fall, she admitted wryly. But that had come later. She'd been halfway gone by the time they'd made love.

307

Whatever had happened between Taylor and Rafe, she couldn't fight the ghost of his late wife. She *wouldn't* fight it. She needed a man who would choose her over all others, and she would settle for nothing less.

The young medic handed her two aspirin and a bottle of water. "Perhaps this will help, sí?"

"Thanks." She downed the pills in one gulp, thinking she'd settle for nothing less than acceptance from her father, too. If he couldn't handle her taking on more responsibility for Travini Vineyards, preparing herself to inherit the business, she'd send to Chile for new vine clippings and start her own damn vineyard. The T & T Vineyard, she'd call it—in memory of Terry. She'd grow the finest grapes possible, produce the best wines with the smoothest taste. Win blue ribbons at every damn county fair in the country.

And she knew exactly how to market her product.

The boat rocked as Rafe and his friend returned from the submarine.

"Take a look at him now," she said to the medic. "And use lots of antiseptic."

The young man's flirty eyes lit up with mischief. "As you wish, señorita." He grabbed up his supplies, hurrying to intercept Rafe before Rafe could escape his ministrations. "Señor, if you will sit here, *por favor*."

Rafe tried to resist, but Donovan insisted. "Don't be a sissy, Big Mac. You bleed just like the rest of us."

Taylor smiled to herself. She could learn to like Donovan. He didn't take any guff.

Without sitting down, Rafe shed his bloody shirt, and Taylor drew in a sharp breath. A reddish-brown slash cut across his side halfway between the ragged scar on his shoulder and the one on his abdomen—the marks of a hero.

He didn't once flinch as the medic worked on his wounds. Instead, his gaze was on her, a sensual caress that captivated Taylor and made her long for what couldn't be. She forced herself to look away.

"Looks like we took down a pretty big conspiracy," he said. "Landry tells me the authorities are already rounding up the conspirators who were behind the hijacking, including those mafia wannabees in the black jackets who were after you in Santiago."

"I followed up on Igor's murder," Landry explained. "About the time you decided to phone home on the terrorists' radio, the authorities had begun to uncover a conspiracy that went almost to the top, including the Chilean Minister of Internal Affairs."

"What about the manager at Hotel Magdalena?" Taylor asked, shuddering at the thought of that creepy little man. "Was he in on it?"

Landry nodded. "A bit player. He was the one who fingered you when you came looking for your brother. The police captain was a part of it, too. We don't know all the details yet, but they'll talk. Chile has a long history of conducting effective interrogations."

Taylor knew he was talking about torture, but that didn't bother her in the least. The men involved with the conspiracy were responsible for her brother's death. She wanted them to suffer.

Waving off the medic, who wanted to examine his leg wound, Rafe pulled his bloody shirt back on over his bandaged chest. "Landry's arranged a ride to Punta Arenas for you. From there you can hop a plane back to the States. If that's what you want."

Her throat tight with emotion, she glanced from Rafe to his friend. "Thank you. I'd appreciate that. I need to get home to tell my father what happened." Was Rafe really going to simply let her walk away? Did she mean so little to him that he didn't feel some regret that she was leaving? Her head began to throb, and she lifted her chin. "I gather you'll be staying here in Chile."

"For a while. I have some loose ends to tie up."

"Of course."

Overhead, the roar of the returning helicopter increased in volume, throbbing in Taylor's chest, and the wash of the rotors kicked up waves in the otherwise still water. She took a step to leave with Landry, but Rafe's hand on her arm stopped her. She might have pulled away, but the intensity in his gray eyes held her, a depth of emotion she hadn't seen there before. She thought for a moment he would ask her to stay. Or say that he was coming with her.

"You can join my army anytime, Legs. Thanks for watching my back."

"You're welcome. But I think my fighting days are over." She wouldn't fight his ghosts, real or imagined. She had her own battles to win.

Hovering, the helicopter lowered a sling to the PT boat. Rafe's hand slipped down Taylor's arm to her fingertips in a lingering caress, while Landry adjusted her harness. The colonel signaled the helicopter to take her up. As she rose toward the helicopter, she spun in lazy circles. The scene below her, Rafe on the small boat deck looking up at her, made her dizzy, sick to her stomach with grief and heartache.

Strong hands grabbed her and pulled her into the helicopter, directing her to a canvas seat in the back, and a crewman strapped her in. The roar of the engine made it impossible to think, only feel, and she sat numbly staring ahead, seeing nothing until Landry arrived.

The helicopter banked to the left in a move that compounded the queasy feeling in Taylor's stomach, and then headed northeast to Punta Arenas.

Landry signaled her to put on her earphones, which muffled the noise and allowed them to communicate.

"For the record," he said, "I think my buddy Big Mac is a world-class jerk. If it had been me, I never would have let you go."

She smiled, but windblown tears stung her eyes. "Thanks. Sounds like the perfect epitaph to me."

"How 'bout the next time I see him, I carve it into his chest for you?"

She thought about Rafe's broad chest, with that intriguing cross of brown hair and the scars that already marked him, and said, "I think he's been hurt enough." And his wounds went so deep, he might never be able to heal them.

Rafe stood on the deck watching the helicopter become nothing more than a tiny speck in the cloudless sky, then vanish altogether. His throat ached, and he had trouble swallowing. His chest felt like he'd taken a blow that had knocked the wind out of him. He couldn't draw breath.

Taylor could be annoyingly stubborn and far more independent than any woman should be. But it felt like she'd taken some vital part of him with her in that helicopter. A part he wasn't sure he could do without.

That scared him spitless.

With his hand he shaded his eyes, trying to catch a last glimpse of the helicopter. But it was gone.

So was Taylor.

In Santiago, Aguilar Mendoza twirled the knob on the safe hidden behind the heavy credenza in his office. Intelligence officers had picked up another of his operatives for questioning. He was beginning to feel the hot breath of the government on his neck and had no intention of being caught before his plan became operational. A matter of hours now, not days.

He pulled a stack of thousand-peso bills from the safe, stuffed them in his inner coat pocket, and was just reaching for his Glock when the door to his office flew open.

"Señor Mendoza!" his secretary cried from the reception area outside his office. "I could not stop them."

From his crouched position, he turned to find Archie Vanderholt, Chief of Military Intelligence, standing in the doorway, a wiry man with thinning hair and obscenely thick glasses. Behind him stood two members of the military police.

Mendoza's hand trembled as he cautiously reached for his Glock.

"I expect you to come peacefully," Vanderholt said. "Any other choice would be the equivalent of committing suicide."

Mendoza considered that option. It might be better than spending the rest of his life in prison. Then again, as long as he still breathed there was hope for the future.

In the end, he left the pistol where it was and stood to face his enemy. "How dare you burst into my office unannounced, Archie," he said with disdain. "Didn't they teach you any manners in toy-soldier school?"

Responding to Archie's unspoken command, the two police officers handcuffed Mendoza and led him out of the office. Members of his staff stood agape, their eyes wide with surprise as he passed by.

But there was no need for them to worry, he assured himself. He had survived Pinochet's downfall and had risen nearly to the top. With his connections and an army of operatives at his beck-and-call, he would survive this minor inconvenience as well.

His personal fortune-teller had never been wrong!

Archie Vanderholt followed along behind Mendoza, a smile threatening to break through his stern demeanor. Mendoza's unbridled ambition was the noose that would soon hang the arrogant prick. The whole of Chile would be better off without him.

CHAPTER FORTY

Four months later

Despite the fog bank that lay just beyond the coastal range, waves of midday heat rippled above the rows of grape vines and the air smelled ripe with the growing fruit. Workers in long-sleeved shirts and straw hats hoed the weeds that had crept in between the rows, threatening to steal nourishment from the vines that the rich soil of northern California provided. Over the rest of the summer, clusters of the now tiny grapes would absorb the heat of the sun, turning it to sugar as they grew plump and juicy. This would be a good year for Travini Vineyards.

It would be a good year for her, too, Taylor told herself as she strode beside a row of vines that led to the house on the hill. Built in the style of an Italian villa, it had a red tile roof, arched entrances and a long porch shaded by overhanging eaves. Giant crimson and purple bougainvillea bushes splashed their colors across the beige stucco, creeping up over the roof, and slender hollyhocks stood at attention beside a wire fence that separated the house from the vineyard.

She'd come from her office in the nearby winery, which was open to the public for tasting and sales, and she carried a manila folder with her latest marketing concept for Travini Vineyards. As president of the company, she carried many responsibilities now, including day-to-day operations, but marketing was still her first love.

She found her father sitting in his usual wicker rocking chair on the porch. Although he still held the title of CEO on corporate documents, he was a shadow of the man he had once been. The loss of his only son had thrown him into a spiral of grief. His cheeks were gaunt, his former mane of white hair had thinned, and age spots had appeared on the backs of his hands almost overnight.

It hurt Taylor to realize how much his son had meant to him and that, at some level, he blamed her for Terry's death.

"Hey, Dad." She stepped up onto the porch and pulled another wicker chair next to his. "How's it going?"

He glanced at her, then returned his attention to the field of vines as though the rooted plants would get up and leave for greener fields if he didn't keep an eye on them. "This weather is good for the grapes."

The wicker chair creaked as she sat down. "We're going to have a great harvest this year."

"Careful with your predictions or you'll jinx yourself."

Suppressing a sigh, she opened the folder. "I've had a great idea, Dad. Something that will make the wine critics stand up and take notice of Travini Vineyards."

"The critics have always liked our wines."

"Yeah, I know. But this is going to knock their socks off."

315

His bushy, unkempt eyebrows, as white as his hair, lifted. "You want I should worry about their socks?"

"Dad . . ." She handed him the top page from the file, the label she'd asked a commercial artist friend of Terry's to design. "Look at this. I want us to create a private label. Aged to perfection. A wine so fine it's worthy of Terry's name. We can call it T-T from Travini Vineyards."

His gaze dropped to the artist's rendering, zeroing in on the background image. "You put his picture on it."

"Do you like it?"

Nodding slowly, he reached over and took her hand. "You're a good girl, Taylor. Your mama would be proud."

"I hope so, but the thing is, I can't create this private label all by myself. My palate is good, but not as talented as yours."

Once again, he nodded in agreement. "You have other talents."

She smiled at that, a powerful admission under the circumstances. "So, anyway, I'm going to need you to select the grapes, work on the blend. This is for Terry, you know, and we don't want to produce vinegar. Right?" What she wanted was to get her father back to being alive. Even fighting with her over her decisions about the vineyard, if that's what it took.

He closed the folder. "You are a very sneaky young woman, Taylor Theresa Travini. But I love you."

Her heart soared. Her father had so rarely said those words, she couldn't help but rejoice. Even if there were another man's voice she had once longed to hear say the same words. A man who hadn't been able to love her back and let her go instead.

"Then you'll help me?"

He gazed off into the distance. "It will take a great deal of work and the perfect grapes. A merlot, I think. Slightly fruity but very smooth. Ideal with any meal. Terry would like that."

"So do I, Dad." Feeling a weight lift from her shoulders, she hugged her father. She sensed that, with a goal to honor his son, he would recover his lost vitality.

"There is a stranger coming," he said, pushing her away as an unfamiliar car came up the dirt road to the house. "He must have missed the turn for the sampling room. You'll have to tell him." Vincent Travini stood, his shoulders hunched, and went into the house. His still raw grief prevented him from dealing with strangers—and often not with his friends, either.

Taylor exhaled, the loving moment interrupted. "Sure."

She strolled down the walkway past the flower beds her mother had planted years ago with nasturtiums, poppies and marigolds. Approaching the sporty Mercedes, not at all a typical tourist rental car, something about the driver caught her eye: the breadth of his shoulders, the shape of his head and the way he focused his attention intently on her. His confident grip on the steering wheel.

Halting mid-stride, she felt her heart rate accelerate. It couldn't be . . .

The car came to a stop. The door opened. A moment later, there was no mistaking the man who exited the vehicle.

Rafe Maguire.

He gave her only a passing look before walking to the back of the car. Lifting the trunk lid, he removed a bundle wrapped in heavy burlap and carried it up the walkway. He was freshly shaved, with no sign of the bruises he'd sustained in Chile. His hair was neatly trimmed, and he wore civilian clothes, a sports shirt and slacks that emphasized his lean hips.

She'd tried so hard to get over him. Had cursed the nights she dreamed of him. Now he was here in the flesh, and she was torn between running into his arms or telling him to get the hell out of her life.

His lips curved into an amused smile. "You're a blonde again."

"The brunette business was expedient."

"Blonde suits you better."

She crossed her arms over her chest. "Why are you here?"

"I brought you a present." He indicated the burlap bundle. "They're from Rudy Huhn. Some of his vine clippings. The airline had a fit about me keeping them wet, but I think they're okay."

Stunned by his announcement, her jaw went slack. "You brought me vines all the way from Chile?"

He shrugged. "You lost the first batch when the *Reina de la Mar* sank. It seemed only right to bring you some replacements. Nice place, by the way." His admiring glance included both the villa and the acres of verdant vines.

Struggling to sort out what was happening, she gestured toward the house. "Why don't you put those on the porch. I'll have Gus Lopez, our foreman, take care of them." Since his heart attack in February, Gus had cut back on his work, letting his son handle much of the load. But officially he was still the Travini Vineyards foreman, and everyone seemed happy with the arrangement.

Rafe laid the bundle down in the shade. "So, how've you been?"

"Uh, fine. I haven't been shot at in months. How about you?"

"I wrapped up my job with the Chilean Special Forces. I'm going to work for Landry."

In spite of herself, she felt a pang of regret. Rafe was still doing his soldier-of-fortune thing. He hadn't changed a bit.

"Landry retired from the army last month. He's starting a security firm here in the Bay Area. Primarily for maritime protection and tracking shipments around the globe as part of homeland security. I've signed on with him."

The Bay Area? The one that was less than a hour south of Travini Vineyards? "Interesting. So what's your job going to be?"

"We haven't worked out the details yet. But I'll be based in San Francisco."

Her heart did a funny fluttery thing that was as annoying as hell. Had he just popped in to tell her they were about to be neighbors? "San Francisco isn't far from here."

"Sausalito is even closer." He took a step towards her, close enough that she could see the pupils flare in his gray eyes. Despite his casual manner, he wasn't unaffected by her. "I'm thinking of buying a boat there, living on it for a while."

She swallowed hard. "Sausalito has a very nice marina. Upscale."

"I suppose that means I'll have to get something a little fancier than our old *Reina de la Mar*." He moved into her personal space, crowding her and making her achingly aware of his overpowering masculinity—the deep tan of his face, the squint lines at the corners of his eyes, the muscular set of his shoulders.

She licked her lips. "Much nicer than that."

"In that case, owning a big boat, I'll be looking for a roommate. A permanent roommate. With privileges, of course." Slowly, he lifted his hand and stroked his knuckles in a familiar gesture along her cheek that sent sensual shivers down her spine. "I thought you might be interested."

"I have the winery to run. Dad hasn't been well. He's taken a backseat as far as operations go. I'm the company president now."

"Good for you." Genuine pleasure showed in his eyes. "You'll be damn good as president. I figured your dad would finally recognize your smarts. Which is why I checked out Sausalito. Seemed like a good compromise location for both of us."

Her thoughts spun. She couldn't leave either her father or the business. But in Sausalito she'd be close. And Rosa Lopez, Gus's wife, had been her father's housekeeper for years. She'd take good care of him. But she wasn't going to make it that easy for Rafe.

"I don't get it. It's been months without a word, then you show up here asking me to move in with you. That's a lot of nerve when you didn't even bother to kiss me good-bye when you sent me off with Landry in that helicopter."

"I was afraid to."

"Afraid?" she scoffed. "You're the hero who runs through fire and a rain of bullets to rescue damsels in distress. As nearly as I can tell, you've never been afraid of anything in your life."

"I'm afraid of love. It scares the hell out of me. And if I'd kissed you back there in Chile, there was no way I would have let you get on that chopper. That wouldn't have been fair to you, Legs."

"Fair to me?" How about the tears she'd tried so hard not to shed? The sleepless nights she'd spent since she returned home to the vineyards?

"You had some issues you had to work out with your dad. I figured by now you'd either be company president—which you are—or you would have walked off into the sunset to start your own vineyard. Besides, I couldn't wait any longer. Not seeing you, not being with you, was driving me nutso."

"Is that how you really feel?"

"It is. For years, since I lost Lizbeth, I didn't want to have anything to do with love. It hurts too damn much to lose someone you love." Gently, he tucked a stray hair behind her ear. "Then you came along, smart and courageous and sassy as hell. The way I feel about you terrifies me. But I couldn't stay away." He shrugged. "I guess you could say I'm waving a white flag. I surrender."

Surrender? Oh, Lord... With her heart in her throat, she said, "In that case, I'd be willing to consider the possibility of being your roommate."

He looked so relieved, she almost laughed—or cried tears of happiness.

"We had a pretty good partnership going on the *Reina*," he said.

"I'd insist this time we take turns being captain."

His lips hitched into another smile, this one provocative. "I can live with that."

Unable to resist, she palmed his face, his cheeks free of the stubble she'd grown used to seeing. His arrival had been so unexpected. She'd given up hope, but the seed of her love had sprung to full bloom the moment she'd seen him step out of the car, despite her best efforts to suppress the emotion.

"I've got another present for you." Slipping his hand

into his trouser pocket, he retrieved an oblong box covered in blue velvet. "A belated birthday present."

Surprised, she carefully opened the box. Inside lay a sterling silver necklace with two aquamarine stones nested together in a pendant. Her chest squeezed so tight, it hurt. "It's beautiful."

"I had it specially made. I thought you'd like to think that in some way you and your brother will always be together, and the necklace would help you remember that."

Lifting the necklace from the case, he linked it around her neck. His warm hands brushed against the sensitive column of her throat in a gentle caress.

No other gesture could have meant so much or showed the depth of his love more clearly. That he understood she'd always be Terry's twin spoke volumes about the kind of man Rafe Maguire was and always would be.

To this point, their relationship had been driven by an abundance of adrenaline and danger. They needed a chance to know each other in more ordinary ways, the day-to-day life of a man and woman living together. The ups and downs. The commitment to discover all the parts of a whole that made up their pasts and their future, and see if together they could become more than they'd been alone.

What he'd offered wasn't a promise of marriage; neither of them was ready for that step yet. Taylor understood that. But this was a promise she would gladly accept, and in her heart, she knew it was only the beginning.

"Thank you," she whispered. "For the necklace and for understanding about Terry. There's nothing I'd like more than being your roommate . . . and your lover."

With infinite care, he brought his lips to hers. At first

he coaxed her with gentleness, molding and shaping their lips together. When he deepened the kiss, she melted into him. She wrapped her arms around him, threading her fingers through the hair at his nape as he pulled her body against his, and she gave herself over to the familiar sensations he aroused.

This was meant to be. In some mysterious way, by searching for Terry she had found herself and the one man she would love forever. For that, she sent up a prayer of thanksgiving to her brother.

Then she lost herself once again in Rafe's kiss and the future they'd have together.

MARJORIE M. LIU
SHADOW TOUCH

Don't miss the sequel to *Tiger Eye*,
the romance *Publishers Weekly* called "a first-rate debut."

"I didn't just like this book, I LOVED this book!"
—CHRISTINE FEEHAN

Elena Baxter can work miracles with her hands. She can coax bones to knit, flesh to heal. She can mend the mind. She has been doing such work for almost all of her twenty-eight years. That is why she will be taken.

The media calls it a rampage of terror, the recent murders. But fighting crime is why Artur Loginov joined Dirk & Steele. The international detective agency specializes in the impossible. Dirk & Steele gave the Russian émigré purpose, protection, community...and refuge from his past, for who can trust a man who can start a fire with his mind, or shape-shift, or read others' thoughts as easily as drawing breath? For his similar talent, Artur will be taken.

- -

FADE *the* HEAT

COLLEEN THOMPSON

Someone is setting fires in the Houston *barrio,* and Dr. Jack Montoya is the first intended victim. Is there some connection between the torching of his apartment and the gorgeous blonde from his past who appears at his clinic on the same day? For sure, Reagan Hurley turns up the flames of his libido, but these days the beautiful firefighter is more interested in putting out conflagrations than fanning old sparks. Yet when a hotly contested mayoral race turns ugly, when Reagan's life is threatened and Jack's career almost destroyed, when desire sizzles uncontrollably between them, it seems that no one will be able to . . . *Fade the Heat.*